MERCENARY MAGE

STAR MAGE SAGA BOOK 4

J.J. GREEN

INFINITEBOOK

Copyright © 2020 by J.J. Green

All rights reserved.

No part of this book may be reproduced in any form or by any electronic or mechanical means, including information storage and retrieval systems, without written permission from the author, except for the use of brief quotations in a book review.

ISBN: 9798622215766

❀ Created with Vellum

CONTENTS

1

Carina Lin crouched at the corner of a stack of crates and peeked out of the cargo bay. Her gaze was fixed on a domestic starship that had just finished refueling. The ship was probably privately owned by a local magnate but it looked like business hadn't been going well lately. The vessel was overdue a paint job. Its name, *Zenobia,* was barely visible emblazoned on the side and in some places metal gleamed dully through the carmine coating. Passages through planetary atmospheres and interstellar space had taken their toll.

Carina felt Bryce ease up close beside her and slip an arm around her waist. She didn't object.

"Is that the one?" he asked, following the direction of her gaze with his own.

"Fits the brief," she replied. "What do you think?"

"It'll do, I guess."

Carina scanned the bay. Portage bots trundled along the aisles, transporting freight onto and off of storage shelves. Not a single human figure could be seen, though that didn't mean a thing. Security surveillance cameras would cover the place, even on a poor, backwater planet like Pirine. And the portage bots would be recording everything that occurred within their vicinity.

Carina wasn't too worried about being captured by the Pirinian authorities—a quick Enthrall Cast would soon ensure their release. What did concern her was the Dirksens. The clan's military remained on the planet, searching for mages, and showed no signs of leaving.

If the Dirksens caught Carina and her siblings escape would not be easy. It could even prove impossible.

Looking back over her shoulder, she said, "All set?" The five children nodded.

She had rehearsed the operation with them many times. Stealing the *Zenobia* should go like clockwork, but Carina knew from her days as a merc that reality usually inserted at least one surprise to upset even the best laid plans. She wondered what it would be this time.

She took another quick scan of the bay. Most of the bots were in the farther reaches of the place, out of sight. She wouldn't get a better chance.

"Darius," said Carina, "Cloak us."

Her youngest brother's big brown eyes were grave as he sipped elixir from a metal flask. Then he closed them to concentrate on making the Cast. A moment later his eyelids lifted again. "I did it."

"Great," Carina said. "Let's go. Remember, everyone stick together."

She stood up and lifted her stolen Dirksen weapon to her shoulder. Bryce did the same. Behind him Carina's brothers and sisters formed a tight knot. Time to move.

As always, it was impossible to tell if Darius's Cast had taken effect. If it was working, they should be invisible to all human and electronic onlookers. However, to the Cloaked, everything looked the same, which made stepping out into the open unnerving.

Carina led the group along the aisle between boxes of freight toward the *Zenobia*. Beyond the wide entrance to the cargo bay, directly ahead, the sun was setting. Carina squinted to see better and wished for a light-reactive helmet visor. Long, black shadows ran out from the *Zenobia*.

The refueling crew had departed and the immediate area around the ship was empty. Carina doubted the vessel was locked but even if it was a quick Cast would solve the problem. With any luck the pilot and air crew wouldn't have boarded yet.

Carina reached the open doors. It was just another thirty meters or so to the ship. Once they were aboard Darius would Cast again to Cloak it, she would hopefully figure out the controls, and then they would be gone. Two long weeks of dodging Dirksen guards would be over and they would be on their way back to Ostillon. From there they would begin the long journey home.

"What's that?" Bryce asked.

Beyond the long lines of shuttlecraft and starships, a vehicle was approaching, fast. A military vehicle. Even at the distance Carina could see the occupants' uniforms were not the dark green of Pirinian troops. The figures were clad in deep gray.

"Shit," said Carina. "Dirksens."

"Are they coming for us?" Parthenia, Carina's eldest sister asked.

"I don't see how they could know we're here," Carina replied. Infiltrating the spaceport had gone smoothly. They hadn't triggered any alarms. On the other hand the Dirksens were all over every spaceport on the planet, like scalobites on a nest of kruekins, determined to block all avenues of escape. The soldiers *were* there for the mages. The only question was, were they there for Carina and her family in particular?

"Hurry up," said Carina. The sooner they were aboard the ship and out of potential sight of the Dirksen guards the better.

They reached the *Zenobia* as the upper rim of the setting sun disappeared. Though the starship was small, compared to most of the vessels at the spaceport it was huge. The engines took up two-thirds of the ship, bulking out each side. And, unlike most interstellar craft, the *Zenobia* was streamlined. A slim nose poked out in front then the vessel flared, rounding out over its engines, in order to smooth its passage through atmospheres.

Carina and her companions passed into the darkness under the massive engines. Meanwhile, the military vehicle sped closer, its headlights blaring bright light and the guards sweeping the spaceport's standing area with their gazes, weapons at the ready. It neared the ship.

Then it stopped and stood beyond the *Zenobia's* engines.

"What the hell?" Bryce muttered. "Why's it stopped just there? They can't see us, can they?"

"Not unless Darius's Cast didn't work," Carina softly replied. It was unlikely. Her brother was the most powerful mage among them—possibly the most powerful in the sector, now that the old Spirit Mage had died. Yet the fact that the Dirksen soldiers had chosen exactly that spot to stop seemed too much of a coincidence.

"Stay cool, everyone," Carina said. "Carry on with the plan as if they weren't there."

The soldiers were climbing out of the vehicle.

"Just be careful not to bump into any of them," she added.

Her little troop emerged from underneath the *Zenobia* into the dusky light. Suddenly, the spaceport's floodlights snapped on. Oriana gave a small scream.

A soldier's head swiveled in the direction of the sound.

"Oh, I'm sorry," Oriana whispered, her voice high with regret and fear.

"Never mind," Carina muttered. "Stay close."

The soldier began to walk toward them.

Carina turned to look up at the *Zenobia.*

"*Shit.*" All the vessel's doors were shut tight, there was no way to board it. No regular way at least.

"We'll have to Transport aboard, guys," said Carina. She would have preferred to walk onto the craft so they knew where they were going.

The Dirksen soldier was directly approaching them.

"Under the engines again," Carina said. "Now."

"No," said Bryce. "Look."

In the shadow of the enormous ship, the other soldiers could be seen scouting the area.

"Can they smell us or something?" asked Carina.

"Well," Bryce said, "I hate to mention it, but..."

Carina stuck an elbow in his side. "We'll just have to Transport from here. Darius, can you move all of us together and put us in the..." She had no idea about the interior layout of the ship. From what she knew, the Transport Cast somehow avoided moving an object inside another object, but she didn't want to take any chances. She needed a wide space. "Into the hold."

"Where's that?" asked Darius. He spoke at his normal volume, which, while he didn't have a loud voice, was loud enough for the approaching guard to hear. The man's body stiffened as he registered the sound. He halted. Probably because he was alerting his CO.

"Uh, about there," Carina replied, pointing to an area at the bottom of the ship near the front. It was a guess, based on the doors she'd spotted in the hull.

The guard was only five meters distant, but Darius wouldn't be able to Transport them if they moved to get away.

"Do it," Carina told her brother, who was frowning as he tried to figure out where she wanted him to send them.

The little boy dutifully took a swallow of elixir.

The guard strode toward them. Another two steps and he would crash into Parthenia.

Darius's eyes closed.

"Quick, Darius!" Oriana squeaked.

2

Pitch darkness surrounded Carina and the air was cold and damp.

Darius had done it. They were inside the *Zenobia*, hopefully in her hold.

"Oh good," said Oriana. "Now we're safe." Her voice echoed from the surrounding walls.

"No, we aren't," said Carina. "Not yet. We don't know if anyone else is aboard, so keep your voice down. And those Dirksen guards knew something was up. Their CO will probably order the ship to be searched. They might even disable its engines. We need to get to the bridge and—"

"We need to find our way out of here first," said Bryce. "Can one of you Cast Light or something?"

"No," Carina replied. "There's no such Cast."

"I could try and make one," said Darius.

"Not now, sweetheart," Carina said. "And I don't want anyone to even *think* of Casting Fire. We'll set off the alarms and the entire spaceport will be all over the ship. Come on, let's look for a door."

She set off blindly into the dark. Before she'd taken more

than a few steps the hold's lights blinked on, activated by her movement. They were inside a space about twenty meters square surrounded by plain unadorned metal, and the ship's cargo.

"Whoa," Ferne said. "Look at all this stuff. I wonder what it is?"

Boxes and packets of all shapes and sizes formed tall stacks, secured to the floor and walls by netting.

"I don't know," said Carina. She was puzzled by the odd cargo too. She'd taken the starship to be a means of transportation for a rich owner, not a merchant vessel. And if it were a merchant vessel she would have expected more uniformity in the freight, perhaps only three or four types of cargo. This was more like... She had no idea. "We don't have time to find out. Come on. This way."

Carina had spied the smaller, internal door that would lead to the main body of the ship. She raced over to it and tried the handle. It was unlocked.

After waiting a moment for the others to catch up, she set off down the passage that led from the hold.

"Do you know where you're going?" Bryce asked as he caught up to her.

"Not at all," replied Carina. "You?"

"Nope, but upward and forward is my best bet."

"Mine too." A sign caught Carina's eye as she passed it. "Wait. What was that?" She turned and ran back a few paces.

The sign said *Service Access.* She pushed on the adjacent panel and it popped open, revealing a ladder. "We'll go this way," she said to the others, who had stopped to see what she was doing.

"Elevator too fancy for you?" Bryce asked.

"A ladder is less trappy," replied Carina, grabbing the rungs.

She ran up the ladder, then thought twice about it and slowed her pace. Darius and Nahla wouldn't be able to go so fast. She paused and looked down the narrow tunnel. Some way below, Nahla clung to Bryce's back as he climbed, and Carina thought she could see Parthenia carrying Darius. She continued to ascend, though at a slower rate.

Had they already triggered the ship's security system? Were the spaceport authorities already on their way, about to team up with the Dirksen guards to gain entry to the ship? From what Carina had seen in the cargo bay the *Zenobia* was not what she seemed, but neither was she a military vessel. It was entirely possible that only forced entry would trigger an alarm. The security measures might not extend to the ship's interior.

Whatever the truth was didn't really matter. If they were to stand a chance of getting off Pirine, they had to find the bridge fast.

The signs next to the tunnel exits were no help. They only stated the levels. Carina passed level two and level three. When she reached the exit to level four, she pressed the release. The door clicked and opened a fraction. She waited for Bryce and the others to catch up and then motioned them to be quiet.

She listened. All she could hear was the silence of an empty starship at rest. Pushing open the door, she peered out. Dim standby lighting illuminated a plush corridor. This was more like what she'd been expecting to see: a carpeted floor, somewhat worn, and walls painted green and gold.

They had clearly arrived at the passenger section. It was here the owner and his family, friends, and business associates would reside while the *Zenobia* was in flight. But this section wasn't for the crew. It was too nicely decorated.

Carina looked up. The service ladder continued to another level. She pulled the door closed and continued her climb. Level five soon appeared. Carina opened the door and saw scuffed floor tiles and white, grubby walls. *This* was a crew area. After checking for signs of occupation again and hearing and seeing nothing, she climbed out into the corridor and set off at a run.

Doors flashed past. Carina didn't worry about leaving the others behind now. She needed to get to the bridge and start the ship's engines. Too much time had passed since Darius had Transported them onto the ship. The Dirksen guards could be aboard and searching it already. And the ship had just been refueled, which meant passengers would be arriving any minute.

Carina slid to a halt, realizing she'd run right past reached the bridge. She doubled back.

The bridge doors didn't automatically open as she approached. It made sense. Here, if anywhere, on board security would be vital. But a locked door posed no problem to a mage. She pulled her elixir bottle from the pouch that hung at her side and unscrewed the lid. Between pants to catch her breath, Carina took a swig and closed her eyes. She swiftly wrote the *Unlock* character in her mind and sent it out. As she opened her eyes again she heard the soft scrape of the door opening.

"There she is!" someone shouted. "Shoot!"

Carina jumped to the side, but not fast enough. A pulse round caught her shoulder. She fired back randomly as she reached the cover of the wall, barely registering the scene on the bridge. Soldiers in Dirksen uniforms had formed a semi-circle around the door. She also caught a glimpse of her eldest brother, Castiel.

"Carina!" Darius yelled as she fell.

Her shoulder felt like it had been punched by a giant, which was a good sign. The soldiers' weapons were set to stun, not kill. Of course, the Dirksen clan wanted to keep her alive and enslave her for her abilities, like they had enslaved Castiel. Luckily, her dominant arm hadn't been hit.

Carina dragged herself away from the open doorway. A

second stunning round impacted her ankle and sent spirals of numbing shocks up her leg. She wouldn't be able to stand until the effects wore off in ten or fifteen minutes. She rested the butt of her weapon against her hip and cradled the rest of it in her remaining working arm.

She heard Bryce urge, "Transport the soldiers away, Darius." He was running up the corridor with the others.

"I can't," Darius replied. "I have to see them."

That was Carina's problem too, or she would have performed the Cast herself. But if she looked into the bridge again she would be stunned in a heartbeat.

Carina continued to scoot backward, hauling her dead leg as she went, maintaining her aim on the entrance to the bridge. As if on cue, a muzzle appeared through the door, but all she could see of the person holding it was a gloved hand. Carina shot and missed. A second shot came from along the corridor. Bryce was covering her. The pulse hit its mark. With a muffled yelp, the owner of the hand dropped the weapon.

"Darius," Carina shouted, "Cloak the ship!" Now the Dirksens knew she and her siblings were aboard there was no point in any further subterfuge. But Cloaking the ship would make it hard for more soldiers to board. And until Castiel could see his brother he wouldn't be able to use Repulse to cancel Darius's Casts.

A helmeted head appeared in the doorway. Carina shot at it but it was gone as soon as she pressed the trigger. Someone had been assessing the situation. Bryce had also fired. He and her siblings had reached the other side of door and he was holding out an arm, gesturing them to move to the wall.

With surprise, Carina registered that not all of them were there. What had happened to Darius and Nahla? Then she realized what she was seeing: Darius's earlier Cloak Cast was still working, and Nahla had to be standing close enough to him to be covered by it. Carina had only been visible to the soldiers because she'd run ahead, out of the Cast's influence.

Elation surged within her. If she couldn't see Darius, neither could anyone else. Carina had to let go of her weapon to gesture to Bryce, trying to convey her message through hand signals. She couldn't speak to Darius out loud and tell him to stand in the doorway to see the soldiers and Transport them away. If they knew what he was doing they would simply blanket the space with fire.

A muzzle flashed out. Carina snatched up her weapon. Too late. Parthenia took a hit to her stomach and dropped like a stone. The shot had been aimed at where Bryce had been standing, but he'd moved.

That was dumb. All the mages were far more dangerous than Bryce, even though he was armed.

He was feeling along the wall, trying to find Darius by touch. He'd guessed what she'd been trying to convey with hand signals! Bryce disappeared. He'd found the little boy and come within the influence of the Cloak.

When another soldier darted out to fire, Carina's finger closed reflexively on her weapon's trigger. Her round hit the man square in the back. Her gun was not set to stun, and at the short range if he hadn't been wearing armor he'd be dead. As it was, he only fell and was quickly dragged away by his fellow troops.

Bryce reappeared. Where was Darius? Bryce's eyes told Carina he'd understood and done what she'd asked. Now they only had to wait and hope the little boy didn't get hit by random fire.

Painful tingles emanated from Carina's shoulder and arm. The stun was beginning to wear off.

All of a sudden, soldiers burst from the doorway, spraying fire. Carina rolled but a round hit her unstunned leg, rendering her completely helpless. Her weapon was caught underneath her. Desperately, she willed her unresponsive legs to move.

Lying on her front, she waited for the coup de grâce.

It didn't come.

Silence fell.

Carina lifted her head and looked over her shoulder. The soldiers had gone. Darius had Transported them. Bryce lay on his back, motionless. Carina also saw the upturned soles of Oriana and Ferne's boots. The soldiers had stunned everyone.

"Where are you?" said a voice. "Where are you, you little shit?"

Castiel stomped out from the bridge, his head turning from side to side as his gaze swept the corridor. "Come out and face me! We'll fight it out and I'll beat you. I'm a much better mage than you!"

His glare alighted on Carina. His angry expression switched to a smirk. "Not so high and mighty now, are you, sis? I ought to Split you all and have done with it. Except you and that little asshole could be useful to me yet. Never mind. He's given me my freedom at least." He swigged from an ornate metal flask and closed his eyes. "See you around."

In another second, Castiel was gone.

3

Carina selected coordinates in an area of deep space and input them into the *Zenobia's* navigation system before unfastening her safety harness and slumping in the pilot's seat. They'd done it. They'd left Pirine and soon they would be out of its system altogether. When they were beyond the heliopause she would input another set of coordinates and, as their journey to Ostillon progressed, several more sets. She would also ask Darius to Cloak the ship regularly so that its trace would be difficult to detect. That, coupled with the arbitrary headings, should make it hard for the Dirksens to follow them.

Might their pursuers guess they were on their way back to Ostillon? Carina doubted it. As far as she knew, the Dirksens had no idea of the planet's significance to mages. They had no interest in the local culture. All they wanted was to override it and stamp their own mark on the place. They couldn't know about the conflict that raged thousands of year previously between mages—the original human inhabitants—and newly arrived colonists.

The Dirksens would never have guessed the importance of

the Characters that the newcomers' religious acolytes now burned. The clan didn't understand about the Map, which the Ostillonians also burned, or the libation of elixir they poured into the ground.

No. The Dirksens would never in their wildest dreams imagine that Carina and her small family would return to the place they had fought so hard to escape. But if Earth was to be their final destination, Ostillon held the key to the planet's location, and so to Ostillon they must go.

A pair of hands grasped her shoulders and began to knead.

Carina sighed with satisfaction and relaxed.

"Feeling better?" Bryce asked. "Stun effects worn off?"

"Yes, thanks," she replied. The painful tingles in her arm and legs had abated while they'd been making their getaway from Pirine. After Darius had evicted the surprise party organizers, flying the *Zenobia* away from Pirine had been easy. The best gunner in the world couldn't shoot down an invisible ship, so even if the Dirksens had artillery stationed at the spaceport, preventing the ship's escape would have been impossible.

The clan had done the right thing by enlisting Castiel to help catch them. Who better to catch a mage than another mage? He must have been alerted to the suspicious sounds of disembodied human voices near the ship and Transported himself and a couple of squads to the bridge. But her eldest brother was no match for...

"Where's Darius?" Carina asked, turning around.

The little boy was sitting in the captain's chair, where Bryce had clearly put him. But the honor hadn't pleased him. He was gripping the seat edge and swinging his legs, looking downcast. Carina got up and walked over to him.

"Can I squeeze in there too?" she asked.

Darius slid from the center to the side of the seat. Carina sat down beside him and wrapped an arm over his narrow shoulders. She was deeply concerned about her little brother. He was a Spirit Mage. His power came from others' emotional energy, which made him intensely sensitive to the emotions of everyone in his vicinity. The former Spirit Mage had said Carina's own long-standing sorrow and grief probably caused him distress, and she ached with guilt over the fact.

Darius was possibly the only Spirit in that galactic sector. Maybe the only one in existence. His destiny had been to memorize the lore and history of the mage clan, to Summon young mages to the Matching, and goodness knew what else.

Yet he was also only a boy, far too young for such responsibility.

Bryce joined them and perched on the arm of the captain's chair.

"How's our little weapon of mass destruction?" he asked, ruffling Darius's hair.

"Yeah," said Ferne, who was squatting down and rooting through his open backpack, "great job, Darius. If it wasn't for you we would've been captured."

"Please don't call him that," said Carina to Bryce. She knew he was only joking, but she'd been forced into being an actual weapon of mass destruction herself. It had been an appalling experience and she didn't want her brother to think of himself in that way.

"I'm going to investigate the ship," Oriana announced. "Who's coming with me? Nahla? Parthenia?"

"Yes, I'll come," little Nahla replied.

"I'll come too," Parthenia said, "if only to keep you out of trouble, Oriana."

"Pfft," Oriana scoffed. "If you're going to police me you can stay here. Ferne?"

"I'll be along in a minute," her twin brother replied. "I just want to check I brought something. I'll Locate you."

"Suit yourself," Oriana said, "but if I find the master suite I'm calling dibs."

"I think there's gonna be nice rooms for everyone on this trip," Bryce said.

"I don't want you going anywhere except the passenger deck," said Carina. "And be careful. Until we search the ship top to bottom we can't be sure we're the only ones aboard. Take plenty of elixir and you take one of the weapons, Parthenia. Whatever you do, don't go into the hold. We have no idea what's down there."

Carina resolved to take a look at the mysterious packages later. She had a suspicion the *Zenobia* held secrets it would be wise to know.

The three girls left.

"Ugh," said Ferne. "Why did *I* have to be the one to bring the dirt? It's gotten over everything." He pulled out an item of underwear and shook it, scattering earth on the deck.

"Don't do that," said Bryce. "We don't want to see your drawers, do we, Darius?"

The little boy giggled.

Carina rolled her eyes. "Put them away, Ferne. And clean up that soil and put it back in your bag. Then find a safe place to stow it. We'll make a good supply of elixir before we go to sleep."

"But we have loads already," Ferne protested.

Carina had made sure every mage had a full canister before they made the attempt to steal a ship. "We can't ever have too much," she replied. "And stop whining. I don't want to spend the next few weeks with a bunch of bratty kids."

Ferne scowled, shoved his underwear into his backpack and stalked off the bridge.

As the door closed behind him, Carina sighed and rubbed her temples. "Whoops. I didn't handle that too well, did I?"

"To be fair," said Bryce, "he was being bratty. But there are probably better ways of stating it."

Out of all Carina's mage siblings, Oriana and Ferne seemed

to be having the hardest time adapting to their new life. Carina sometimes wondered if the twins took turns at being petulant. They'd grown up surrounded by luxury, and though their monster of a father had been harsh with them, Carina guessed that Ma had overcompensated with well-meant kindness and attention.

"I'm not being bratty, am I?" asked Darius.

"No," Carina replied, hugging him. "You couldn't be bratty if you tried. How are you feeling?"

"Okay," he replied. But his eyelids hung low and his little face was pale and shadowy. He was clearly on the edge of exhaustion.

"Would you like something to eat before you go to bed?" asked Carina.

"Uh huh."

"What do you say I take you to look for food?" Bryce said. "A ship like this is bound to be well stocked. And then we can find a cabin for you. Maybe we'll beat the girls to the master suite."

"I want to sleep in Carina's room," said Darius. "Can I?"

"Of course you can," Carina said. "You, me, and Bryce. How does that sound?"

"Good. I'd like that."

Bryce took Darius's hand and helped him down from the chair.

"Are you going to be all right here alone for a while?" he asked Carina.

"Yes, I'll be fine. Please be careful. I know it's unlikely, but I meant what I said to the girls. There's a chance we could have unwanted passengers."

"What'll we do with them if we have?" Bryce asked.

"Stars, I don't know. Lock them in a cabin, I guess. We'll cross that bridge if we come to it."

Bryce led Darius out, and Carina rested her face in her hands. The elation she'd felt when they'd successfully stolen the *Zenobia* was melting away and being replaced by worry. Her sharp remark to Ferne had been borne from anxiety and guilt.

Disaster threatened their quest—*her* quest—to find Earth, the birthplace of humanity and mages. They could be captured by the Dirksens, become lost in deep space, or attacked by outlaws.

It would be safer to find an out-of-the-way planet, well away from the Dirksen- and Sherrerr-controlled areas, and live out their lives in safety and peace. That had been the mage way for thousands of years: hiding their abilities from non-mages, living simple, isolated existences, and quietly passing on their traditions to their children.

But for what? Mere survival? Mages had to hide in the shadows simply to exist? What kind of a life was that? It was not one that Carina wanted, or one that she felt she deserved. She was not like Castiel, yearning for everyone to bow down around him, but neither was she prepared to hide what she was any longer. She wanted to live somewhere she could walk down the street without fear of public attack or ambush.

Would she find that on Earth? It seemed unlikely, considering that mages had been persecuted and forced to leave it. But that had been thousands of years ago. Perhaps things were different there now. Whatever she found on her clan's origin planet, Carina wanted to lay her eyes on the mountain home of her ancestors and breathe the air they had breathed.

She yawned as exhaustion suddenly swept over her. She wondered where the others were and if Bryce had found food for Darius. They all needed to rest, but she would stay awake for a few hours while Bryce slept. Then he could take the second watch. Until they were positive they were alone, she didn't want to risk having everyone asleep at once.

When she'd rested, she would go and check out their cargo.

4

Carina woke to the sensation of limbs pressing against her. She turned over. Darius was starfishing again. With his arms and legs spread out, somehow his small body managed to take up most of a bed large enough for two or three people.

She stretched and sat up. Bryce was gone. She'd woken him after four hours, as they'd agreed, so he could take over patrolling the ship while she slept. She'd spent her watch searching every level for stowaways, but the place seemed empty.

How long had she been asleep? She turned and activated the screen set into the wall next to the bed. Six and a half hours? She hadn't meant to sleep so long. And that meant Darius had been asleep for over ten hours. He clearly needed a long rest.

Carina used the screen to turn on the light at a low level and climbed out of bed. She hadn't had much of a chance to look at the room Bryce had found for them. Now that she had time for closer scrutiny, she found it was luxurious and decadent.

Curtains hung from the ceiling at the corners of the bed where Darius lay sleeping. As Carina looked upward, she noticed the screen above the bed for the first time. It was as large as the bed itself, and she could take a good guess as to its purpose. She cringed as she wondered what had gone on in the spot where her brother currently rested.

Similar curtains swathed the walls, giving the room the appearance of the interior of a huge tent. The rug she was standing on was so thick her bare feet sank into it. A musky but not unpleasant scent hung in the air, supplied by invisible means. The place seemed bare of everything except the bed, but Bryce had told her before he left that the room had an en suite.

Carina walked to the curtained wall and felt for a parting in the fabric. She found a gap and pulled the material apart to reveal a door. When she opened the door, however, she discovered it didn't lead to the en suite. She was facing a closet filled with racks of clothes and stacks of shoes.

It was a handy find. Clothes had been the last of her worries while they were trying to escape from Pirine. None of them had brought along any more than the clothes they stood up in. Carina ran a hand along one of the lines of hanging clothes. It didn't take much further investigation to realize the garments were *expensive*. The fabrics were sumptuous and richly textured.

She began to feel a weird disconnect between her first impressions of the *Zenobia* compared to what she was finding in this cabin. The ship appeared to belong to someone with cash flow problems, yet this wardrobe would cost years of a regular worker's salary, and it was only for the owners' use while they were away from home.

Carina inspected the clothes more closely. Men's clothing hung on one side of the closet and women's on the other. She tried to find something she could wear, pulling out items to look at them. The women's clothes seemed totally unsuitable: floor-length dresses and long over jackets in sizes that would look ridiculous on Carina as well as hamper her movement. Then she found a pair of wide pants, a tunic, and a belt. These would do, with some adjustment.

A second attempt to find the en suite met with success. The room was almost as large as the bedroom and held a shower, tub, massage table, and sauna. Here, the scented air smelled floral and fresh. Carina showered, washing away the grime that had built up while they'd been sleeping rough on Pirine. Then she put on her new clothes, rolling up the pants legs and tying the belt to both hold up the pants and pull in the baggy tunic. None of the shoes had fit her so she put on her old boots.

By the time she emerged, the bed was empty and the door to the corridor was open. Darius had woken up and wandered off. Carina stuck her head out of the door.

The corridor was empty. The tension that had dissipated during her shower returned.

She picked up her elixir, intending to ask Bryce if he knew where Darius was. Then she remembered that Bryce wasn't a mage and couldn't be contacted via a Cast.

She wasn't thinking straight. Carina took a deep breath and exhaled.

She could Send to Parthenia instead, but she didn't have anything of her sister's to use to Locate her. Finally, the answer hit and Carina slapped her forehead. She was aboard a starship. With a comm system.

She strode to the interface next to the bed and figured out how to comm the bridge.

Bryce answered. "You're awake? Did you get enough sleep?"

"Yes. Is Darius there?"

"Nope. I thought he was with you."

"He isn't. He went off somewhere while I was in the shower. He could be anywhere!" Carina's heart was racing.

"Calm down."

"Calm down? He's six years old."

"He can't have gone far," said Bryce. "I'll ask the other kids to look for him."

"All right, but tell them to stay in pairs. I don't want to lose another one."

Carina ran into the corridor. Where could her little brother be? What if he'd gone down into the hold? They didn't know what was down there yet. Foreboding settling over her, she darted back into the room to collect her weapon before setting off to find her young brother.

He was a smart kid who had experienced more than enough danger for a lifetime. It was out of character for him to wander off alone without telling anyone where he was going. Carina couldn't think what might have prompted him to leave the suite.

She opened the first door she came to and scanned the lavish quarters. She spied a couple of backpacks that told her the twins had taken the place for themselves. How typical it was that, despite the extensive accommodation available and their constant bickering, they'd elected to share a cabin.

But the room was empty.

"Darius!" Carina shouted as she closed the door. "Darius, where are you?"

Opening the next door revealed a dining room, set up like a small banquet hall, nothing like any shipboard refectory Carina had ever seen. She took in the long, wooden table and padded, throne-like chairs. It seemed that the *Zenobia* threw up another puzzle for her at every turn.

And Darius was not here either.

Carina left the dining room and ran on. The corridor ended at an elevator. Should she turn around and search the other rooms on that level? Carina guessed that if Darius was nearby he would have heard her calling. She shouted his name again and then, when he didn't reply, called the elevator and waited for it to arrive.

When the doors opened, Darius was standing inside.

"Stars!" Carina exclaimed. "There you are! Where have you been? You frightened me nearly to death."

In answer, Darius burst into tears.

"Oh, I'm sorry," said Carina, hugging him. "I didn't mean to scare you."

Between sobs, Darius said, "When I woke up I was all alone, so I tried to find you. But I couldn't so I took the elevator, but I couldn't remember which way to go or where the bridge was, or..."

"I was in the shower, that's all. I didn't leave you alone. I wouldn't ever do that. Look, let's forget about this and go to see the others, okay?"

Carina told the elevator to take them to the bridge. If Darius had simply done the same he wouldn't have gotten lost, but maybe he'd been panicking too much or his home on Ithiya hadn't contained any elevators.

They walked onto the bridge to find only Bryce there.

"Hey, Darius," he said. Then to Carina, "Where did you find him?" His eyes took in her new costume. "And what are you wearing? You look like a bandit."

"He was in the elevator," she replied. "I found some clean clothes in the closet in our room. You should take a look. Maybe it's time for a style update. Where are the others?"

"I don't think they've gotten much farther than searching this level. Hold on a minute." Bryce was sitting in the captain's chair. He opened the interface on the armrest and leaned over to speak into it. "Comm to all crew. This is your captain speaking. All hands to the bridge immediately."

As he spoke, Carina faintly heard his voice echoing in the corridor outside.

He closed the interface and grinned. "I've always wanted to

do that. Here, take this." He tossed her a comm button. "I'd prefer our conversations to be more private."

Carina fastened the button to her tunic with an uncomfortable familiarity. She hadn't worn a comm button since she'd been forced to join the Sherrerr military. How long ago had that been? Only a few months, but so much had happened since then it felt much longer.

Parthenia, Ferne, Oriana, and Nahla burst into the bridge.

"Woohoo!" Ferne said. "Here he is. Where did you get to, Darius?"

"I was looking for Carina."

"Ha!" said Ferne. "And *she* was looking for *you*."

"Right. But now we're finally all together," Carina said, "I want to tell you what we're doing today. First, we have to make plenty of elixir, using the—"

"Already on it," said Bryce. "I've deactivated the smoke alarm in the captain's study so the kids can make a fire in there. They were about to start when you comm'd me about Darius."

"Oh," Carina said, feeling somehow deflated. "In that case, after you've made some elixir, you can—"

"*Please* don't give us any more chores," said Oriana. "Making elixir is enough for today. We want to have fun. We haven't had any fun since the Matching."

"Yes," Ferne said. "We want to explore."

Carina hesitated. They were kids, after all. Even Parthenia was only fifteen.

"Okay," she relented.

Ferne and Oriana whooped. Even quiet, reserved Nahla looked pleased.

"But only after you've made ten liters of elixir," Carina added. She turned to Bryce. "I noticed we seem to have some real wood aboard. That'll come in handy if we need extra ingredients."

She recalled a chore she'd set for herself that day: to find out what was inside the packages in the hold.

"Can I leave you to supervise the kids for a while?" she asked. "I want to check the cargo."

"Sure," Bryce replied. "But go and eat something first. You'll be amazed at what you find in the stores."

5

Carina took an elevator down to level zero, the hold. The elevator panel also displayed levels minus one and minus two, which housed the engine rooms. She'd taken a brief survey of them during her watch, and she hoped she would have no need to pay a return visit. While she could fly a starship in a pinch she had no idea how to fix a starship's engine—or any other type of engine for that matter.

She would have to rely on the *Zenobia's* owner keeping her engines well maintained. But if the state of the less visible parts of the ship was anything to go by, that was probably the case. The more Carina saw of the vessel, the more she had the impression that someone wanted it to appear more decrepit to a cursory view than it actually was.

The hold looked unchanged from when she had Transported into it. She walked to the center and turned a slow circle, surveying the freight the ship was carrying.

Her comm chirruped.

"Hey," Carina answered.

"I just wanted to check you're okay," Bryce said.

"I've only been gone five minutes."

"Yeah, but like you said, we don't know if someone else is aboard the ship."

"I said that before I'd searched it," said Carina. "Now I'm pretty sure we're the only ones aboard."

"Well, I think it would be a good idea to maintain contact while we're apart. Just in case something bad happens."

Carina smiled. "You know, if you keep this up, the kids will talk about us. I already saw Ferne pretending he was going to vomit when he saw us hug the other day."

"Let them talk. I don't care."

"Wait, where are you?" Carina asked.

"On the bridge."

"So where are the kids?"

"They're here too."

"Are they listening to this conversation?"

"Yup."

Peals of laughter and excited giggling came from Carina's comm button. She smiled again. It was good to hear her siblings being kids again, free from the fear of capture for once, even if the luxury was only temporary.

"They've gone off to make elixir now," said Bryce. "We can talk freely."

"I'm not sure if I believe you. Besides, I can't talk. I need to check out this stuff."

"All right, but leave your button on."

Carina selected a tall, thin package to open first. She couldn't guess what it was from the shape. The netting covering it and adjacent packages ran from the floor to the ceiling, where it hung over hooks. Carina debated climbing up to unfasten it but she didn't want to risk falling. A Heal Cast might quickly fix her broken bones but she would rather not break them in the first place. Perhaps she should Cast Rise on each section of net where it was attached to a hook.

She wondered how the netting had been fixed up there. It

didn't seem possible without gymnastics that she was confident were beyond the capabilities of the average cargo handlers.

Suddenly the answer came to her. She scanned the room again. It had to be here somewhere, unless the handlers took it away when they left. Carina peered into a corner obscured by boxes. There it was: a cargo mech. The machine looked like it had seen better days. Its paint was chipped and its grips worn. Something else to give the impression the *Zenobia* was less upmarket than she was.

As Carina climbed into the machine, scenes of the Mech Battle event on Ostillon came back to her. What a night that had been, and what a finale, when the Sherrerrs had rained down hell on the Dirksen planet.

She started up the mech and grasped the manipulators, giving the grips a few turns to get the feel of them.

"What's that?" said Bryce.

Carina jumped a little. She'd forgotten he was listening in.

"Just a cargo mech," she replied.

"Ah, okay. Don't get into any fights in it."

"Har har."

Carina walked the mech out to the center of the bay and over to the netting that held the tall, thin parcel. She extended the grips all the way up to the ceiling and used the fine tips to lift the netting off the hooks. The thick, knotted ropes fell down, and, released from pressure, the tall package slipped to one side. Carina grasped it and laid it on the floor before turning off the mech and jumping down.

The wrapping was white and fibrous. Carina rolled the package over, looking for a label or anything that might tell her what was inside, but she found nothing. She took out her knife and cut a long slit. The wrapping was several layers deep and one of the layers was different from the others—a dense material flecked with metallic elements. Something to deflect or confuse scanning waves?

Carina paused. Did the package contain contraband? And if so, what kind? The first thing that sprang to mind was explosives, or perhaps the package contained a weapon. It would be a very unusual weapon. Despite digging down through five or six layers of wrapping the object inside still felt soft to the touch. Explosives could be soft but she'd never seen them packaged in such an odd way.

She proceeded with more care. To avoid further poking and prodding, she cut across each end of the slit and then peeled back one side. A final layer of the white material lay between her and the package's contents. She pushed in the knife tip and gently drew it along the edges of the space she'd created.

"You're awfully quiet," said Bryce.

Carina nearly leapt out of her skin. "Stars, do you have to keep doing that?"

"Sorry. Just checking in."

"Look, I'm going to turn off my button. I'll let you know if I find anything interesting." She closed the comm.

Carina put down her knife and lifted the corner of the layer she'd cut. Underneath it lay a dark blue substance decorated with orange swirls. She ran her fingertips along the surface. It felt exactly like…a *rug*.

She cut away at the wrapping, exposing more of the interior. The swirling pattern continued to spread out over the dark blue background.

A freaking rug! And she'd been worried it might be explosives.

The rug was probably a cultural artifact prohibited from export or perhaps it contained a substance banned from use in manufacturing. She knew that applied to some dyes made from poisonous plants.

Or maybe the rug wasn't the contraband. Was it hiding something more illegal?

She cut off the remainder of the wrapping and rolled the

rug out on the floor of the hold. Nothing was hidden inside it, though that didn't mean it wasn't hiding anything. She'd heard of smugglers soaking materials with banned pharmaceuticals in order to sneak them through customs. She bent down and sniffed the rug but she couldn't detect anything unusual in its scent. It smelled old which probably meant her initial guess that it was a cultural artifact was correct.

Carina sat back on her heels and looked around at the other parcels stored in the hold, wondering what interesting items they might contain.

She rose to her feet. It was time to find out.

A COUPLE OF HOURS LATER, Carina was surrounded by opened packages. She'd discovered animal parts, both dried and bottled; jewelry; paintings; ornate furniture; technology she didn't recognize; and a host of other eclectic items. More importantly, stashed inside some she'd also found pills and powders she guessed were illegal drugs. This was not the baggage of a rich family traveling between the stars. The *Zenobia* belonged to a smuggler.

Carina had no strong feelings one way or the other about smuggling. In the past she'd even contemplated joining the trade to get herself out of a tight spot. Trading in stolen and illicit items probably wasn't the most moral activity, but people like the Dirksens and Sherrerrs did far worse things. Smugglers were only trying to make a living, not subjugate entire populations to their will.

But the revelation posed a serious problem. The *Zenobia's* owner was not a local businessman, who would report the ship's theft to the authorities and just claim on the insurance. This ship and her contents probably represented a significant portion of her owner's wealth, and there might not be insurance to claim. The smuggler would be furious at the loss of the vessel and its precious cargo. He or she would stop at nothing to get it back and punish the thieves who had taken it. What was more, the ship was probably fitted with a powerful tracking beacon for the exact eventuality that had befallen it.

Carina comm'd Bryce.

"You're talking to me again?" he asked.

"I think we may be in trouble."

"What? Why?"

"Are the kids there?" she asked, suddenly remembering their earlier conversation.

"No. They're all gone. They made the elixir and then they went off to explore. What kind of trouble?"

"The big kind. I found—"

The chatter of excited voices came over the comm. The children had returned to the bridge and they were talking over each other, trying to be the first to tell Bryce something. Carina couldn't make any sense out of their babble.

"Quiet down," she heard Bryce say, followed by, "Parthenia, tell me what this is about."

Carina heard her sister say in a soft, serious tone: "We think someone else is aboard the ship."

6

"Someone *did* move it!" Ferne exclaimed. "They did!"

Carina was skeptical. The children's claim that they'd spotted signs of a stowaway was turning out to be less than reliable. Bryce had remained on the bridge so she wasn't sure how much he knew regarding the evidence for their assertion.

"I put it in the corner," said Ferne, "but now it's next to my bed."

Carina looked at the object of contention. The backpack's appearance was no different from the last time she'd seen it. Why would an intruder bother to move an old, weather-stained bag from one side of a room to another? It made no sense.

"It's true," Oriana added, her arms folded to convey her earnestness. "He definitely put it in the corner. I saw him. And when we came back after making the elixir it had moved."

Ferne and Oriana had picked a suite with twin beds for themselves. The room was similarly opulent to Carina and Bryce's, though a little smaller.

Carina surveyed the room. She was surprised her brother and sister could tell the place was any different from how they'd left it that morning. They'd discovered the hidden wardrobe and seemed to have transferred most of its contents to the floor and bed. The door to their en suite. stood open, and the mess inside was just as bad.

"All right," said Carina. "Let's say we accept that your backpack mysteriously ended up in a different place from where you put it. Did you check inside? Is anything missing?"

"I had a quick look," Ferne replied. "But everything seemed to be there."

Carina restrained herself from rolling her eyes. If a stowaway were aboard ship it was a serious matter. She had to investigate the possibility thoroughly before she dismissed it.

"If you want me to explain why they moved it, I can't," Ferne said, his cheeks coloring. "But I'm one hundred percent positive it was moved, and Oriana agrees with me."

"That isn't the only thing, Carina," said Parthenia.

Carina turned toward her sister. At fifteen years old, she was a more convincing witness than the others.

"Did something move in your room too?" Carina asked.

"No, but..." Parthenia glanced at Nahla, who hung her head. Then the teen looked back at her older sister.

"Can I show you?"

"Sure," Carina said. "Lead the way."

Parthenia went ahead and the group passed several doors in the corridor. Eighteen or twenty passengers could live aboard the *Zenobia* comfortably. Parthenia stopped at a door like all the others.

"Ferne and Oriana have to stay out," Nahla said in an uncharacteristically forceful tone.

Little Nahla, only a couple of years older than Darius and the only non-mage of the siblings, was usually also the quietest and most self-effacing.

Oriana raised her eyebrows at her twin, who shrugged. "Okay. We won't come in."

"What about me?" Darius asked.

"You wait outside too," said Nahla.

Darius accepted his exclusion pragmatically.

Parthenia touched the security panel and the door opened.

"You activated the room security?" asked Carina.

"I did after I saw what had happened while we were gone."

Parthenia had taken Nahla under her wing since they'd boarded the *Zenobia*. Their room was similar to Ferne and Oriana's but much tidier. Here, it wouldn't be hard to tell if something was out of place.

The only messy area in the room was one of the beds. The covers hung off of it, as if the occupant's sleep had been restless.

Something was bothering Nahla. She'd buried her face in her hands.

"It's okay," said Parthenia. "No one believes it was you."

Her words didn't have their intended effect as the little girl began to cry.

"What's wrong?" Carina asked.

Parthenia walked to the messy bed and silently gestured at the under sheet. A wet patch sat in the center, the edges drying to a faint yellow stain.

"I didn't do it!" Nahla wailed.

"Did you make the beds this morning?" Carina asked Parthenia.

"Only mine. Nahla made her own. But I'm sure I would have noticed if..."

"But when you came back this bed had been unmade?"

"That's right. And Nahla was with me the whole time we were away. She couldn't have snuck back, and if she had, why wouldn't she just use the bathroom?"

Carina squatted down in order to give Nahla a hug. "It's okay, sweetie. Don't be sad. I believe you." She actually hadn't quite made up her mind about it but she didn't want the girl to feel bad. Kids sometimes did weird things, especially when they were upset or worried.

Nahla's sobs eased, and Carina left her to tell Oriana and Ferne to go to the dining room, where she would meet them in a few minutes for lunch.

The twins tried to peer around her into the bedroom when she opened the door, but she blocked their view. When they'd left, she said to Parthenia, "Help me put this dirty laundry in the chute. Then I want you and Nahla to pick another room. We'll move your things over before we join Ferne and Oriana."

As they worked, Carina tried to imagine the reason behind the strange occurrences in the children's rooms. The obvious answer pushed its way to the forefront of her mind but she tried to ignore it, attempting to believe the more prosaic solutions: Ferne was mistaken about where he'd left his backpack and Nahla had wet the bed and then tried to cover it up.

If only.

The events that preceded the departure of the *Zenobia* led her to a different conclusion. She resolved to speak to Bryce about it privately before saying anything to the kids.

FERNE AND ORIANA'S discovery of a printer in the ship's galley had driven all their earlier excitement about the possible stowaway from their minds.

When Carina entered the dining room, Oriana ran to grab her hand and tug her to the galley. She guessed what her sister wanted to show her. She'd spotted the device during her search of the ship while the others slept.

"We didn't even have one of these on Ithiya," said Ferne, gaping at the machine. "I've seen pictures but I've never seen one in real life. And we have it all to ourselves!"

"I guess it is pretty cool," Carina said, finding his delight infectious despite her nagging worries about the *Zenobia's* smuggler owner and the hidden unwanted passenger. "Do you know how to work it?"

"No," answered Ferne. "Do you?"

"We used to have one aboard the *Duchess*," Carina replied. "It belonged to the owner, and the cook wasn't supposed to use it for anyone else. He did, though. You just put some gloopy stuff in and tell it what you want." The cook had been taking a risk feeding the soldiers from the owner's precious printer, but he hated the woman as much as everyone else.

Carina opened a cupboard above the machine. The rows of packets inside appeared similar to the ones she remembered from her days as a merc.

"Was the *Duchess* another ship you were on?" Parthenia asked as Carina retrieved a few packets of gloop.

Carina paused, unsure how much to say right then. The girl was old enough to hear the entire story of Carina's life before she was taken captive by Stefan Sherrerr, but the other kids were a little young yet.

In the end she said simply, "It was the ship I took Darius to after I rescued him. Do you remember it?" she asked her brother.

"I remember seeing you in a hospital," he replied.

"Yes," said Carina. "We talked in the sick bay." It had been there that Darius had proudly told her he'd seen her Cast, and put her in fear for both of them.

"I wish we had all your friends with us," Darius said. "Then we wouldn't have to run away all the time. They would protect us."

"My friends?"

"The other fighters, like you," explained Darius.

"Oh." Carina wondered what Darius had made of her fellow mercs. When he'd first seen her he'd been terrified—understandably considering what the Dirksens had put him through—but it appeared he'd lost his fear of her and the other soldiers. Probably not wise; even she had found them scary.

"We would have to pay them *a lot* of money if we wanted them to protect us." Then she changed the subject. "So, you put the base ingredient in here," she said, lifting the lid on a reservoir. "Do you all know what you want yet?"

"I want custard," Ferne announced.

"For lunch?" Carina asked.

"Yep."

"Okay," she said. "Just this once. That should be easy. But if you want it a certain way you'll have to tell the machine."

"I would love an apple," Parthenia said. "I haven't eaten an apple in ages."

"You might be disappointed," said Carina. "It'll make something that looks like an apple but you'll probably find the structure isn't quite the same."

She left the kids to play with the meal printer and walked out into the empty dining room to comm Bryce.

"I was just about to tell you I'll be down to join you for lunch," said Bryce when he answered.

"Can you wait a while? I don't think it's a good idea for the bridge to be left unattended."

"You mean because of our stowaway? You think the kids are right?"

"I think *something's* going on, and it's more than likely it isn't one of the kids who's doing it. Which only leaves one conclusion." Carina couldn't deny the facts any longer. There could only be one person who would be interested in the contents of Ferne's backpack, and who would pee on Nahla's bed.

"No kidding," Bryce said.

"Yeah, and I think I know who it is."

"Huh? How? Have you been reading the ship's data files?"

"I don't need to. This person doesn't have anything to do with the *Zenobia*. It's Castiel."

7

When Carina arrived on the bridge, Bryce had a holo of the ship's interior up and running.

The *Zenobia's* decks and rooms were clearly outlined in glowing green, with fixtures contrasted in red.

"Cool," said Carina. "That'll help us find him."

Before she could say any more, however, Bryce strode over to her and took her in his arms.

It was a pleasurable while before his lips parted from hers. They hadn't kissed since that unfortunate time at the Matching when Carina had sought to numb her emotional pain with an intimate encounter. Bryce had quite rightly refused her but she was over the embarrassment now.

"I've wanted to do that for ages," said Bryce, still holding her.

"Mmm, me too," Carina said. "We never seem to get a moment to ourselves, do we?"

"It isn't easy with the kids around all the time, and there's always something more important to do."

"Like find our stowaway," said Carina.

Bryce released her and, hand in hand, they walked over to the holo. "What makes you think it's Castiel?"

Carina explained about how Ferne's backpack—containing the soil needed to make elixir—had been moved. Then she explained about the urine in Nahla's bed.

"I have to admit," Bryce said, "we could explain away Ferne's backpack by saying he's mistaken, but pissing in Nahla's bed sounds exactly like something Castiel would do. He probably hates her most out of all of them because she went over to their side. But how did he know the bed was hers?"

"I guess he saw her old clothes on it." All the children had quickly availed themselves of the luxurious adult garments stored in their rooms, coming up with imaginative outfits for their smaller bodies.

"What an asshole," said Bryce.

"He's more than that," said Carina. "He's dangerous. We're lucky the kids have gotten into the habit of always carrying their canisters of elixir with them, or he would have been able to steal it from their rooms. At least he has to make his own, though now he has the soil he needs."

"And water and metal are easy to come by." Bryce said. "You were saying you found real wood on the ship..."

"So he only needs fire, and if he understands how to short an electrical circuit that won't be difficult."

"And then we're screwed."

"Exactly." Carina studied the holo of the ship. "I take it this isn't an internal scan?" She couldn't see any figures or objects or the contents of the hold.

"No," Bryce replied. "I guess the ship must have one but this is all I could bring up for now. It's only a blueprint."

"It's still useful. I'm confident we've searched every area of the ship. I can't figure out how I missed him last night...Or maybe I can." Carina added. "I didn't know about the closets in the cabins. He could have hidden inside one of them."

"But why is he even here?" asked Bryce. "I thought he hated you guys. Why isn't he staying with his new friends, the Dirksens?"

"It isn't really that strange," Carina replied. "Remember how he was handcuffed to Reyes when they surprised us at that old woman's house? He even said he couldn't command the soldiers. It's pretty clear to me he hadn't achieved the status among the Dirksens he imagined he would and they were treating him like a servant, or even a slave. And remember what he said when he Transported after the fight to take the ship? He said Darius had given him his freedom."

"But he had elixir then," said Bryce, "or he wouldn't have been able to Cast. Why does he need to make more?"

"I guess the Dirksens only let him have a little at a time. Maybe he Transported off the ship and then back onto it again after he realized he was better off leaving Pirine with us, so he's used most of—*Damn!*" Carina had just recalled her revelation about the *Zenobia's* hidden purpose.

In response to Bryce's questioning look, she said, "I forgot to tell you, we're in deeper trouble than only having a Dark Mage aboard. I think we stole a smuggler's ship."

"Ah," said Bryce. "All those weird packages in the hold. What did you find?"

"A lot of stuff, mostly illegal from what I could tell. The *Zenobia* is masquerading as private interstellar transportation so it won't be subjected to the usual cargo inspections of commercial craft. The owner must be greasing the palms of customs officials to avoid spot checks too."

"The good news just keeps coming today," Bryce said.

"No kidding. When I was a merc I didn't have much to do with smugglers," continued Carina, "but they were in the same shady line of business as merc bands. One thing I learned was that you never mess with them. The money stakes they deal in are high and if you cost them a trade—by accident or otherwise

—they'll soon tell you about it. And they really don't take it well if someone steals their stuff. This ship is sure to be fitted with a high-powered tracker."

"Won't Darius's Cloak block the signal?" Bryce asked.

"Your guess is as good as mine on that," replied Carina. "One thing's for sure: that Cast doesn't last forever. In between Darius's Cloaks that tracker is going to be yelling at the top of its lungs all the way back to Pirine and for hundreds of light years all around. I'm taking the long way back to Ostillon, with plenty of course deviations, but the owner of this vessel is going to find it eventually."

"With any luck we'll be long gone by then."

"I hope so, but to be on the safe side we'd better leave the cargo intact. Then, if the *Zenobia's* owner discovers our identities, he or she will understand we were never trying to steal their stuff. Whether that'll make them deal with us more leniently, I don't know. Smugglers are an unpredictable bunch. Some are worse than the most psychotic mercs I've ever known."

Bryce puffed up his cheeks and exhaled. "All right. One thing at a time. Let's find your evil shit of a brother. Then we can worry about a smuggler's vengeance."

"Yeah," Carina agreed. "We should divide up the ship into sections. When the kids have eaten, they can...Wait. Where's the elixir they made?"

"Over there." Bryce pointed to two twenty-liter containers on the floor near the pilot's seat.

"Good," said Carina. "I was worried they'd left it unattended. Castiel won't dare approach them to steal theirs while they're together. He wouldn't be a match for them as a group, and especially not as long as they have Darius with them. What was I saying? Oh, yes. When the kids have eaten we'll split into two search parties and secure the bridge so Castiel can't access any of the ship's controls or that elixir. Then, we find him."

"And then what?" Bryce asked. "What do we do with him?"

"I haven't decided yet. The wisest option would be to space him, but even if I *could* do that to my own blood, knowing how Ma loved him in spite of what he is, I couldn't do it in front of his brothers and sisters. What would that do to them?"

"What'll he do to *us* if we don't?"

"This ship must have a brig or something similar. If we lock him up, without elixir, he should be powerless for the rest of the voyage."

"And then?" asked Bryce. "What happens when we land at Ostillon?"

"Like you said, one thing at a time."

Carina studied the holo of the ship closely. The passenger areas were already familiar to her but Castiel was unlikely to be hanging around them during the active period aboard ship. He was probably in the crew section, or he might even have gone down to the hold.

"Does the ship's operations data show when the elevators are in use in real time?" Carina asked.

"I'm not sure." Bryce turned to the interface on the arm of the captain's seat.

Carina watched him as he checked for the function. Bryce's physique had matured since they'd first met. His body had thrown off the effects of the Ithiyan plague and he'd gained bulk, but not in an unpleasing way.

Despite the threatening situation they were in, Carina couldn't resist taking hold of his arm and pulling him toward her, going in for another kiss while they had some rare, precious time alone.

The bridge door opened. "Yuuuuuck!" exclaimed Ferne as he burst onto the bridge. "They're smooching," he said in a disgusted tone to his siblings behind him.

The five children crowded in the open doorway.

"I think it's romantic," said Oriana.

"It's *private*," Parthenia said. "Sorry we busted in. We'll leave you alone and come back later."

"No, it's fine," said Carina. "I need to explain a few things to you anyway. We have an important job to do, and I'm not sure how you'll feel about it."

The children came all the way into the room.

Carina went on, "I think we—"

A piercing whistle interrupted her. She winced and put her hands over her ears. "What's—"

"Fire alarm," yelled Bryce, his gaze on the captain's interface. "Crew's galley." He lifted his eyes to make contact with Carina's. "We've found him."

8

Carina sprinted from the bridge to the nearest service ladder access point, shouting to Bryce, "Take the elevator!"

Castiel would be leaving the galley in the crew's section, two levels below, now that his attempt to start a fire had triggered the alarm. Carina couldn't guess what direction he would take, but if Bryce approached from another angle they doubled their chance of catching him.

She tore open the door and jumped into the tunnel, grabbing the side rails of the ladder. Dropping several rungs at a time in her haste to reach the crew's quarters, the rails slid through her hands as she descended. Level four flew past and level three soon approached. Carina unhitched the door and leapt out.

But which way was the galley? She paused as she recalled the ship's holo then ran left. Another sound was rising above the alarm, a hissing sound. Carina saw clouds of powder in the passageway ahead. She arrived at the galley, but the air inside was thick with white powder, puffing out from overhead fire extinguishers.

She coughed, choking on the dry dust. She pulled her tunic up over her nose, swung her weapon forward and, squinting, entered the room. Metal worktops and cupboard doors loomed from the translucent atmosphere. The powder was settling on everything, dulling the shiny surfaces.

Had she arrived in time to catch Castiel? Probably not, but he might still be hiding somewhere in there. If Carina were in his situation, she might have remained in the galley, out of sight, guessing that her pursuers would think she'd left.

She coughed again, deeply. The white powder was also stinging her eyes and making them weep. She would have to leave for a moment.

As Carina stepped back through the doorway, she met Bryce. The children were running up.

"Sorry it took us a while," Bryce said. "I had to make sure the bridge was secure before we left."

"No problem," said Carina. "Good thinking."

"Any sign of him?" he asked.

"Not that I can see," she replied, "but it's hard to see anything in there."

"He must have left as soon as the alarm sounded."

"Maybe, but—"

"Did you catch Castiel?" Oriana asked as she reached them. "Is he in there?"

Bryce had clearly told the others about Carina's deduction that their brother was the stowaway.

"Let's move away from here," Carina suggested, shepherding the children down the passage. If Castiel *was* still in the galley, she didn't want him to overhear her telling them that might be the case.

A few meters from the doorway, they stopped.

"Are we going to search for him?" Ferne asked Carina.

"Yes. But we have to be methodical about it. I don't want anyone deviating from the plan or he could slip through our fingers. And you must be careful. Castiel may have elixir with him, though probably not much or he wouldn't be trying to make more."

"I wish we had something of his," said Parthenia. "It would be so much easier to Cast Locate."

"Wishing isn't going to help us," Carina said, "but we can catch him. It's five mages against one. As soon as you have him in your sight Cast Enthrall. Then he'll come quietly."

"Then we can make him do whatever we want," said Ferne.

"Except we aren't going to do that, are we," Carina said. It wasn't a question. "We treat even Enthralled people with dignity, right?"

"He doesn't deserve any dignity," said Ferne. "He knew the Dirksens were going to massacre the mages and he didn't care."

"Our treatment of him isn't about him," Carina said. "It's about us." She waited a beat for her meaning to sink in. "If Bryce or I see him first we can stun him. Parthenia, are you okay with leading a search party? One person will have to restrain him to give the other time to Cast Enthrall."

When her sister nodded, Carina continued, "I'm going to Lock the elevator doors and the doors to the service tunnels. We'll Transport between the decks and search each room thoroughly, one by one. When he's found Castiel will try to bolt."

She ran her gaze over the waiting children, considering how best to divide them up. She wanted to keep Darius with her because he was so little. On the other hand, she and he were the two strongest mages and if he stayed with her it would leave the others more vulnerable.

A sudden movement from the direction of the galley caught her eye.

"There he goes!" shouted Ferne.

Castiel had burst out of the room and was pelting down the passageway.

"Enthrall him, Darius," Carina called as she aimed her weapon at him.

Castiel was heading for the service tunnel she had used to come down to the crew's section. He was nearly there.

She fired but missed. When she fired again, Castiel had slammed open the door, and her round hit it. Then he was gone.

"He was too fast," said Darius.

Carina was already running toward the service tunnel. As soon as she reached it she leaned inside, angling her weapon downward, but she could only see a short distance.

"Dammit!"

She climbed inside and onto the ladder. The top of Castiel's head was below her, growing smaller as he hurriedly descended. Clinging to the ladder with one arm, she fired at it. In the narrow space the flash of the pulse round blinded her.

When she could see again, Castiel was gone.

She'd heard a door open in the distance. Her brother must have exited the tunnel on another level, most likely the level directly below, but she couldn't be sure.

She climbed out of the tunnel. "At least we know one thing," she said to the others. "He's short on elixir, if he has any at all, or he would have Transported out of the galley and not risked being captured. But that's also going to make him desperate and dangerous. We all know how little he cares about anyone except himself, so please take care as we go after him. Parthenia and Darius, help me Cast Lock on all the exits on each level, then we'll all Transport to the level below us and start our search there."

She re-entered the service tunnel to Lock the doors from the inside, but as she did so she heard a door below her open. A couple of levels down, Castiel appeared.

Hastily, Carina aimed at him. But it was hard to shoot straight one-handed while hanging off a ladder. Again, her shot went wide, dissolving harmlessly against the tunnel wall and Castiel disappeared.

But now she knew exactly where he was.

Carina spoke to the others through the doorway, reluctant to leave the tunnel in case Castiel moved again. "He's in the hold. We'll approach it from both tunnels and the elevator, Locking all the exits as we go down." She quickly divided them up: Parthenia and Nahla, Bryce and Darius, and Ferne and Oriana, who were to come with her. They would meet up outside the hold and enter it together.

Aside from worrying about the children's well-being, she hoped the inevitable fight wouldn't damage the smuggled goods badly. She'd left them strewn over the floor of the chamber, intending to repackage them at a more convenient time.

A couple of minutes later, Carina climbed out of the service tunnel with Ferne and Oriana into the passageway to the hold. Bryce and Darius emerged next, and then Parthenia and Nahla. No one had spotted Castiel moving between the levels. He was still there, somewhere amongst the artworks, luxurious furnishings, drug shipments and the rest of the various stolen and illegal cargo.

After a brief discussion, they had their plan. Bryce would remain at the hold's only exit after Carina Locked it. As well as being a second gun, if Castiel managed to Cast Unlock, he would be a physical barrier to the Dark Mage's escape. Carina and the children would form a line and walk slowly across the chamber, searching the hold. They should be able to capture Castiel easily.

The hold looked the same as it had when she'd left it. The place was a real mess. She hadn't tried to be tidy as she'd unwrapped the many packages. She'd been too keen to discover what they contained. Among the many objects, empty boxes, netting, and discarded packaging, there were many places to hide. In the corner stood the mech, its operator compartment empty.

Carina gestured to her siblings to spread out along the nearest wall. Parthenia went to one corner and Ferne to the other.

When they had all formed a line, Carina swept her arms forward. They all began to walk across the room. The white carpet wrapping lay across Carina's path. She lifted it with the toe of her boot and peered beneath it. Nothing.

To her right, Oriana overturned a box. It was empty. Parthenia pressed lumps in the carpet with her feet. Ferne peered into the foot well of a desk. Darius looked behind a painting propped against a trunk.

The searchers worked in silence, moving items quietly to avoid giving Castiel notice of their close approach. Tension stretched taut in the hush, the gentle rustle and scrape as objects were moved the only noise.

By the time they'd crossed half the room, Carina's heart was in her mouth. Each passing second she expected Castiel to leap from his hiding place and try to make his escape. Or had he already Transported?

As she advanced, she was holding her weapon in one hand and her open elixir flask in the other. Castiel was spiteful and evil enough to Cast Split if he was cornered, and Carina dreaded not being able to Repel it in time.

Suddenly, a flurry of movement disturbed the mess of cargo. Nahla screamed. In another second, she was gone, dragged down by her ankle into a jumbled pile of boxes. Carina flew toward the spot and ripped away the boxes. She saw Castiel holding Nahla around her waist. In his other hand he held a canister. His eyes were closed.

"No!" Carina yelled. She lunged at the two of them, but her hands snatched empty air.

9

They crowded into the elevator. Bryce had made the sensible suggestion that their priority now was to protect the bridge. The hub of the ship's operations, it was the place Castiel could do the most harm. Carina was uncertain Castiel knew how to fly and navigate a starship but she couldn't deny the potential damage her half-brother could do from there.

The thought of Nahla as the creep's captive made Carina sick to her stomach. The sweet girl had been the butt of all Castiel's bitterness and rage, built up over the years of growing up without any special powers in a family of mages. Who knew what he was currently doing to his younger sister? Taking out his revenge on her, not only for her abandonment of him but also all that he probably suffered at the hands of the Dirksens.

Darius began to sob. He pushed his face into his little, chubby hands and wailed.

"Hey," said Bryce, squatting down and hugging him. "Don't worry. We'll get her back."

"He's feeling everything we're feeling," Carina explained. "All of us. Even you, I think."

The knowledge that Darius was a sponge to all the despair and sadness among the group made her feel wretched but she didn't know what to do about it. Except to make Castiel give Nahla up. Then they would deal with him.

The elevator stopped and the doors opened. The bridge door was closed but that didn't mean a whole lot. When Carina approached it didn't respond.

"I set it to only open for me," said Bryce. He pressed his palm against the panel and the door slid to one side.

The bridge was empty.

"Thank the stars for that," Bryce said, walking immediately to the captain's interface. "I'll restrict access to—"

"Where's the elixir?!" exclaimed Parthenia.

Carina swiveled to face the spot she'd seen the container. It was gone. She groaned. Castiel must have used his last mouthful of elixir to Transport himself and Nahla to the bridge, probably intending to take over the ship, when he'd come across an unexpected prize.

For the first time in all her encounters with Castiel, Carina began to feel afraid. From the looks on her siblings' faces, they felt the same fear. A Dark Mage with a large supply of elixir could wreak havoc.

Ferne clapped a hand over his mouth and his eyes widened. "The soil!"

"That's right," said Carina. "He knows where it is. Go and get it Ferne. If he takes it all we won't be able to make any more elixir. Then we'll never beat him. Go with him, Oriana. I don't want anyone moving around the ship alone."

Ferne and Oriana left. Even as a pair Carina was concerned about them. Should they all travel around as a group in case Castiel struck again? She was confused, unnerved by the amount of power Castiel now had over them.

"I don't think he'll hurt any of us," said Parthenia. "He wants us to work for him, the same as Father did."

"If he hurts Nahla I'll kill him," said Carina.

"Will you, Carina?" asked Darius, his teary eyes blinking. "Are you going to kill Castiel like Mother killed Father?"

The comment froze Carina's heart. Parthenia began to weep.

"No," Carina said. "Not like that." She'd never been sure how much Darius had seen of his father's death aboard the Sherrerr flagship, the *Nightfall*, when Ma had Split her rapist and torturer in two. Too much, clearly.

Yet the problem of what to do with Castiel if she caught him resurfaced., and catching him was the absolute priority now. He might spare the mages due to their usefulness to him but the same didn't apply to Nahla or Bryce. Their only value lay in emotionally blackmailing the mages to do Castiel's bidding—threatening to hurt them in order to exert pressure, exactly as his father had done. Yet Castiel could use the mage siblings themselves for that.

"But what *will* you do?" asked Parthenia.

"Let's just concentrate on catching him first," said Bryce.

"I know he's a terrible person," Parthenia persisted, "and I know he's hurt Nahla, but I don't think you should kill him."

"You don't think he deserves to die?" asked Carina. "What about all the people he killed when he went to war with the Dirksens?" She herself had seen a shuttle Split during flight, to crash in flames.

"Haven't you also killed people in battle?" Parthenia asked in return.

Carina couldn't answer. She had been responsible for more deaths than she could count. But that had been when she'd been a merc. She hadn't used her mage powers to kill then, and when Stefan Sherrerr had forced her to she'd felt dirty and disgusted with herself. Somehow, killing as a soldier felt cleaner and more honest. It felt fairer.

But if she tried to articulate her reasoning to Parthenia she was sure it would sound like a cop-out.

"If the tables were reversed," Carina asked instead, "do you think he would spare you? You know his only concern for you is what you can do for him."

"I don't know," said Parthenia. "I really don't know. Maybe the fact I'm his sister might count for something. But whatever the truth of it is, you can't execute someone for a crime they might commit."

"Dammit!" exclaimed Carina. "I only want to protect you all. You know how evil he is."

Ferne burst onto the bridge, gripping his backpack in both hands. "I've got it!" he panted. "He didn't take it."

Oriana was behind him.

"That's something at least," said Carina. "Now we need to figure out a plan to catch him. It won't be easy now he's taken the elixir you made, but there's still only one of him and five of us."

"Please don't kill him," begged Darius, his lower lip trembling and tears running down his cheeks again.

"Are you going to kill Castiel?" Ferne asked Carina, his eyes round.

In some ways, the siblings' attachment to their malevolent brother was touching. In others, it was extremely frustrating. "I haven't decided what I'm going to do. At the moment it's beside the point."

"I don't know about everyone else," Oriana said, "but I believe that would be wrong."

"Yeah," said Ferne. "It's not about *him*, Carina. It's about *you*."

She glared at her brother.

Then she gasped, "I know how to find him."

Without another word she ran out of the bridge and along the corridor to the elevator. As the doors opened she sprang out. She couldn't afford to waste a second. If Castiel realized the mistake he'd made he could fix it easily. He already knew where Nahla's cabin was.

Carina sped through the open door into the room. Warm relief flooded her when she saw that Nahla's old clothes, which she'd worn in the weeks since leaving Langley Dirksen's estate, remained neatly folded on her bed.

Silently thanking the stars that the little girl hadn't put the garments down the garbage chute as they deserved, Carina picked them up. Holding them under one arm, she opened her flask and took a sip of elixir.

The Locate Cast zoomed in on a cabin in the crew's quarters. Carina didn't need to know if Castiel was there too. If he'd tied Nahla up and left her there, he would be back eventually.

Carina opened her eyes. Now all she had to do was to Transport herself there.

But something made her hesitate. Was it a trap? Had Castiel thought ahead and deliberately left Nahla's clothes alone, knowing Carina would use them to find her?

But so what if it was? Castiel could only Cast, whereas she had a gun.

She sipped elixir again, and Transported.

Arriving in the cabin, Carina only had time for the briefest assessment of the situation. First, she saw Nahla, tied to a bed, a rag filling her mouth. Bruises besmirched the little girl's soft, clear skin. The rest of the room seemed empty. Except...Nahla's gaze broke from Carina's and turned upward.

There he was. Castiel crouched just below the ceiling, one foot on the open door of a cupboard and the other on the corner of the door jamb. One hand was pressed against the wall for support and the other held a flask. His eyes were closed.

Carina had the opportunity for one good shot. It was all she'd ever needed.

She fired. She did not miss this time.

She made no effort to break his fall and relished the sound of his bones breaking as he hit the floor.

10

Castiel was not a quiet or compliant prisoner. After carrying him to the brig and reluctantly Healing his broken arm, Carina avoided setting eyes on him as much as possible. She asked Bryce to take charge of feeding him and seeing that his other basic needs were met because she didn't want any of her brothers or sisters to visit him. She was worried their shared history might soften them to his wiles. Perhaps he would persuade one of them to set him free or give him elixir, which amounted to the same thing.

All she could do to prevent that from happening was keep a close eye on her siblings' activities so she knew where most of them were most of the time. She didn't want to outright forbid visits to their eldest brother in case it had the opposite effect and encouraged them to defy her. Oriana and Ferne were of an age where they liked to be contrary just for the sake of it, and though Parthenia seemed to have forgiven Carina for Enthralling her, any further attempts at exerting control would not be well received.

Rather than using heavy-handed tactics to keep her siblings away from Castiel, Carina was trying to employ softer means.

She was trying to make their lives aboard the *Zenobia* as it traveled its slow, zigzagging journey to Ostillon pleasant and fun and a distraction from their brother's deservedly isolated and lonely time in the brig.

It wasn't easy. Her capacity to act as a replacement for Ma was limited. Since Nai Nai had died, her life had been hard. Living on the streets between the ages of ten and sixteen, she'd received no kindnesses or affection, heard no gentle words. Her days had been spent skulking in shadows, avoiding detection and the brutal treatment usually meted out to gutter rats.

And after Captain Speidel had rescued her and inducted her into the Black Dogs, things hadn't improved much. She'd been guaranteed a full belly and creds at least, but mercs were a tough lot, often bordering on psychotic. If you didn't give as good as you got they would crush you for your weakness. No one wanted to be in a firefight with someone with no guts.

Her experiences had left her messed up, she knew. She loved her siblings dearly—with the exception of Castiel—but sometimes she struggled to show it, especially when they were being exceptionally annoying.

One activity she'd instituted to build bonds between her and her little family was to tell them all she knew about mages. It was important they understood why they were going to Ostillon and what she hoped to discover there.

Another activity she encouraged was for everyone to sit together for the main meals of the day. Though sometimes the bickering and whining, particularly of Oriana and Ferne, made her grind her teeth, she did her best to not react. However, she would catch Bryce smiling in response to the faces she pulled.

One dinner soon threatened to test her patience again. She had just asked Darius if he'd remembered to Cast Cloak over the ship that day when Oriana dropped her cutlery with a clatter and suddenly burst into tears.

Ferne, exhibited his characteristic brotherly love by rolling his eyes and saying, "For stars' sake, what is it now?"

It took several moments for Oriana to compose herself sufficiently to speak coherently. "I know it's stupid, but I don't know how old I am."

This comment drew a confused silence around the dining table.

"You're twelve, the same age as me, you idiot," said Ferne. "What's wrong with you? Are you getting space sick?"

"Are we twelve, though?" Oriana asked. "I'm sure our birthday was weeks ago. Now we've left Ithiya how can we tell how old we are? Ostillon and Pirine both take longer to circle their suns. Their years were longer, though their days were shorter, and they had different names for the months."

Though Oriana was over-emotional about it, her meaning was sound. Carina herself had kept only a rough tally of time passing after she'd left her home planet. Aboard the *Duchess* it hadn't been too hard to track the days and months according to ship time, but after she'd resigned to pursue her quest of discovering the mages on Ithiya, things had become trickier. Even she wasn't certain if she was now nineteen.

People who spent most of their lives aboard starships lived according to ship time. Most other regular folk rarely left their home planet. But those who lived on and off ships existed in a confusion. If they wanted to know their biological age they could ask a splicer but as far as Carina knew, they rarely did.

Why did it matter how old you were? Why wasn't an approximation good enough? Carina's gut reaction to Oriana's outburst was similar to Ferne's. She wanted to tell her sister off for being self-centered and silly, but she swallowed the harsh words that sprang to her lips. Perhaps there was more to Oriana's complaint than she was stating.

Carina said, "I guess back at your home on Ithiya birthdays were a big thing?"

Oriana nodded glumly. "We would have a party and a cake, and Father would give us so many presents."

"It was about the only time he was nice to us," said Ferne wistfully.

Carina could only imagine how Stefan Sherrerr's pleasure at the anniversary of his children's births, the products of rape, would have made Ma feel, but she kept quiet. It takes a great deal of cruelty and abuse to crush a child's love for its parent, and she guessed that by the time her siblings had grown old enough to notice what went on in their household, Stefan's behavior had moderated somewhat. Despite all that he'd done to them, there was a part of his children's hearts that missed him as well as the luxurious life they had led in his care.

"I have an idea," Carina said. "Let's have a birthday party now."

"What?" Parthenia said. "For whom? How do you know whose birthday it is?"

"Let's make it all our birthdays." Carina shrugged. "You can be sixteen, Bryce and I will turn nineteen, the twins can become thirteen, Nahla will be nine and Darius will be seven."

"Woohoo!" Darius exclaimed, "I'm seven!"

Parthenia went to speak, as if to pour cold water on the idea, but then her mouth closed and she smiled. "I think I'd like to be sixteen."

"The let's celebrate," Carina suggested. "Let's print a cake."

"Cool!" exclaimed Oriana. "We'll put all our names on it. We can design it together."

"I want chocolate," said Ferne.

"No, lemon butter cream," Oriana said. "You know I hate chocolate."

"But everyone else likes it."

"That doesn't matter. It's my birthday and I can have what I want. That's the rule."

"The rule you just made up. Oriana, we're *twins*. We can't

both have what we want if we share the same birthday, and today it's everyone's birthday anyway."

"I'm pretty sure you can program the printer to make a cake in multiple flavors," Carina pointed out.

Oriana and Ferne's jaws dropped open and their eyes popped.

"Multiple-flavor cake would be great," said Parthenia. "Let's go and make it." She got up from her seat at the dining table and led the other children to the galley.

When they'd gone, Carina said to Bryce, "Thank the stars for Parthenia. I don't know what I'd do without her."

"She really does a great job of looking after the other kids," said Bryce.

"She understands them better than I ever can," Carina said. "She grew up with them in that mansion-prison on Ithiya, and she probably had it the worst of all of them—saw Stefan at his worst, I mean."

Bryce touched her arm as it rested on the table. "Don't underestimate how much you mean to your brothers and sisters too. You're the missing piece in their lives. You're their source of knowledge about their magehood. You're the one who can teach them how to use their powers responsibly."

"I suppose so, but even my knowledge is limited. I'm sure Nai Nai knew ten times more than I do. She just didn't live long enough to pass it all on. I sometimes wonder if trying to return to Earth is a fool's quest. I'm not even completely sure what I should be looking for on Ostillon, let alone where."

"Maybe it wasn't such a good idea to split up from Jace," said Bryce tentatively.

Carina's lips tightened. The decision to part ways with the high-ranking mage had been argued over long and hard before her wishes were followed. "As I said at the time, it was too risky to remain in his company. He was too noticeable." The tall, broad man with his black, shaggy hair and beard was too attention-grabbing in her opinion.

"Well, he's probably found a way back to Ostillon too by now," Bryce said. "Maybe our paths will cross again."

"But what about you, Bryce?" Carina asked. "You've thrown in your lot with us mages despite all the risks. What about your family on Ithiya? Won't they be wondering what's happened to you?"

"I've sent a packet telling them I'm going on a long voyage. They won't worry about me." He took her hand. "I haven't thrown in my lot with a bunch of mages for no reason. I'm here for you. The kid magicians are just a bonus."

Carina smiled and leaned forward to kiss him.

It wasn't long before they were interrupted, as always.

Parthenia headed the delegation just come from the galley. "Nahla wants to put Castiel's name on the cake."

"Nahla?" said Carina. *The same Nahla who Castiel beat and tied up only a few weeks previously?* she thought but did not say.

"She says even though he's a bad boy, he's still our brother and it's still his birthday."

Nahla could be seen peeking around Parthenia, watching for Carina's reaction. The rest of the children clustered behind her.

"Right," Carina said. "And what do the rest of you think?"

Parthenia shrugged. "I stopped thinking about Castiel as a brother a long time ago."

Ferne stepped forward. "I don't care but I'll do it if it'll make Nahla happy."

"I say no!" Oriana exclaimed. "Castiel's an asshole."

"I don't think we should either," Darius piped up. "I can feel him and he's not sorry for anything he's done."

Carina agreed with the general sentiment. She called Nahla forward and took the little girl's hands in her own. Was she hankering for the days when it was her and Castiel against their mage siblings? Carina had never considered how Nahla felt about being the only one of the brothers and sisters who had no mage powers. She hoped it wouldn't make her sister twisted and bitter as it had Castiel.

"It's nice of you to think of Castiel," Carina said. "One day, if he becomes a better person and apologizes for hurting you, he can be with us as a family again. But today isn't that day. Do you understand?"

Nahla looked at her toes. "Yes," she whispered.

Their dispute settled, the children went back to making their cake.

"You handled that well," said Bryce.

"Did I?" Carina asked. She wasn't so sure. She worried that Nahla's childish, confused loyalties would get them all in trouble.

"Have you decided what we're going to do with the prick when we get to our destination?" asked Bryce.

"Nope."

Carina had returned to the problem again and again since putting Castiel in the ship's brig, but she was no closer to a solution. And she didn't have long. In another three days they would arrive at Ostillon.

11

Months had passed since they'd been on Ostillon. As Carina sat at the pilot's station inputting the final set of coordinates that would put the *Zenobia* in high orbit around the Dirksen-controlled planet, she wondered what had happened there while they'd been gone. They had left behind a war-torn, ravaged world, struggling to rebuild after barely repelling the Sherrerr invasion attempt. Had the Dirksens aided in the planet's recovery or had they abandoned it, deciding the expense was not worth the potential profit?

Carina hoped it was the latter. It would make her job so much easier.

Darius wandered onto the bridge, as he often did when the children were practicing their Casting. Carina had taught them all she knew during their trip and Darius had soaked it all up with ease. She knew the practice sessions bored him so she didn't mind too much when he played hooky.

Nahla was already there too. She'd taken to investigating the *Zenobia's* data base while the other kids practiced their mage skills, immersing herself for hours. She particularly seemed to love gazing at the blueprints of the ship. Carina sometimes wondered if the little girl was finding places to hide in case Castiel turned on her again.

Darius stood beside Carina and draped an arm lazily over her shoulders. "What are you doing?"

She was seated, and as she glanced at him standing over her Carina could have sworn the boy had grown five or six centimeters in a few weeks. He would have his father's height and he was a negative of Stefan Sherrerr's coloring, but luckily he hadn't inherited the man's temperament.

"I'm setting our final heading," she replied.

Darius heaved a sigh and rested his head on her shoulder.

"What's up?" asked Carina. "Are you sad our trip will soon be over?"

"Kinda. It's been fun living on the ship all together."

"It has, hasn't it?" Carina gave her little brother a hug.

"If you forget about the beast in the brig," said Bryce from the captain's seat.

"Yeah." Now it was Carina's turn to sigh.

"I liked learning all about what it is to be a mage," Darius said. "So much of what the Spirit Mage taught me makes sense now. All the old stories and the lore. I hope I can take her place one day and pass on what I know."

"You do?" Carina asked. "I think there's a lot she didn't tell you. She said you would have had to live with her for years so she could train you to take over from her."

"But maybe I can learn the rest of it on Earth," said Darius. "If that's where we come from, I bet the stories are still there. The mages must have left some things behind when they left. Information on systems."

"That was thousands of years ago," said Bryce. "It's hard to recover data that old. It's even hard to find data from a few decades ago."

"Then maybe there will be books," Darius said. "Like the religious book on Ostillon you told us about, Carina."

"Maybe," she said. "Maybe mages are living there still. I'm not sure they all left. It's even possible more have appeared within the population and if they found the historical sources relating to the mages who were driven away, they might have learned how to Cast."

"They might have invented new Casts like I did," said Darius.

"I thought you only invented one," Carina said. "The Cloak Cast."

"I've invented another one." The little boy looked away. "I know I was supposed to be practicing, but..."

"It's okay," said Carina. "I don't mind. What did you invent?" She wistfully hoped it was a Cast for disappearing Dark Mage brothers, but she doubted it.

"I call it Guise," said Darius. "It's kind of like Cloak in that it hides you, but it hides you by making you look like someone else."

"Uh huh," said Carina, sitting upright and turning widened eyes to Bryce. "Can you give us a demonstration?"

"Sure." Darius removed his elixir flask from the belt around his waist and sipped the liquid. His eyes shut, he took one step backward.

For a moment nothing happened. Carina began to wonder if Darius's new Cast was all in his seven-year-old mind. She didn't doubt his ability but in every other way he was still a young child.

Then he turned into Bryce. It wasn't a gradual transformation where he grew taller and his face changed shape. One moment he was himself and the next, a perfect copy of Bryce.

The real Bryce was so astounded he stood up.

Carina laughed with delight. "Say something, Darius."

"What do you want me to say?" He sounded like himself so she figured the Cast only extended to the mage's appearance.

"How long will you stay like that?" she asked. "Can you turn it off when you want?"

"No," Darius replied. "I stay like this as long as the Cast lasts. Just a few minutes. I can't control when it stops. And I have to be able to see the person to do it. I know because I tried to turn into different people when I was alone in our cabin. I thought about how they looked, but it didn't work. I have to make a copy of someone I can see right then. I tried it out by peeking at you guys around a corner and then Casting."

The restriction fit in with the natural laws that seemed to apply to Casting. Though it wasn't always impossible to Cast at something you couldn't see or had no tangible relationship to, it was hard and sometimes it *was* impossible. Darius might eventually refine his skill so that he could create a Guise of someone he couldn't see but he clearly hadn't developed the ability yet.

"Can you do a quick lap?" asked Bryce. "I'd love to see how I walk."

Darius took a stroll around the bridge, producing fits of laughter from Carina and Bryce.

"Not bad," Bryce said. "But of the two of us, I think I'm better looking."

The bridge door opened and Oriana and Ferne burst in.

"Whaaaaa…?" said Oriana, holding Ferne back with one arm, her mouth remaining open. Her gaze switched between the two Bryces.

"I'm the real one," said Bryce.

"No, I am," piped Darius.

"This is too freaky!" Ferne exclaimed.

"It's Darius's new Cast," said Carina. "It should wear off soon."

"That is *so* cool," Oriana said. "You have to teach us how to do it."

"I can try," said Darius. His attempts to teach the Cloak Cast had failed. Even Carina couldn't learn it. All the mages could write the Character but when they sent it out nothing happened. Carina didn't know why that was so, but she suspected the same would be true of Guise.

"We finished today's practice," Ferne said to Carina. "Can we go to lunch now?"

"Yes. And while we're eating we can talk. We only have a few hours until we arrive at Ostillon and I want to tell you all what will happen then."

"Don't we get to decide anything?" asked Oriana, pouting.

"We've talked about this stuff for weeks," Carina replied. "I've listened to everyone's opinions but I'm making the final decisions and that isn't negotiable, sorry." She was aware the children may think she was overbearing but she was happy to have that reputation if it meant she kept them as safe.

Oriana snorted her disapproval and stomped out of the bridge. Ferne tutted and followed her, his hands clenched at his sides. Carina wondered which of his bossy, difficult sisters bothered him the most.

THE CHILDREN HAD BECOME adept at using the food printer and they'd thoroughly familiarized themselves with the copious supplies aboard ship. They made two main meals per day together in a chaotic mess of banter and minor bickering that nevertheless resulted in delicious dishes everyone liked.

Bryce took Castiel his meal while the children laid the table for what would be their penultimate meal aboard the *Zenobia*. There was no question they must leave the ship behind when they arrived at Ostillon. Carina had searched the place high and low—even venturing into the accessible sections of the engines—but she'd been unable to discover the tracker. If they didn't leave the ship its smuggler owner would catch up with them eventually, and Carina would rather face the Sherrerrs or the Dirksens.

This was the first decision Carina had explained to her sisters and brothers and it was met with predictable complaints. After weeks of moving from place to place, hiding out from their pursuers, the children had settled into living aboard the starship and had probably come to feel like it was home. This sense was probably heightened by the *Zenobia* also mimicking their first home in terms of luxurious fittings and supplies.

Yet the disgruntlement over leaving the ship was soon forgotten, however, when Nahla asked, "What's going to happen to Castiel?"

The conversation paused and five pairs of eyes focused on Carina. Just the mention of the kid's name made her angry and fearful.

"I've thought about this a lot," she said. "My first idea was to abandon him on an isolated planet. He's a mage so he would survive. But I didn't want to divert our journey any more than I already was and I realized I was only postponing the problem of his existence. All the habitable planets in this sector are settled, as far as I know, so wherever we left him he would find a way to leave the place in the end. He would return to the Dirksens or Sherrerrs or perhaps he would create his own evil organization and come after us when he has more backup. So that idea was out.

"The only other option that allows us to get rid of him is to hand him back to the Dirksens and hope they limit his influence. They certainly don't seem to hold him in high esteem. But they hate mages. They proved that on Pirine. They would encourage him to find us, so the second option gives the same result."

Carina took a breath and said glumly, "I've been forced to conclude the safest way of dealing with Castiel is to keep him with us. We'll have to do our best to keep him restrained and deny him any access to elixir."

"For how long?" asked Parthenia.

Carina couldn't tell how her sister felt about the decision. Parthenia had learned to hide her emotions as a survival strategy while growing up in a dysfunctional, abusive household. Yet all along it had been she who had wanted to capture Castiel and prevent him from hurting anyone, so Carina thought she would be pleased they would be doing exactly that. But then, who would be happy about spending what could be the rest of their lives in their evil brother's company?

"For as long as we must," Carina finally replied. "Maybe when we get to Earth we'll find a way to remove his powers. That would be the best solution. But I don't know if it's possible."

Parthenia seemed satisfied, at least, because she didn't say anything else. The others appeared shocked, as if Carina's decision had been the last one they'd thought she would make.

Bryce returned to the dining room. He took one look at the expressions on everyone's faces and said, "I guess you told them Castiel's coming along for the ride?"

12

Preparing to leave the *Zenobia* had taken much longer than Carina had anticipated. Everything in the hold had been returned to roughly its original state, but they also had to take clothes, supplies, and elixir to last them several weeks on the surface. If they could find what they needed to set them on the right track for Earth without having to take jobs to survive, that would be ideal.

Nevertheless, though gathering everything they would need took several hours, Carina had been pleased with the speed and efficiency with which the children completed the task. She'd expected more bickering and attachment to favored but non-essential items. Yet they seemed to be overcoming their pampered upbringing at last.

Not only that, their mage powers had improved considerably on the journey. Carina guessed this was in part due to the habit of meditation she had instilled in them, something Ma had entirely—and necessarily—neglected. They knew all about the Elements, the Seasons, and the Strokes and their daily recall of them had honed their Casting skills.

The ritual surrounding the Map had been the hardest part.

Carina knew only too well how challenging the task was for young minds, but though her brothers and sisters' lives on Ithiya had been soft in many ways, their regular education had been rigorous and this experience seemed to help them with memorizing the star points within a 3D frame.

All in all, Carina anticipated a better experience for them all than they had known before as they undertook their search. Her group wasn't only a family, it was a skilled team, each member lending their strengths to aid in achieving their purpose: to find the true home of mages.

Now all was packed and ready. The *Zenobia* only carried a couple of emergency shuttles and they were too small to fit everyone and their baggage, so Carina was preparing to fly the ship itself to the surface. She'd contemplated asking Darius to Transport them down but she worried that something might go wrong. She didn't want them to become separated, especially somewhere other people might be roaming about and could spot one of them materializing from nowhere.

As long as Darius's Cloak continued to work the ship wouldn't be observed as it descended, but the effects of landing a large ship anywhere other than the specially prepared surface at a spaceport would be unmissable. As soon as the *Zenobia* landed they would need to get away from it as fast as they could.

The children were on their way to a section near the ship's exit that contained safety seats for passengers. Bryce was with them but he would take a detour to collect Castiel from the brig. He'd fashioned a pair of handcuffs for the Dark Mage to wear. It wasn't much but it was the best they could do to keep him under control. Once they were on the surface Carina and Bryce would be forced to sleep in shifts to keep an eye on him.

Carina picked a spot fifteen klicks or so from the capital city where she'd first discovered the religious cult that held the secrets to mage history on Ostillon. They would Transport to the outskirts of the city as soon as they landed.

When Darius's Cloak wore off and the starship appeared in the middle of nowhere, questions would be asked, but that was not Carina's concern. Nothing remained aboard that could link the ship with her, her siblings, or Bryce.

Carina moved to activate the descent sequence. She'd deliberately chosen an area of air space that was free of traffic. The chances of something colliding with the invisible ship were slim but still not worth taking.

The pilot's interface flashed a message. A hail had arrived. Carina's hand froze over the console. Who could be hailing them? The originator field on the message was blank. Who could have seen through Darius's Cloak? She didn't think it was possible for even a mage to penetrate the Cast. Could it be Jace? Carina had never plumbed the depths of his mage abilities. He belonged to the Mage Council, but that was all she knew.

But if it was Jace, why didn't he say so in the message? Unless he wasn't sure who he was hailing.

Carina opened the message but only as audio from her side.

A round-faced man wearing a bright blue hat with an iridescent sheen appeared on the interface.

"I am disappointed," said the man in a rich, deep voice. "I was looking forward to seeing the thief who stole my ship. You are wise to keep your identity secret, but your efforts are in vain. I will look upon you soon enough. Until then I will bide my time thinking of the slowest and most painful way to kill you. If you do not resist boarding, perhaps I'll be kind and do it quickly."

The interface screen turned black.

For a beat, Carina only stared at it.

The smuggler had found his ship, but how? Had the tracker penetrated even Darius's Cast? And why had the smuggler given a warning he was about to board? If he anticipated a fight to take back the ship he'd lost the advantage of surprise.

The *Zenobia's* short-range scanners reported a starship bearing down on them fast.

Carina could only guess the smuggler wasn't confident he had the numbers to take the ship. He had no idea how many were aboard or who he might come across. The ship could be carrying a couple hundred mercs for all he knew. He'd opened a parley to avoid a fight. After all, it was his own ship he was trying to take back so he had a good reason to try to avoid damaging it.

Whatever the smuggler decided to do, it was clearly time to abandon the ship. Carina took out a pouch filled with small items. In preparation for their return to Ostillon, she'd told the children to gather things they could use to Locate each other in case they became separated. She took out a shoelace and wrapped it around her hand.

Darius was in the elevator. Carina couldn't Send to a quickly moving target so she'd have to wait for Darius to leave the car.

An high-pitched alarm sounded. Carina could hear it coming from outside the bridge too, blaring throughout the ship. The interface stated 'Proximity Alert' and switched to a map showing the *Zenobia* and a second ship approaching it fast. The display stated thirty seconds to contact. The kids and Bryce were heading to the exact place the *Zenobia* would be boarded and they had no idea what was going on and no time to prepare a defense.

"Carina?" said a voice in her head. Darius was Sending to her. "What's that noise?"

"We're about to be boarded. The ship's owner has caught up with us. Can you Transport us all to the surface?"

All the mages had the ability to Transport themselves but

without a frame of reference they would all end up in different places.

"Oh, okay," was all Darius said, though his mental tone betrayed his anxiety.

"We're above open farmland right now," said Carina. "Try to keep us together if you can."

Her bag containing her belongings and flasks of elixir was next to her seat. She leaned over to grab it. As her fingers reached out, she felt herself Transported. The next second, she fell and hit the ground with a bump. She was sitting in a hay field in bright sunshine, her hand gripping her bag. Relieved she'd managed to bring it with her, Carina stood up.

Where were the others? Shading her eyes with her hand, she swept the field with her gaze. In the empty, flat landscape it didn't take her long to spot figures standing in the tall grass even though they were some distance away. Perhaps due to their separation aboard the ship, Darius's Cast had flung her three or four hundred meters away from her companions. She slung her heavy bag over her shoulder and set off toward them.

This area of Ostillon reminded her of the prairie on Pirine, where the mages had held their Matching, only this was a farmed landscape. She was wading through grass and wildflowers, but grain crops grew in other fields and an autonomous harvester sat on the horizon. If she had her bearings right the city lay to the north, behind her. The sun sat in a clear blue sky to her left. They had about an hour until sunset, when they would have to find somewhere to spend the night.

Somewhere above her, the *Zenobia's* owner and his crew would be searching the ship. Eventually they would wonder what had happened to the thieves who had stolen her, flown all the way to Ostillon, and vanished into thin air.

13

"It's okay," said Carina. "Really."

Darius was distraught. He was so upset, Carina felt like a Spirit Mage herself because she could almost *sense* the waves of negative emotion coming off of him.

"I just forgot," he repeated. "I could have Transported him, but he wasn't with us, so…"

"We were surprised and in a hurry," Carina said. "It's no one's fault." If it was anyone's fault, it was hers. Darius was seven. *She* was the adult. It was her responsibility to remind him if something was important. "Let's walk a little before we go to the city."

She wanted to wait until dusk before their next jump to the city's outskirts. Transporting into an unknown area held the risk of their sudden appearance being noticed by bystanders. The failing light would hide them somewhat and still allow time to find somewhere to sleep. Everyone gathered their bags before the group set off walking north.

Carina didn't blame Darius for failing to Transport Castiel from the ship but the fact that he remained there worried her. The round-faced smuggler would have discovered him by now, and she had no idea what Castiel would tell the man to explain his presence. Knowing Castiel his story would be self-aggrandizing, despite his incarceration in the brig. He would probably make up something about overwhelming forces attacking him, not his big sister picking him off like a bug on the ceiling.

But what would he tell them about mages? Had he learned from his experiences with the Dirksens?Would he keep the knowledge of his powers to himself?

Carina couldn't guess. His capacity for boasting seemed infinite and might overwhelm his instinct for self-preservation. Not that she cared the slightest for his welfare, but his blabbing could endanger all of them.

If the smuggler learned what Castiel could do and that more people with his abilities had magicked themselves down to Ostillon, the man would probably come after them. Smugglers didn't only deal in artifacts, they were also known to traffic humans.

Bryce gave her a sideways hug. "I hope our prospects aren't as bad as you seem to think."

"Do I looked that stressed?"

In answer, he placed his thumb against the skin between her eyebrows and gently rubbed.

Carina smiled and felt her face relax. "I think we'll be okay. No one saw us Transport here. That's a good start."

"Don't tell me you're worried about that little shit we left on the ship," said Bryce.

"Not about *him* exactly," said Carina, "but the danger he poses to us."

"Can't Darius Transport him here in that case? I mean, I'd rather not, but if it helps..."

Carina shook her head. "A moving ship is too hard to target. I doubt even Darius could do it. If Castiel tells the *Zenobia's* owner about us and that guy decides to track us down."

Bryce frowned and peered at the spot between Carina's

eyebrows again. He lifted his hand, but Carina laughed and pushed it down.

"I get it," she said.

"We'll have plenty of time for worrying about it *if* the smuggler comes after us," said Bryce. "Anyway, how would he find us?"

"It might be hard but it's not impossible. I didn't anticipate the possibility of leaving Castiel behind. We might have left something on the ship he could use to Locate one of us. I mean, we did a pretty good job of removing or cleaning everything we used, but we were aboard for weeks. It isn't easy to live somewhere for so long and leave no trace of your presence."

Carina let out a deep breath. "But you're right. There's no point in worrying about it now. We'll have to face that problem if we come to it. I got a good look at the guy's face and I'll recognize him if I see him again."

They walked on in silence toward the gray line on the horizon that was the edge of the city. Carina's anxious mood began to ease. It was good to be planetside again, surrounded by grass and feeling the sun on her skin. Perhaps everything would go smoothly. They would find what they needed without too much trouble and embark on their new journey quickly, leaving Ostillon, the Dirksens, the Sherrerrs, and Castiel behind forever.

An hour or so later, when the children were beginning to murmur about resting and eating and the sun had disappeared below the horizon, Bryce suddenly said, "Is that smoke?"

In the oncoming dusk it was hard to tell whether he was right or if it was only low clouds, but a gray pall hung over the city.

"I don't know," said Carina. "Maybe." If it was smoke, it wasn't a good sign for the state of Ostillon.

In their hour of walking the only living things they'd encountered had been bugs, lizards, and a single grazing animal who appeared to be lost. Machines for weeding and harvesting stood in the fields, idle and likely broken down. The farm work had been automated, the Dirksens having stolen the Ostillonians' land and not even provided them with jobs in return. Yet Carina was surprised by the absence of people. The fact that they'd encountered absolutely no one, considering they were close to a large city, implied that Ostillon hadn't begun to recover from the Sherrerrs' attack.

"Let's Transport the rest of the way," Carina suggested.

"Thank the stars for that!" Oriana exclaimed. "My feet feel like they're about to drop off."

"Then you won't mind volunteering to Cast for all of us," said Carina.

"Huh? All six of us?" The whites of Oriana's eyes stood out in the deepening gloom as she displayed her surprise. "I can't do that."

"I think you can," Carina said. "It's the same as Transporting one or two people, just with greater *oomph*."

"Oomph?" said Bryce. "Is that a special mage word?"

"Why can't Darius do it?" asked Oriana.

"Yeah," said Ferne. "I'm not sure I trust Oriana to Transport me anywhere."

"Shut up," Oriana said. "I bet I can Transport more people than you."

"No way!"

"Both of you shut up," said Carina, wondering to herself what she'd been thinking earlier when she'd imagined her siblings had matured. "Oriana, this is a good opportunity for you to practice Transporting several people. If you get it wrong we can Locate each other easily with our collections of personal items."

"Hmph," Oriana said, narrowing her eyes at Ferne. "I'll try. Where do you want me to aim for?"

Carina indicated a position near the city but still several

hundred meters from its edge, though the distance might not be necessary—as night approached no street lights had come on that might betray their sudden appearance out of the blue.

"Right," said Oriana, opening her elixir canister. "Everyone, hold your stuff tight. Ready?"

The next instant, the scene jumped and Carina found herself looking at a scene of utter devastation.

Oriana whooped. "I did it!"

Carina swung around and jumped on her sister, clamping a hand over her mouth. "Be quiet, you idiot," she hissed.

Oriana's eyes were apologetic above Carina's hand. When Carina released her she whispered, "Sorry."

Carina returned her attention to the destroyed city. Not a building she could see remained whole. In some cases, only piles of rubble stood in their place, detritus at the bottom of a gap in the street's facade. The places that were standing did so precariously, aslant, as if about to topple any moment.

And Bryce had been correct: over it all hung a cloud of smoke from a distant conflagration.

Carina could smell the stench of burning plastic and stars knew what else in the air. She recalled the state of the city when they'd left, which had been bad enough, but somehow things seemed to have gotten worse in the intervening time. Had the Sherrerrs returned to finish off the number they'd done on the Dirksen planet?

She didn't comment on what was evident to everyone. "Come on. Let's go. It's getting dark and we don't have anywhere to sleep yet."

The group began to trudge across the short distance of wasteland that lay between them and the ruined houses. Their pleasant walk through the countryside had come to an end. Now they walked toward darkness and destruction. Carina wondered what had happened to Langley Dirksen and her two-faced son, Reyes. Did their estate still exist or had the Sherrerrs bombed it to smithereens? Knowing how self-serving Langley was, she and Reyes were probably long gone.

She surveyed the destruction. The scene in front of her was depressing enough but she had a greater concern: how could they expect to find information about the origin of mages in this wrecked and chaotic place?

14

As they walked down the center of a main street that appeared to lead toward the city center, avoiding bricks, broken concrete, and other remains of buildings that littered the sidewalk, Carina became aware of their first mistake.

Not many people were about but those who were found her group very interesting. They were attracting attention wherever they passed, and it wasn't a good kind of attention. She saw hungry, envious looks coming from the shadows where Ostillonians lurked.

Bryce had noticed them too. "Looks like we're famous or something."

"I don't think it's that," Carina replied. "At least, I hope not."

It wasn't impossible that the Dirksens might have thought the mages could return to Ostillon but it seemed very unlikely. A move like that would be mad if it weren't for the information on mage clans the place contained and the Dirksens couldn't know anything about it.

"It's our clothes," she decided.

They were all wearing clothes taken from the *Zenobia*. The children had altered theirs to make them fit, but they were essentially the same: made from rich, costly fabrics. By contrast, everyone else in that residue of a city was dressed in rags. Either they had nothing better to wear or they weren't stupid enough to dress expensively in a place full of starving looters.

"Shit," said Bryce. "You're right. But it isn't just the clothes, it's our bags. Look at everything we're carrying out in the open, like we're asking for it all to be taken off our hands."

"Are those people following us?" Parthenia asked.

Carina looked back. A handful of men and women had joined their path down the center of the street. They were looking directly at her group, making their intent clear.

Carina turned to face ahead again. The street stretched onward without a bend or corner. Running into one of the derelict buildings would be madness. They would be trapped —if the building didn't fall on them.

Neither could they Transport out of the situation. The Dirksens were probably unaware the mages had returned, but the first report of a group of strangely dressed people vanishing into thin air would soon alter their misconception.

"Bryce," Carina murmured. "I think it's time we showed our admirers what they're up against." She reached into a long bag she carried so he would get her meaning. He was carrying a similar bag.

She took out the Dirksen pulse rifle. She turned around and began to walk backward, aiming at the goons on their tail while Bryce his focused on the road ahead.

"Carina," said Nahla nervously.

"It's fine," she replied. "Don't worry. Everything's going to be fine."

One minute passed and then another. They'd hit upon a major thoroughfare that showed no signs of coming to an end, and though after catching sight of the guns their followers hadn't drawn closer, others had joined them.

It was crazy. As far as Carina could see none of them was armed. The Dirksens had done a great job of disarming the local population. If they attacked some were sure to die yet they seemed willing to take the chance and hope it wouldn't be them. Things had gotten desperate on Ostillon.

"So...how long do we do this?" Bryce asked.

The city was darkening as night fell. Dark clouds scudded across the indigo sky, shading out the starlight. Soon, everyone would be navigating mostly by sound and if it came to a firefight Carina didn't want to risk accidentally shooting one of the kids or Bryce.

"We just need to find somewhere to stay the night," she said.

"I don't think these good people are interested in letting us sleep," Bryce muttered.

Carina wracked her brains for an idea on how to get out of the situation. She was fast realizing it would have been safer for them to sleep out in the open beyond the city outskirts than enter it at night.

She glanced over her shoulder. They were coming up to a side street. Perhaps if they could get off the main drag they could escape down the warren-like lanes she remembered carved through that part of the city. Even if they couldn't escape they could lose their pursuers long enough to Transport without being seen.

"We're taking the next left," she said.

Despite the gun muzzle staring them in their faces, the people following had begun to edge closer. In the shadowy light, Carina saw looks of tense, fearful anticipation on some of the faces as if the individuals were steeling themselves to make the first move. It wouldn't be long until one of them worked up the courage. Carina's glance forward and saw Ostillonians walking slowly in front of them too.

If things were different Carina would be tempted to take out a member of the crowd with a stun shot just to warn them off—but she had a feeling the city dwellers were so starved and desperate firing on them would break the tension and trigger an attack.

They turned onto the next street. Narrower and darker, it concentrated their pursuers into a knot of people who had drawn so close the mages would not have time to stop and Cast before they were set upon.

Carina began to mentally curse. She didn't want to kill anyone and neither did she want to draw attention to themselves but it was looking like she didn't have a choice. All her other options involved risking the kids' safety.

Bryce seemed to have read her thoughts. "It's time we made a stand."

"You're right. In another ten paces, we stop."

She counted down her steps. When she reached zero, she halted. The Ostillonians were so close each face was distinct to her in the low light. They were dirty and unkempt and their eyes sunk into their sockets.

"Get back," Carina told them firmly, "or we'll shoot."

"Give us your stuff," said a man wearing a black hat pulled down low over his eyes, "and we'll leave you alone."

"You've got food in those bags," a woman wrapped in a shawl said. "I can smell it. Share some with us. That's all we want. We're starving."

"We don't have enough to share," said Bryce. "We only have enough for ourselves."

"If you won't share," the man in the hat said, "we'll take it. All of it. And you'll have nothing."

Despite the man and woman's words it was clear the mob would take every scrap of food they had the minute Carina and

Bryce lowered their weapons, and probably hurt or even kill them in the process.

"If any of you take a step closer I'll shoot to kill," said Carina. "Leave us alone. I'm sorry you're hungry but it isn't our fault. Go ask the Dirksens why they aren't helping you."

The woman spat. "We haven't seen those bastards for weeks. They don't give a shit about us. I have kids at home who'll die soon if I don't get them something to eat. If you kill me at least I won't have to go home and face them empty-handed."

"Maybe we should give them something," said Parthenia.

The woman's words had moved Carina too. If it weren't for the certainty that the mob would overwhelm them she would have already helped the woman. But she couldn't. She also had kids to protect.

She didn't reply, only took aim at the crowd.

"These people are under the protection of the Temple of Lomeq," said a woman's voice, clear and strong. Carina turned toward the speaker. A woman in priestess robes stood there, her back to the mages and her hands raised, facing the mob.

"Step back or face her wrath."

Not a soul moved.

"I command you to step back!"

The crowd shifted and murmured.

"But we're hungry and they have food," a voice shouted. "Why has Lomeq provided for them and not us?"

"It is not your place to question her ways," the priestess replied. "But if you wait I will bring out what little we can spare. Be patient. Do not fight each other. Show dignity and grace or Lomeq will not hear your prayers."

The priestess gazed at Carina's group for a moment and then turned and walked into the building behind her. Carina recognized it as the same kind of place she'd slept at after escaping from Langley Dirksen. The entrance was open and she could see garish religious paintings on the walls in the lamplight within.

"I guess we're supposed to follow her," said Bryce.

"That would seem like a good idea," Parthenia agreed.

The priestess's words hadn't had the desired effect on everyone in the crowd. As Carina moved to go with the others into the temple, the man in the black hat flew at her. She heard his quick footsteps and saw him run up.

She'd have time to get off a shot but her gun was set to kill and she didn't have time to change the setting. Instead, she turned the rifle around, waited a beat for the man to reach her, and then cracked the butt against his skull.

As he hit the ground, she cast a glance at the remaining Ostillonians. No one else was feeling brave any longer.

Carina walked into the temple.

15

When they were out of sight of the crowd and within the inner temple where the walls and floor were plain and rough and torches flamed for lighting, the priestess turned and lowered her hood. "If you have food you must give it to me. Not all of it, but some. If I don't take some food out to them they will attack."

"What about the wrath of Lomeq?" Bryce asked.

"Her wrath will descend in the next life," replied the priestess, "not this one. Sometimes people's viewpoints are short-sighted, especially when they haven't eaten for days."

"We're happy to give you what we can spare," said Carina. "I didn't realize things were so bad."

"You didn't?" The priestess sounded incredulous. "Where have you been living for the last few months?"

An uncomfortable look passed between the members of Carina's group.

Instead of answering, Carina directed her attention to her siblings. "Let's give the lady some food. Everyone's carrying some. Give her half of what you have."

"Half?" said Ferne. "But what if we run out?"

"If we run out we'll find some more," she replied.

This answer didn't satisfy Ferne but, like the others, he dropped his bag onto the floor and began to look through it. They quickly made a pile of random packages.

Carina noticed Parthenia taking most of the food out of her bag.

"No," she said, touching her sister's arm. "Put some back."

"I don't need it," Parthenia insisted. "I don't eat much. I can go for days without feeling hungry."

"No you can't," Carina said. "Put some back. I need you strong and healthy."

"But those people are—"

"Those people are not our problem or our responsibility," Carina said with finality. "I know it sounds harsh, but it's true. All over the galactic sector people will be starving due to this war between the Dirksens and the Sherrerrs. Are you going to feed them all? We give what we can but we look after ourselves too."

Parthenia wore a defiant look that Carina hadn't seen for a while, but she did as Carina asked and reluctantly took some of the packages back, angrily thrusting them into the depths of her bag.

When they'd divided up their food and donated half, the priestess put it into two bags which she lifted to carry out to the crowd.

"Do you need protection?" Carina asked her.

The priestess smiled. "They won't hurt me. They know Lomeq will punish them."

While the woman was outside distributing the food, Carina and the others repacked their lightened bags. Losing half their food was a blow but it was true that the mages had more options than the regular folk.

"Is this where we're sleeping tonight?" Oriana asked, always the one to consider the state of her feet.

"I hope so," replied Carina. "I think the priestess will feel obliged, and we'll need somewhere to stay until the crowd disperses. I wouldn't put it past them to wait until we leave so they can take the rest of what we have. But we're also in the right place to find out some more information about mages."

She'd told the children about the connections she'd found between the Ostillonians' religion and mage lore.

"Yes," said Darius. "We can ask to look at their Map."

"It won't be that easy," Carina said. "We have to tread carefully. The Map and the Characters are religious items to them. Maybe sacred items. If we push too much we might be kicked out. And, tonight at least, that's something we need to avoid."

When the priestess returned it was she who made the suggestion that Carina's group stay the night.

"We only have this room to offer you," she said. "We have taken in a number of orphaned children and the weak and elderly, but it will be safer for you to sleep here than on the street tonight."

"This room will do us fine," said Carina. "We appreciate it."

"Then I will show you were you can wash up."

"You can show Ferne and he'll tell us later," said Carina. "The rest of us will prepare our bedding."

Ferne went with the priestess and the others pulled out the sleeping bags they'd made from the fine fabrics available on the *Zenobia*. Carina suggested they sleep next to each other in one corner of the inner temple for warmth and for protection. She and Bryce would take turns keeping watch, just in case some starving Ostillonians lost their religious sentiment.

When Ferne returned they ate a small meal, not knowing how long their halved rations might have to last. The priestess didn't visit them. Carina guessed they were alone for the night and her inquiries about the Temple of Lomeq's religious artifacts would have to wait for the morning.

"Can you tell us some more stories about mages before we go to sleep?" asked Nahla.

"Shhh," said Carina. "Remember, we can't speak freely. We aren't alone anymore, even though we might appear to be."

"I don't think anyone is listening," said Oriana, who had just returned from the restroom. "The corridor is empty."

Carina looked at the eager, expectant faces of her siblings. It probably wouldn't hurt to tell them something as long as she didn't use the word 'mages'.

"I can tell you what Ma told me when we were on the *Nightfall*."

"I'd love to hear that," Parthenia said, her eyes shining in the torchlight.

"Okay." Carina took a breath. "Ma said that when our ancestors first came together as a group they went to live on a remote mountaintop. There, they could practice their skills in peace and quiet away from the rest of humankind. They learned about the different...things...they could do. Maybe they even invented new ones, like Darius does."

The little boy beamed.

"What was it like living on the mountain?" Nahla asked.

"I don't know," Carina replied. She recalled her time at the Sherrerr mountain stronghold. "Cold, I guess."

"Very cold," said Bryce, sharing a look that told Carina he knew the subject of her thoughts.

"The problem was," she continued, "the secret about where they were staying got out. People would journey into the mountains to try to find them, hoping to join them or receive instruction on how to do what they did. So our ancestors began to test everyone who turned up. If the visitor failed the test they had to leave, and some perished on their way back. That was what began the true hatred for our kind. They were blamed for the deaths."

"But why didn't they let them in?" Parthenia asked. "It wouldn't have hurt them."

"Because if they had more would come," explained Bryce. Though he didn't know the story, the answer was obvious. "Then your ancestors would have had to house and feed them all and teach them and deal with their disappointment when they finally understood that they didn't have the ability they desired. All your ancestors wanted was to be left alone to live their lives."

"I guess that's kind of similar to the reason we can't give all our food away," Parthenia said.

"That's right," said Carina, relieved her sister was finally getting it. "We have as much right to survive as everyone else. It feels selfish but unless we have more than we need we have to keep some back for ourselves."

"I wish I hadn't given away the cookies I made," Ferne said wistfully. "They were delicious."

This brought a chuckle from the others.

"Don't worry," Carina said, "I'm sure you'll get a chance to make some more one day."

"Will we find the mountain where the...our ancestors... lived?" asked Oriana.

"It's been so long since they left Earth it might not be possible," Carina replied. "Things will have changed a lot. Even the climate. Magda, the Spirit Mage, said the climate had undergone a huge upheaval before our ancestors fled. But who knows? Maybe we will find that mountain home and traces of the people who lived there. But that's going to be a long time from now after a long journey. It's time you guys got some sleep."

Bryce volunteered to take first watch, so Carina lay down and shut her eyes. She listened as, one by one, the children fell asleep, their breathing altering to a deep, regular pattern. But sleep would not come to her.

She opened her eyes and turned over. Bryce faced away from her toward the outer door, sitting cross-legged with his rifle across his lap, his figure dark in the flickering light from the torches, which were burning low.

He must have heard her move because he looked over his shoulder and then got up and walked to her side. He lay down, moved his head close to hers, and whispered, "Can't sleep?"

Carina gave a slight shake of her head. "I'll take this watch if you'd like."

"I don't think I'll be able to sleep either," he said.

The glow from a torch illuminated his face and Carina saw an emotion that she shared. The two of them had not gotten to spend a single night alone together in all the weeks since the Matching, when by an unspoken agreement they had chosen each other.

Bryce put a hand on Carina's waist and moved closer to kiss her. As their lips met, the room exploded in a cacophony of noise and light.

Someone screamed, "Get up! Get up!"

Before Carina could figure out what was going on, large, muscular hands grabbed her under her armpits. She snatched for her weapon but she was dragged away from it and hauled to her feet. Men in odd clothes were grabbing the children, manhandling them out of their sleeping bags and kicking their elixir flasks out of reach. Bryce was wrestling with bald, wiry man.

Carina spun around, swinging her fist behind her, but her blow was deflected, hard, by the butt of a weapon. She heard a crack and feared her arm was broken. Nevertheless she let her impetus carry her around and brought up her other fist to punch her assailant in the stomach. Her hand was caught in a larger one and crushed. She gasped with pain and saw her attacker for the first time. He was a giant, dressed in baggy, rich clothes like the rest.

Through her pain, the source of the attack finally clicked in her mind. These were not starving Ostillonians or Dirksen troops and neither did they look like priests of the temple. These were the smuggler's men. It was the only answer that made any sense.

The giant released his bone-crushing grip on Carina's hand, grabbed her shoulder, turned her roughly around, and shoved her front against the wall. Behind her she could hear the frightened sobs and cries of her siblings but there wasn't anything she could do to help them: the smuggler's man had her pressed so hard against the wall she thought her ribs would break. The cold, rough stone grated the skin off her cheek and jaw.

She couldn't breathe and felt herself losing consciousness.

She registered her wrists gathered together and secured by thin rope that dug into her flesh. Then, mercifully, the pressure on her back eased. A hand dragged her around again and pushed her backward. The giant bent down to run his hands over her legs, searching for weapons.

Carina jerked her knee up, smashing it into the man's nose.

His head snapped backward at the impact. When he rose, his face was a mask of blood and rage. His massive hand grabbed Carina's jaw and twisted it, tugging at the skin and grinding her teeth together. He moved so close their noses nearly touched, then he thrust her head sharply backward, bashing her skull into the wall.

Black edged into Carina's vision as pain exploded at the point of contact. She staggered and dropped to her knees.

"Carina, stop," Bryce pleaded. "You're going to get yourself killed."

She was aware of warm blood trickling down her head onto her neck. She sagged forward. Bryce was right. They were outnumbered and she was no match for this gigantic thug.

"Get up," said the smuggler's man.

When Carina didn't comply fast enough he heaved her to

her feet with one hand. The children were already being forced out of the room, looking scared. Bryce was next to be pushed toward the doorway. His hands were tied behind his back too.

Carina was the last to leave, her captor's hand heavy on her shoulder as he forced her out.

16

The van the smuggler's men put them in was windowless and smelly and the ride was bumpy as they drove away, fast, through the city streets. The vehicle did not use the a-grav engine the Dirksens had introduced to the planet. It was an older model the men had dredged up from somewhere.

Darius curled up close to Carina. She put an arm around him while trying to steady herself from the rocky movement with the other. Her head was pounding from the wound she'd sustained and blood continued to trickle down her neck.

"Where are we going?" asked Oriana.

"What's happening?" Ferne asked. "Who are those men?"

"We'll find out soon enough," Carina said, "but I think Castiel is behind this and the men are from the *Zenobia*."

"Why can't he leave us alone?" Parthenia asked.

"He probably wants us even more now," said Oriana. "We locked him away for weeks. He wants to get his revenge."

"So do I," Carina said. "He kidnapped and hurt Nahla, and that was *after* he tried to help the Dirksens catch us. He's lucky I didn't space him. I won't make the same mistake again."

The van hit a pothole and lurched, sending them all crashing into each other. Nahla squealed in fear.

"It's okay," Bryce said. "It's just a bump."

"The people in the street will be happy we've left," Darius said. "They'll get all our food now."

His words seemed to throw a dark cloud over their already miserable situation. No one spoke, and all Carina could think of was how every time they tried to escape from people who wanted to exploit them for their powers, something happened to drag them right back again. It was doubly terrible that it was their own blood who was responsible for it.

She couldn't understand why Castiel would think things would go differently for him this time. Had the smuggler promised him wealth and power in return for giving them up? It would have been clear to the *Zenobia's* owner that an interesting story lay behind the ship occupied by only one person, who was locked in the brig. What tale had Castiel spun for them?

Had the Dark Mage bargained for his freedom in return for his siblings'?

The van rumbled on and Carina began to feel sick. Her headache, the stuffy air, and the darkness all contributed their part to her nausea. She tried to plan ahead, to think of a way to escape before the men could bundle them onto the *Zenobia*, assuming that was where they were going, but nothing came to mind. She was too befuddled. Yet if she didn't think of something and they were forced aboard the starship their options for escaping would be drastically narrowed, especially if the ship left orbit.

Mental exhaustion suddenly hit her. Was this how things were going to be forever? How many more times would she have to find a way out of captivity? How many more times would she have to fight to free herself and those she loved? Was this the destiny of mages who refused to live in secrecy and solitude?

Carina felt Bryce's arm slide around her. She rested her head on his shoulder, wondering how long she could carry on.

The van hit rougher ground and jostled the captives. Carina hung onto Darius as the vehicle swayed and bumped. She guessed they were traveling outside the city. Had the smuggler landed the *Zenobia* somewhere outside a spaceport in an attempt to avoid detection? That had been her plan too. But unless Castiel had learned how to perform Darius's Cloak Cast, the ship would not go unnoticed for long.

The van's driver certainly seemed to be in a hurry. The rough ground didn't deter him or her from driving fast. The passengers were bounced so violently they crashed into the walls and floor.

Carina finally lost her temper and thumped the wall separating them from the driver with her fist, shouting, "Slow down!"

Her words had no effect. Fifteen minutes or so later the driver slammed on the brakes, flinging the captives forward. Seconds later the doors opened and hands reached in to drag out the children, Carina, and Bryce. The night air hit Carina like a cold wave. She saw starlight and the black silhouette of a starship before she was rushed aboard along with the others.

The interior that greeted her was depressingly familiar. They were back aboard the *Zenobia*.

The men pulled Carina and Bryce away from the children and forced them into an elevator. Darius and Nahla wailed and reached out their arms but there was nothing Carina could do. The giant had her wrists firmly in his grasp and was lifting her arms upward. One movement and he could dislocate her shoulders.

"Just do what they tell you," Carina called out. "Don't fight them. We'll get you out as soon as we can."

The men accompanying her and Bryce found this very funny.

For the first time she got a good look at them. The men were all large and heavily muscled with big bony heads and wide mouths. Their beards were carefully styled and a few continued the styling to the hair on their heads. When they laughed their voices were deep and velvety like the owner of the *Zenobia's* when he comm'd the ship.

She had never seen men like them. She guessed they were all from the same planet, somewhere far away, perhaps even outside the sector.

The giant who had captured her was a head taller than the rest. He glared at her for the entire elevator ride, not bothering to wipe the blood ran slowly from his nose, dripping from his chin onto the deeply muscled chest revealed by the open neck of his baggy white shirt.

The elevator stopped and soon Carina found herself back on the bridge. The owner sat in the captain's seat, which barely contained him. His paunch hung between the thick thighs of his spread legs, and his broad body protruded past each side of the back of the seat.

The man was awaiting their appearance, his seat swiveled to face the door. The iridescent blue, cone-shaped hat Carina had seen before remained perched on his head. Unlike his men, he was clean shaven.

He grinned at Carina and Bryce's appearance on the bridge. Carina didn't think she'd ever seen so many teeth. The man obviously took great care of them too. They were the brightest things in the room.

"Come in, come in," he said, waving them forward and acting as if he were inviting guests to a party.

Carina's guard didn't share his boss's welcoming sentiment. He thrust her forward while maintaining his one-handed grip on her wrists, causing her arms to jerk upward painfully. Her resulting grimace made the *Zenobia's* owner grin even wider.

"Sit down," he said.

Carina and Bryce were forced to their knees.

"Good, good," said the man.

Carina looked for Castiel but he was nowhere to be seen. \

The captain rested his hands on his knees and leaned forward, screwing up his eyes as he inspected Carina and Bryce. "It is strange. You don't look any different from regular people. I'm interested in the abilities of your kind. I see some similarity between you, girl..." he jabbed a finger of heavily bejeweled hand at Carina... "and the boy who claims to be your brother. I know now he spoke the truth when he said you were related. I can see the resemblance. Your family customs are strange. If my brother were to betray me..." He drew a finger across his throat, turned toward his men, and laughed. They echoed his laughter.

"Believe me, Castiel will be the first to die when we escape," Carina said.

The smuggler's laughter redoubled. His fat belly jiggled with merriment and he wiped tears from his eyes. His men's mirth increased by the same degree. But when he waved a hand for silence it fell within a moment.

"Do not mistake me," said the smuggler. "Your brave words in the face of insurmountable odds are admirable, if unrealistic. Such courage is rare in this barbaric region of space, where individuals hide within their starships, using weapons to do their fighting for them. You are like the women of my world. I find your attitude deeply stimulating."

"What's your name?" Carina asked.

The smuggler flashed his impressive rows of teeth again. "Why do you want to know?"

"So I can add you to my list of people to kill."

Bryce softly sighed.

Carina thought she saw a flash of anger in the smuggler's eyes, set deep in his fleshy face, but he only smiled—his lips closed this time—and nodded, as if understanding a new truth. "I am Berami Lomang. Place me at the top of your list. I will accept no lesser position, and I look forward to our encounter."

"The top?" Carina scoffed. "No. That place is reserved for my brother."

17

Castiel was so predictable. Carina and the others hadn't been in the *Zenobia's* brig longer than half an hour before he arrived to gloat.

The guards had separated the group into two: males and females. The brig only contained two cells, which faced each other across the passageway. They were only intended for single occupants.

Carina was sitting with her sisters on the bunk, trying to think of a way to escape when Castiel turned up.

The brig walls and door were transparent. Castiel sauntered into view, one hand on his hip in an apparent attempt to emphasize his nonchalant superiority. If Carina hadn't been so angry with him she might have laughed at his act.

"How does it feel?" he asked. "Not very nice, is it? Shut away, confined against your will, having to sleep, shit, and piss where everyone can see you?"

"No one watched you shit, Castiel," said Bryce from across the way. "Stars, why would any of us want to see that? But don't let that stop you from wallowing in self pity."

"You deserved all you got," Carina said, "and more. Much more."

"I never deserved any of it," spat Castiel. "I didn't ask to be born into this lousy family, growing up with my brothers and sisters showing off their 'special powers' in front of me, acting like they were so much better. Making me feel inferior every single day of—"

"It wasn't anything like that!" Parthenia exclaimed. "You were Father's favorite. None of us got any attention or praise. It all went to you."

"That's because he was trying to make up for our bitch of a mother—"

"Don't you *ever* speak about Mother like that!" Parthenia was on her feet and at the wall, her fists pressed up against it.

"I'll speak about her however I like!" Castiel yelled. His young face transformed into a snarl. "She was a bitch who wanted our father for his wealth and power, but as soon as she got what she wanted she refused to give him the only thing she had to offer in return: her mage powers. She just wanted to take, take, take. Beautiful dresses and jewelry, a mansion to live in, all she could desire. But when it came to fulfilling her side of the bargain? No. She wouldn't do it, so Father had to make her. That's the truth, but none of you will admit it."

As far as Carina was concerned, Castiel had signed his own death warrant when he'd given them up to the smuggler, Lomang. Calling Ma a bitch only meant his death would be slower than he might have liked. Yet she was mildly interested to hear Castiel's take on his parents' relationship. Was that what Stefan had told him, or had he concocted the false narrative himself?

"How can you even think that?" Parthenia asked. "Are you insane? Mother hated Father with every bone in her body. He was cruel and evil. You think being behind these walls for a few weeks was a bad experience? Father held Mother captive our *entire lives*. And not only that, he..."

The horrible memories were too much for Parthenia. She covered her eyes and sobbed.

Carina walked over to her sister and hugged her.

"Go away," she said to Castiel. "You've said your piece. Now go."

"Do you really think you can boss me around?" Castiel sneered. "You can't tell me what to do. I'm the one with the power now. You're all going to have to do what I say, pretty soon."

"You're as dumb as you are arrogant," said Carina. "What makes you think the smuggler is going to treat you differently from the Dirksens?"

Castiel reddened. "The Dirksens treated me well. They were going to give me a high-ranking position."

"Yeah, that's why you couldn't wait to get away from them," Carina said. She turned to Bryce in mock curiosity. "What was it he said after Darius Transported their troops off this ship?"

"Something about giving him his freedom." Bryce was watching the exchange from the opposite cell.

Castiel's color deepened. "I didn't say anything like that."

"You're a liar," Carina said, "but that's no surprise. You think you've done something clever by handing us over to that man? All you've done is make things worse for yourself. Do you think Lomang is going to see you any differently from us? I'm surprised you aren't already in the brig now that he's got us, like you promised him. He probably wants to keep you happy for another couple of days, until he's learned what he wants to know.

"In some ways I pity you," Carina went on. "One of the first things I learned about being a mage is you never, *ever* tell a non-mage what you can do. Because sooner or later they're going to want to exploit you for their own ends and if you refuse they'll make you. As soon as a non-mage learns about your powers you cease to be a person to them. You're just a freak who deserves to be used however they want. But Ma never taught you that. She never had to. She didn't think you had any powers. What amazes me, though, is that now you've learned that once the hard way, you've made the same mistake again."

Castiel's hands balled into fists at his sides. "That isn't how it's going to be. I've joined Lomang's crew and I'm going to receive a percentage of his profits—profits that are going to increase now that he has me and all of you working for him. And if you don't do what I say I'll hurt Nahla."

"You touch one hair of that little girl's head and I promise you, Castiel," Carina hissed, "I will Split you like Ma Split your father."

"Carina," warned Bryce.

"Back off!" she yelled. "I'm sick and tired of everyone making excuses for this evil little runt. He's his father's child, he doesn't have a trace of Ma's sweet nature in him. You should have let me kill him while we had the chance."

Parthenia stepped back from her. "No," she said gravely. "He's still our brother."

"How can you say that when he's just put you back into captivity?" asked Carina.

"You don't understand," she replied. "You didn't grow up with us. You weren't part of our family." She seemed about to say more but closed her lips and looked away.

"And I never will be?" demanded Carina. "Is that what you were going to say?"

"No. It wasn't that."

"Then what was it? I'd *love* to know."

"It doesn't matter." Parthenia strode the few short steps to the bunk and sat down, her arms folded. She continued to avoid Carina's gaze.

Carina couldn't help but think she'd guessed correctly. It was true, she hadn't been a part of their childhood. While her half-siblings had been living in luxury with their monstrous father and Ma, she'd been trying to avoid starvation on the streets of her backwater planet. She hadn't been a part of that dysfunctional family's existence and she would never share that bond they had, no matter how much she protected and cared for her brothers and sisters—with the exception of the asshole who stood in front of her. "I thought I told you to go away."

Castiel's expression had changed from embarrassment to a smirk. "It's good to know my brothers and sisters will save me from you in the unlikely event you ever have any power over me."

"I wouldn't be too sure of that," Ferne called out from his cell.

Castiel ignored him. "In case you hadn't noticed, we've left Ostillon and we're heading into deep space. Lomang is rendezvousing with a business client there. I will be present in order to Enthrall the client so he agrees to terms that are wildly unfavorable to him. However, in case I need assistance, Parthenia will be coming with me, and Nahla too, so Parthenia does as she's told. Until then, you will all remain here."

"We can't all sleep in here," Oriana said. "There isn't room."

"You'll manage," replied Castiel.

"Hey, Bryce, when Castiel ends up in your cell," Carina said, "make sure he sleeps on the floor."

"Oh, you can be sure of that," Bryce replied.

"I'm *not* ending up in the brig," said Castiel, his smirk turning to annoyance.

With another scowl, he finally left.

Carina slumped against the wall. Parthenia's comment had hurt. She'd risked her life for those kids, more than once.

She felt a gentle touch on her shoulder.

"Carina," Parthenia said. "I'm sorry. I didn't mean to—"

"It's fine," she replied. "I'm fine." She straightened up. "Let's think of a way out of here. It sounds like you're going to be the first one out of the brig. Maybe there's something you can do." As she spoke she noticed something on the ceiling above the bunk. "Oriana, stand up."

"Huh? Why? I'm tired."

Carina rolled her eyes. "Just do it."

After the girl surrendered her seat she climbed onto the spot. A small, faint anomaly marked the smooth ceiling. Carina could only just reach it. She brushed the surface with her fingertips and felt a cross hatch of ridges.

"Shit." They could forget about discussing escape plans, at least not out loud.

She waved to get Bryce's attention, then pointed at the ceiling before cupping her ear. He understood immediately.

Parthenia also understood. She whispered first to Oriana and then to Nahla. They gazed upward at the tiny grille leading to a recording device. Carina climbed down from the bed. The inability to speak freely was another impediment to their already limited prospects of escape.

She sat in Oriana's place, mulling over their situation. The mental exhaustion she'd felt in the van returned and she put her head in her hands. She began to wish, crazily, that her mother and father had never left her with Nai Nai; that they'd taken her with them on the trip that resulted in Stefan Sherrerr capturing them. Maybe he would have just killed her, but maybe she would have grown up in his family, not separated from Ma. Would her siblings have seen her as one of them then?

"I hope they bring us something to eat soon," said Oriana.

But much to their disappointment Lomang's guards didn't reappear, with or without food. Hours later, when they'd given up even bothering to talk about food, or water, or to whisper about escaping, the lights suddenly went out.

The immediate darkness without warning brought groans of dismay from the children. It was a signal they would have to endure their hunger and thirst over the quiet time aboard the ship.

They had already discussed sleeping arrangements. If Parthenia slept at the foot of the bunk, Oriana and Nahla could squeeze together at the top. Parthenia's feet would be in their faces, but it meant only Carina had to sleep on the floor. She'd done that often enough in her life for it to not be a major discomfort.

She folded her arm under her head to act as a pillow, told the girls to stop complaining at each other, and closed her eyes. She hadn't slept at all the previous night, her head still hurt from her wound, and her psychological fatigue hadn't abated. Despite the girls' continued whiny chatter, she fell asleep.

When Bryce woke her, it took her a moment to remember where she was. At first, she thought he was waking her to take her watch at the temple. She sat up in utter darkness, confused. Her surroundings were nothing like the temple on Ostillon.

"Carina," Bryce whispered urgently. "Move. We have to get out of here."

Then it all came back.

"What are you doing in here?"she asked as Bryce fastened a hand around her bicep to help her stand.

"Shhh," he replied. His lips touched her ear. "Castiel came back. He's helping us escape. Come on. We have to hurry."

18

They huddled in a storage room near the brig, conversing in low voices about how to take over the ship. Their familiarity with its layout would be an advantage but Castiel was hazy about the number of crew members and where they were stationed.

Carina watched Castiel tell them what he knew, not believing for a minute that he had come over to the mages' side, even though he'd handed them each a canister of elixir. He had some other, long-term plan, and he needed his siblings' help to enact it, that was all. Perhaps her telling him that Lomang would turn on him eventually, had made him change his mind about keeping them in captivity, but whatever his motivation was it was self-serving. She had no doubt about it.

"I'm pretty sure most of the crew are in the crew's quarters and only Lomang is in the passenger section," Castiel said. "We should just space them all as soon as we see them, Transport them outside the ship."

"No," said Carina. "That would be cruel and unjust and not something a mage should do. Though they haven't exactly been kind to us…" she reflexively touched the clot of dried blood on the back of her head… "we did steal their ship."

"What?" said Castiel. "Weren't you the one talking about Splitting me a few hours ago?"

"It isn't unjust to punish people as they deserve," Carina replied.

"What have I done that means I deserve to die in agony?" asked Castiel, his tone rising.

"Cut it out, you two," said Bryce. "Let's focus on what we need to do now."

Castiel turned away from Carina. "I know which cabin Lomang is sleeping in. I figured it out before I came to release you."

"We can Enthrall him," Oriana said. "The rest of the crew will do whatever he tells them."

"That might work," said Carina, "but only temporarily. Lomang knows about the Enthrall Cast because Castiel's told him he can use it at this business meeting he has planned. Lomang might have told the crew about it and if they receive strange orders they'll suspect something's up. We can't Enthrall them all, either, and even if we could it would be a round-the-clock job to keep them all under."

"We can't put them all in the brig," Ferne said. "There isn't room."

It was true. Just the giant who had captured Carina would take up most of the space in one of the cells.

"Could we put them somewhere else?" asked Bryce. "Somewhere we could lock them up indefinitely. Could we confine them to one level of the ship?"

"Imagine if we put them in the hold for months," said Oriana. She wafted her hand in front of her nose. "Phew!"

"We can't put them in the hold," Carina said. "There are all kinds of things in there. They might be able to make something they can use to escape." She was reluctant to confine

Lomang and his crew to the passenger area for the same reason.

"If we were near a planet I could Transport them to the surface," mused Darius.

Carina ruffled his hair. "You could." She thought for a moment. "Maybe that's what we should do. We haven't been underway for long. If we return to Ostillon, we only have to keep them captive while we fly back. Then we dump them on the surface and leave them there."

"And then they find a way to find us and take back the ship," said Bryce. "They found the *Zenobia* once despite all Darius's Cloaks and your course corrections. They'll find it again."

"And isn't Ostillon where *we* want to be?" Parthenia asked.

"Yes," said Ferne. "We need to do it the other way around. We take control of the ship, fly to Ostillon, then *we* Transport to the surface."

"That's no good," said Carina. "Lomang has some idea of what we can do, thanks to Castiel telling him. He'll come after us because he knows he can use us, and as we found out it isn't easy to lay low on Ostillon right now."

"Then what *should* we do?" Castiel asked tetchily. "I thought when I set you all free you would be of some help. I would have been better off sticking with Lomang."

"Maybe we should space *you*," Carina said. "You're more danger to us than Lomang and his crew put together."

"Stop it," said Bryce. "Arguing among ourselves isn't helping." He paused, listening. "Shit. Someone's coming."

The hard surface of the passageway floor outside the storage room was resounding with the heaving footfalls of running feet, growing rapidly louder.

"Someone's noticed the brig is empty," Carina guessed. "They're going to start searching for us. Wait until they've passed, then we run for it."

"Where to?" Ferne asked.

She didn't know. They still had no plan.

"Lomang's cabin," she decided.

It was the only place she could think of. Perhaps the smuggler would still be there and they could Enthrall him, buying themselves some time.

She stood with her ear to the door, waiting for the noise of the running men to recede. As soon as it did, she opened the door and peeked into an empty passageway.

"Let's go."

She led the others out of the storage room. The passenger cabins were in the level above. Luckily, she knew where the nearest service tunnel lay.

She began to run, the others following.

Carina rounded a corner and smacked her head against a wall of skin and muscle. She looked up right into the giant's face.

He grinned and shouted something in a language Carina didn't understand while reaching for her shirt. Grabbing the material, he lifted her off her feet, but her hand was already on her elixir canister.

She unscrewed the lid and took a drink before the giant had time to realize what she was doing. His eyes widened and he slapped the container out of her hands. It clattered against the wall, the liquid spilling out. She heard the kids shouting as her eyes closed.

The giant's other hand closed around her neck. He squeezed, sending blood into her head so it felt like it would explode, but she stayed calm and wrote the character in her mind. Pressure built up behind her eyes and tongue as she sent the character out. Hands were on her, trying to pull her away from the huge man.

A moment later, the grip on her throat relaxed a fraction. Carina opened her eyes. The giant's gaze was vacant.

"Release me," she gurgled.

The hands opened and she dropped to the floor.

"I Enthralled him too," said Darius excitedly.

"Then he's double-Enthralled," Carina said, rubbing her throat and picking up her elixir canister, which was now nearly empty. "But he called his buddies. We have to go."

The entrance to the service tunnel was only another twenty meters away. As they reached it, however, the smuggler's men appeared. Some of them halted when they saw the giant and spoke to him in their language. Others ran on, spotting the mages as they climbed into the tunnel. Carina waited until everyone was on the ladder heading up to the passenger level before she climbed in herself, closed the hatch, and Locked it. She made it just in time. Immediately after she sent out the Cast, hands hammered on the outside.

Given the commotion going on, Lomang was unlikely to be in his cabin any longer but they didn't dare go more than one level in the service tunnel now it was known they were inside. At the next exit they climbed out.

"This way," said Castiel.

He took off along the corridor. Carina followed with the others, wondering what was really going on in the mind of the dark-haired boy in front.

He took them to the suite she, Bryce, and Darius had shared. The door stood open. Lomang had gone.

"Dammit, where is he?" said Bryce. "He's the key to everything."

The sound of the elevator's chime came down the corridor.

"Quick," said Carina. She ran toward the elevator, already draining her remaining elixir. As soon as she caught sight of Lomang's large form, she stopped, closed her eyes, and Cast.

She opened her eyes. Lomang had turned and was staring at her, his arms raised as if to fend off a blow. He was utterly still.

The elevator doors opened. Carina tensed, waiting to see if

anyone stepped out. She was all out of elixir, though the remaining mages had joined her.

No one emerged from the elevator, and the doors closed again.

She walked up to Lomang. The man's eyes tracked her as she approached but he didn't move. He was wearing a yellow silken robe, fastened around his considerable belly and now that he was no longer wearing his hat, his hair hung down to his shoulders.

He had seemed strong-willed in their previous encounter, so she knew he would throw off the Enthrall Cast fairly quickly. In the meantime, they had a shipful of hostile crew to subdue. Casts alone wouldn't do it. They would need weapons, somewhere to confine the crew, and a plan for what to do next.

"Lomang," she commanded. "Return to your cabin."

"What are you going to do with him?" Parthenia asked.

"I'm not sure," said Carina. "I'm still thinking."

She only had the germ of an idea but it was rapidly taking shape in her mind. Her frustration and exhaustion over their constant need to run, hide, and defend themselves as mages, and her short time with Lomang and his crew, had sparked a potential solution to their problems that was entirely new.

As they reached Lomang's cabin, she asked him, "The *Zenobia's* tracker, can it transmit a message?"

The smuggler replied in a monotone, "Yes."

19

The brig was crammed with as many of the smuggler's crew as would fit inside the two cells. Carina had put the giant in their with the other men who seemed the most dangerous. Others were locked into a few of the crew's cabins—conventionally locked in, not by the temporary effects of a Cast. She had confined Lomang alone in his room on the passenger deck. She didn't want him near any of his crew in case he thought of a way for them to take back control of the ship.

The situation regarding the prisoners was not great. Conditions in the brig were bad, and Carina feared that sooner or later one of the crew would figure out a way to escape. Then he would release the rest, they would all swarm the mages, and everything would be back to square one.

All in all, Carina had counted twenty-five crew. Her own small group was vastly outnumbered and four of them were just kids. Though the young mages could Cast, they couldn't be expected to fight. Only she and Bryce were competent with a weapon, and Castiel was entirely untrustworthy. If he thought it would be to his advantage he would switch sides in a heartbeat.

But a return message had arrived that meant an end to the precarious state of affairs was possible—if only they could hold out long enough.

Carina saw Lomang as the greatest threat. He was the smartest and had the most to lose. He'd certainly demonstrated his high motivation to reverse the fate she'd thrust upon him, promising her all kinds of painful and humiliating retributions for taking his ship from him *again*. It was even tricky opening his door to send in food.

The first couple of times he'd been waiting and had wrenched the door open and tried to escape. He'd even hit Bryce over the head with a leg from the bed. So they decided to Enthrall him the second the door was open. Only they couldn't perform the Cast while he was out of sight, so someone had to stand by, waiting for him to emerge.

Then Lomang had taken to hiding in the room. Despite his size, he managed to remain hidden long enough to surprise both Parthenia and Bryce. He'd grabbed Parthenia and threatened to break her neck, but Bryce had told him about the Transport Cast that could put him outside the ship.

Lomang had demonstrated his intelligence and desire for survival by letting her go. However, Bryce had reported that the man remained angry. Dangerously angry.

Yet Carina was cautiously confident she'd hit upon a strategy that would see an end to Lomang's threats and to the constant threat of capture the mages had labored under for so long.

The kids had been overjoyed to have the run of the ship once again. As the *Zenobia* sped towards the rendezvous point, they had taken over passenger cabins at the opposite end to Lomang's, returned to preparing feasts in the galley, with liberal and imaginative use of the meal printer, and made gallons of elixir.

Carina was down in the hold working through the cargo, trying to figure what everything was worth and putting it all into some kind of order. No expert on contraband, she was sure she was undervaluing some items and overvaluing others. The jewelry was the most straightforward. Lomang could not have made it as a smuggler if he couldn't tell the difference between genuine precious stones and paste, so she assumed that if something looked like a sapphire, ruby, or diamond, that's what it was. The same applied to the thick gold chains, which certainly felt heavy enough to be the real thing.

A few of the illegal drugs were also somewhat familiar to her, not through personal use—Nai Nai had warned her that narcotics and hallucinogens would weaken her ability to Cast—but through her time with the Black Dogs. Mercs could get away with drug abuse in ways that military personnel could not, which was one reason some of them made the switch. As Carina removed the powders, pills, and liquids from their hiding places, she smiled sadly, remembering Smitz. Obnoxious, defiant, and disgusting in his habit of chewing a narcotic herb and spitting his brown saliva wherever was most convenient to him, her fellow merc had given his life in the rescue of Darius from the Dirksens.

As had Captain Speidel, the closest thing she'd had to a father since Ba had disappeared when she was three. Carina sighed and continued her work.

She had rearranged the items into groups ranging from the least to the most valuable according to her estimates. Payment would need to be made so it was important she'd got it roughly right.

When she was nearly finished, she climbed into the cargo mech to move the heavy or unwieldy objects she couldn't manage by herself. She could have asked Bryce to help her but he was in charge on the upper levels, supervising the kids and maintaining security.

She started up the machine and walked it over to the long cylinder of the rolled-up rug. After grasping it with the mech's pincers, she turned it upright and stepped to the side of the bay, where she balanced it against the wall. Next, she extended the mech's arms to grip the netting that lay on the floor, raised the edge to the ceiling, and slipped it over the hooks.

Previously, she had shifted a large, ornate cabinet made from dark, close-grained, heavy wood from its position in order to search it, and had found a cache of uncut gems in a secret compartment. Now she needed to slide the furniture against the wall. As she turned toward it, her comm button sounded.

She opened the comm but before she could say anything, Bryce said, "Some of the crew have escaped! The ones in the brig."

"*Shit*. Where are you? What's happening?"

"Castiel and the kids are with me on the bridge. I'm not sure where the crew is. Take care, Carina. They might reach you in the hold."

"I'm coming up. Are you armed?"

"We have weapons and elixir. We're heading out to round the escapees up before they reach Lomang and the others."

"Okay. Be careful. I'll join you as soon as I can. Let's leave the comm open."

Carina had put down her pulse rifle to use the mech. She scanned the hold to locate it and saw it propped against the wall near the door. She turned off the machine, and heard the snick of its safety cage unlocking.

As she prepared to jump down, the hold door opened and in strode the giant wearing nothing but an open vest and pants. He didn't notice her at first as his gaze roved the cargo greedily. He'd clearly slipped down to steal something while the rest of the crew were attempting to take back the ship.

He was standing between Carina in the mech and her weapon, but she had her elixir canister on her belt. On the other hand, as soon as she moved... She slid her hand slowly toward the canister.

The giant's head whipped up. His eyes focused on hers in a ferocious glare. He was only a few steps from her. She wouldn't have time to unscrew the canister and take a drink before he was on her.

She restarted the mech as the giant reached her, the safety cage locking her in.

The giant snarled and grabbed at her through the bars. He was so tall and his reach so long, the cage was no impediment. He snatched the elixir canister from her waist and threw it across the hold.

Shouts and the fizz of pulse fire came from Carina's comm.

"Carina," said Bryce. "Where are you? They've taken Darius. We stunned or Enthralled most of them but one ran in and snatched him as he was trying to Cast."

Both of Carina's hands were fastened around the giant's thick forearm, trying to prevent him from grabbing her throat. The mech rocked with their struggle. The man's other hand appeared through the bars. Carina squirmed away to avoid his grip but there was nowhere for her to go.

"Carina," said Bryce. "What's happening? Are you okay?"

The giant's hand approached her head, trying to grab her face. She leaned forward and bit it, grinding her teeth into the flesh of his palm. He roared. The man's other hand gripped her head and tried to twist it to break her neck or the hold of her teeth, or both.

Through Carina's comm, Bryce cursed. She heard more gunfire and Parthenia's furious shouts, demanding the return of Darius.

The mech rocked more in Carina's violent struggle with the giant. Suddenly, she recalled another time she'd been in a mech, on Ostillon, when she'd been trying to convince someone to let her fight in the Mech Battle.

She stopped fighting the giant and grasped the controls. Immediately, her opponent thrust both arms up to his armpits into the cage and enclosed Carina's neck in his fists. She pivoted a pincer so that it faced toward her. The maneuver was hard to perform. The pincers were not intended to be used in that direction.

"Shit!" she heard Bryce say. "What's that?"

But the world was closing in around Carina as the giant attempted to strangle her. She tensed her neck muscles, fighting back against the pressure. With a great effort, she pulled in the pincer, fast. The metal smacked against the giant's back. His eyes widened and he shouted in pain but the pressure didn't lessen. She wanted to take hold of her attacker and pull him off the mech but she couldn't see anything except the man's face and arms.

She swung the pincer out and in again.

The second impact made her point.

The giant screamed in pain and let go of her. She stepped back several paces on the mechanical legs and moved the pincers forward.

The giant's face was screwed up in pain and sweat glistened on his forehead. He stooped but his neck craned upward, his eyes fixed with rage.

Dimly, Carina heard the dull clang of metal on metal from above. Something large had impacted the ship and she knew what it was. They were being boarded.

"It's over," she said. "Go back to the brig now and I won't hurt you."

"Ha!" the giant replied. "You'll never hurt me, little woman. Come out of your crate before I rip it apart."

"I won't warn you again." Carina opened the pincers.

The giant clenched his fists, yelled, and ran at her. She

swiped one pincer wide, smacking the man across his chest and sending him careening across the hold. Netting broke his fall. He staggered as he righted himself. A welt was already visible on his chest.

"Don't be stupid," said Carina. "I'll kill you if I have to."

When he didn't run at her again, she thought he'd heeded her warning, she realized he appeared to be thinking. His gaze ran up and down the mech and over the cargo. Then his eyes lifted briefly upward before returning to Carina's face. He began to pace sideways.

If she didn't miss her guess, he appeared to be planning to go around her, climb the netting behind her, and jump onto the top of the cage. He probably thought he could reach in and throttle her from above or poke her eyes out. If so, it was a stupid plan. She wouldn't be able to remove him or make him stop without killing him.

The giant passed to her left and Carina turned the mech to follow him. She wanted to catch him before he reached the netting. She didn't want to kill him if she could avoid it. Remembering Captain Speidel had reminded her he had a different image of her, an image she wanted to live up to.

She stepped forward to cut the giant off. He sped up but the mech was faster. She jabbed a pincer into his path, which he ducked, but she was already moving the other pincer in his way. He lunged in her direction, seeming to intend to run under the prehensile pincer arms. Carina gently closed one toothed grip around his waist. If she squeezed too hard she would cut him in two.

"*Arghhh!*" The giant yelled more words in his own language as he pushed down against the pincer, the thick muscles of his arms and chest bulging with the strain.

"Don't fight it," said Carina. "I don't want to hurt you."

She lifted him up, sending his legs dancing. He glared and hollered, spitting out his fury.

Carina carefully closed the second pincer around the man's hips. She was going to have to leave him there for a while. From the sounds that were coming from her comm she was still needed on the upper decks, though things seemed to be more in hand now.

When she was sure the giant was secure in the mech's grasp she turned off the machine and climbed out. Her captive's ire continued to ring in her ears. Though she had no idea what language he was speaking, it wasn't hard to guess his meaning.

She rubbed her neck and walked toward the hold door.

As she reached it, it opened, and a familiar figure stepped through and grinned. "Your boyfriend said I'd find you here."

"Atoi!" Carina exclaimed. She reached out and grabbed the woman's hand, pulling her into a hug. Atoi was more muscly than she'd been when Carina had hugged her goodbye as she left the Black Dogs.

"Been working out?" she asked as they stepped back.

"You know me, Car," Atoi replied. "What's with all the brats on the upper decks? They belong to you?"

"I'll explain everything later. Is the ship back in our hands?"

"Sure is." Atoi's eyes turned toward the giant, who was now watching them both with a silent glare. "You had your own little fight going on down here I see."

"I wouldn't call him little," replied Carina, "but, yeah. Is Tarsalan still in charge of the Black Dogs? I was surprised she wasn't the one who replied to my message."

"No, she isn't," Atoi said. "We have some catching up to do."

20

Carina didn't think she'd ever seen a more disparate bunch of people. On one side of the room sat Bryce and the mages, on the other sat the remaining members of the Black Dogs. There were nineteen in total, including Lieutenant Colonel Cadwallader. Some faces she recognized, like lithe, fit Brown, Jackson with his prosthetic arm, and the staring eyes of Halliday. Other faces were new. Clearly, the band had undergone a few changes in the year or so since she'd left.

Compared to the scarred, battle-hardened men and women, Bryce and her siblings looked young and vulnerable. They were also still dressed in the expensive fabrics and elaborate styles of Lomang's wardrobes, whereas the mercs wore armor of various styles, ages, and states of repair. The children sat upright and neatly, betraying their cultured upbringing, while the mercs sprawled and some hung an arm over the backs of their chairs. From the looks on everyone's faces each side was curious about the other, but the kids looked a little scared. They were wise to be so. Carina knew her former fellow mercs well. Most were ex-military who had left—or been dishonorably discharged—due to psychological problems, addictions, or lack of control.

One of the few exceptions was Stevenson, the pilot. He was steady and reliable, and Carina was glad to see he remained with the band. She'd never felt confident flying the *Zenobia*. Now he could take over the responsibility it would be a weight off her shoulders.

"So," said Cadwallader, "who goes first?"

"I'll start," Carina said. "There are a few things we need to get out of the way. I had to think long and hard about telling you this. I'm taking a risk but I don't really have a choice about it. If I don't tell you Lomang's men will." She went on to explain, as briefly and simply as she could, about her and the children's ability to Cast.

Some of the mercs smirked and rolled their eyes as though they didn't believe her.

She retorted, "If you think I'm making this up, fine. I don't give a shit. I'm not going to provide you with a demonstration because I'm not a performing animal, and frankly it's in my interest if you *don't* believe me. It doesn't matter, except for the fact that if you decide to back out on the deal I made with Cadwallader and try to take the ship, you'll find yourself spaced before you know it. Then it'll be too late to change your minds."

"You didn't make a deal with Cadwallader," said a man she didn't know. "You made a deal with all of us." Half of his face was scarred as if it had been burned. He reminded her of Carver, who had died in the first attempt to rescue Darius on Orrana. She hadn't had her facial scar fixed because she liked the look.

"Yes," Cadwallader said, his unnervingly pale blue eyes settling on Carina, "things have changed somewhat since you left us."

"For the better!" exclaimed the scarred man.

"The short of it is," continued Cadwallader, "Tarsalan planned to disband us and sell the *Duchess* and all our equipment and armor, which wouldn't have been a problem if I hadn't discovered she was also planning to sneak away without paying the wages that were owed. I couldn't in good conscience allow that to happen. I had already winked at the abandonment of good men and women who had refused the suicidal mission to rescue that young man." His gaze flicked to Darius and then back to Carina. "I wasn't about to look the other way again."

"We mutinied," Atoi said, grinning. "I wish you'd been there to see the look on Tarsalan's face when we forced her off the shuttle on some godforsaken planet at gunpoint, Lin."

"Should have killed her," the scarred man said. "Would have been safer."

"Maybe," said Cadwallader. "But I don't think murdering an unarmed woman would have been a good beginning for our enterprise." He said to Carina, "I've retained my function as CO, but all profits are shared equally, after subtracting expenses. When we received your message I discussed your proposal with the rest of the troops and we took a vote."

"It was a no-brainer to agree when we heard it was you," Atoi said.

Judging from the expressions of some of the other mercs, Carina doubted the vote was unanimous. The newcomers didn't know her. She couldn't expect any special treatment or consideration from the Black Dogs. They had a business deal, nothing more.

"I'm certainly glad you agreed to take the job," said Carina. "As I outlined in the message, I anticipate we'll be using your services for three, possibly four, months. We need to return to Ostillon and while we're doing that we have to keep Lomang's crew under control."

"The men we fought when we boarded your ship?" Cadwallader said. "Was that all of them?"

"I don't know," said Carina, looking at Bryce.

"No, that was only the ones from the brig," he said. "We managed to stop them from releasing the others. Thanks for your help in rounding them up."

"That's what we're here for," said Cadwallader. "When you didn't answer our hail I guessed things might have gone south. I'll take a look at your security arrangements as soon as the meeting's over. We can post a round-the-clock guard. You won't have any more trouble from them."

"You said three to four months," Halliday said. "That's longer than it'll take to get to Ostillon. What happens then?"

"There's information I want somewhere on the planet," Carina replied. "We'll need protection as we search for it."

"Wasn't Ostillon under attack from the Sherrerrs recently?" asked Cadwallader.

"That's right. The Dirksens were using the planet as a hideaway. I'm not sure if they're still there but the place is in turmoil right now. The economy's broken down due to the war and the population is desperate. We need your help to keep us safe."

Atoi asked, "What are you looking for?"

"Honestly," Carina gave a humorless laugh, "I'm not exactly sure. But I'll know when I find it."

"We can shorten the journey to Ostillon for you," said Stevenson. "The *Duchess's* engines are faster than the *Zenobia's*. If we keep the ships tethered the *Duchess* can tow the slower ship."

"Good," Cadwallader said. "The faster we get to Ostillon and you find your information, Lin, the faster we get paid."

"Sounds good," said the scarred man.

"We'll need to maintain a presence on your ship," Cadwallader said to Carina. "I mean soldiers sleeping and eating here, not just guards on duty. If there is a breakout it'll be easier to subdue with us already on hand."

"I can see the sense in that," Carina said, though she'd thought the mercs would mostly keep to their own ship. "There's room and food to spare, but I'd like to remind everyone there are kids aboard. These are my half brothers and sisters and I won't take kindly to anyone behaving inappropriately around them."

Her comment garnered a few smirks.

"I understand," Cadwallader said.

"We'll be on our best behavior," the scarred man said. Suppressed snorts of laughter erupted from various mercs.

Carina clenched her jaw but she didn't say anything.

"I'd like to speak to my soldiers in private for a few minutes," said Cadwallader, "then I'd appreciate a tour of the ship."

"Let me know when you're ready," Carina said, then she left with Bryce and the children.

As soon as they were outside the meeting room, Ferne said, "Did you used to work with those people? That's so cool. No wonder you're good at fighting."

"Don't be too impressed," she replied. "Killing for a living isn't as glamorous as you might think. Now, I want you to take the three rooms at the end of the passenger section near the elevator. Cadwallader will need some of the passenger rooms for the mercs if they're going to sleep aboard this ship."

"And you want to keep us separate from them," said Castiel.

"Yes, I do. Go on. Do what I said."

She watched the children depart and then noticed Bryce was looking stressed.

"Something wrong?" she asked.

"I'm not sure it was a good idea enlisting these thugs to help us."

"They aren't thugs, they're soldiers. I can't deny there are a few similarities but the two aren't the same. What are you worried about? I'm doing what I can to keep them away from the kids."

"It isn't only the kids coming into contact with them that bothers me, it's the safety of our entire enterprise. What if that Cadwallader decides to empty the hold and transfer everything to his ship? We barely managed to contain Lomang's crew, and we had the upper hand. We're no match for trained mercs with a plan."

"Cadwallader's more honorable than you give him credit for," said Carina. "And I've updated the hold security so that only you or I can get in. As to the other mercs...The ones who know me won't turn on me, even if they don't believe my threat about spacing them. I'm sure of that."

"And the rest?"

"If they wanted to be pirates, they could be. But they're mercs, soldiers. They want to do their job and then do the next one and so on. They like things simple and orderly, not messy and undisciplined. It's hard to explain."

"I don't like that guy with the burn marks on his face," said Bryce.

"Me neither," Carina said. "But we won't be using the Black Dogs forever. As soon as I find out how to get to Earth we'll part ways and that'll be it."

Bryce appeared to remain unconvinced. "And what do we do with Lomang and his crew?"

"That I don't have an answer for yet."

The door to the meeting room opened and the mercs started to leave.

Atoi appeared and strode to Carina's side. She wrapped an arm around Carina's shoulders, looked Bryce up and down and said, "Is he spoken for?"

Carina laughed. She'd forgotten about Atoi's predatory sexual habits. Bryce *actually* blushed.

"Um," Carina replied, "yes". Bryce looked relieved. Justifiably so, if he'd known what Carina knew about Atoi.

"Shame," the other woman said. "By the way, I told Cadwallader about that huge guy in the hold. He said to put him in a cell of his own. What did you do with him in the end?"

"Shit!" said Carina. "I forgot about him. He's still down there."

21

When Carina went to the bridge the following day, she found Stevenson sitting at the pilot's controls. Her heart warmed as he looked over his shoulder and raised a hand in greeting.

"I didn't get a chance to speak to you yesterday," he said as she walked over to him. "Long time no see."

"How have you been?" Carina asked, perching on the edge of console. "I wasn't expecting to see you still running with the Dogs."

"What can I say? A better offer hasn't come along."

"You must have been living under a rock if you never received a better offer than ferrying a bunch of mercs from one dangerous situation to another."

"Maybe I thrive on danger," said Stevenson, lifting an eyebrow.

She laughed out loud.

"After you abandoned us on Ithiya," the pilot said, "I didn't expect to see you again."

"Abandoned you? I resigned, that's all. I had something important to do. I ended up finding my family." Carina sighed. "Maybe I was abandoning ship too. Speidel had advised me to leave, and it did seem like the ship was going down."

"It was, until Cadwallader turned things around. We discovered that by not accepting suicidal missions, no matter how high the payment, and sticking to low-fee, easy work, we could make a decent living. Who knew?"

"Tarsalan always did have her eyes on the creds, not the brief," Carina said. "Lucky for me she was pushed out. I wouldn't have liked to deal with her. And lucky for me you were within hailing distance."

"Must have been fate," Stevenson said.

Carina smiled and cast a glance at the controls. "What are you doing?"

"Syncing up the ships' drives. They have to be perfectly aligned or when we start to move…" He mimed ripping something in half.

"That wouldn't be good."

"No." He held her gaze for a beat and then returned his attention to the console.

"Wait," said Carina. "I thought the *Duchess* would be towing us?"

"It turns out the *Zenobia* is faster than I thought," Stevenson replied without looking up. "Was it you who was flying her before we rendezvoused?"

"Yeah. Why?"

"The balances are all wrong. You were wasting a ton of fuel."

"Oops. I only know what you taught me so a lot of guesswork was involved."

"If you were flying this ship based on the few hours you messed around with the *Duchess's* controls, you didn't do badly at all."

"Thanks," she said. "I'm grateful for that little bit of tuition you gave me. Without it we would have been screwed, several times."

Stevenson looked up at her.

"Figuratively speaking," Carina said.

The bridge door opened and Bryce walked in. He paused a moment as he took in the scene before him. "Hey, can I speak to you?" he directed at Carina.

"Sure." She slid off her perch on the flight console. "What about?"

"In private," said Bryce, looking at Stevenson.

"Um, okay. See you later," Carina said to Stevenson.

When the door closed behind her outside the bridge, she said, "What's the big secret?"

"No secret," said Bryce. "I just didn't want to talk to you in front of a mercenary."

"Stevenson isn't really a merc. He just pilots for them."

"Yeah, well, I'm not sure there's a difference, and what I wanted to discuss with you concerns them. Let's go and see the kids. We should talk about Ostillon too."

As they walked to the elevator, Bryce said, "I agreed with what you said at the meeting yesterday, about your soldier friends watching their behavior around the children, but I'm not sure they're taking you seriously."

A heavy feeling settled in the pit of Carina's stomach. *This* was what she feared from the soldiers, not them turning on her as Bryce had mentioned the previous day. "What have they been doing?"

"Nothing, yet," he admitted. "But I've noticed some looks Parthenia's received, and I've overheard comments made to her I didn't like. I don't think she should be alone around them. She's only sixteen."

Carina grimaced. "I was only sixteen too, when I joined up. But I hear you."

Sixteen-year-old Carina and Parthenia at the same age were two very different people.

"I'll say something to Cadwallader," she added.

The elevator arrived and they stepped inside.

"I guess hooking up is a stress relief when you're a mercenary," said Bryce, staring ahead as the doors closed and they descended.

"It is, and they have their needs like everyone else, but that's their problem, not Parthenia's. She's very young, and with the life she's led, in many ways she's naive. Vulnerable. I'll tell Cadwallader to tell them she's out of bounds."

A silence followed. The elevator stopped and the doors opened. Carina stepped out but Bryce didn't follow. When she turned, he had an odd look on his face.

"That guy..." Bryce said. "What did you say his name was? Stevenson?"

"That's the pilot's name, yeah. What about him?"

Bryce appeared to struggle to know what to say. "You two seem to have a history. Am I right?"

"I have a history with the Black Dogs. You know that." Carina's stomach muscles tightened as she wondered where the conversation was going.

"That isn't what I meant," said Bryce. "Don't dodge the question."

"Right," Carina said. "So it isn't only Parthenia you're concerned about in that regard."

"I don't know if *concerned* is the right word."

"So you aren't concerned about me?"

"Stop twisting things. You're being deliberately evasive." Bryce took a step forward, his gaze on Carina intense. "Why can't you just answer me? Was there something between you and the pilot?"

"Why can't you stop being an asshole? What happened in

my past is *my* business. You're not entitled to a list of people I slept with."

"So it's a *list*, is it?! How many more of your old merc buddies are on it?"

"Get *fucked*, Bryce!"

A short distance along the corridor, a door opened and Oriana's head poked out. Carina realized with remorse that she and Bryce were yelling.

"Go back inside," Bryce said to Oriana, his tone lowered. "We'll be there in a minute."

The girl withdrew and closed the door.

Carina locked gazes with Bryce for several moments. Was he expecting some kind of apology or confession? She didn't know but she was damned if she would give him either.

Eventually, he broke eye contact and said, "Sorry. I was out of line."

Carina took a breath. "That's okay," she said, though anger still boiled inside her. Anger, and something like humiliation. She wasn't exactly ashamed of anything she'd done during her days as a merc, but at the same time being reminded of who she'd been then made her uncomfortable. She hadn't realized she'd changed so much—that events had changed her.

"Let's forget about it," she ground out.

They walked to Oriana's cabin, tension stretching out between them. The arrival of the Black Dogs had solved a major problem but introduced a smaller, more personal one. Carina hadn't taken Bryce to be the jealous type. She hoped he wouldn't obsess about her 'history' and allow it to drive a wedge between them.

All of the children had gathered in the cabin Oriana was sharing with Ferne. Even Castiel was there, though he sat apart from the others. The other kids occupied the two beds in various ways; lying on their stomachs, propping themselves against pillows, or sitting cross-legged. Castiel sat alone in a corner, leaning over an interface. All were awkwardly silent after overhearing Carina and Bryce's fight.

"We should put together a plan of what to do when we get to Ostillon," Bryce began, "even if we don't have a lot to go on. We can't employ the mercenaries forever so we need to make the best use of them we can."

"We should go back to that temple," said Parthenia. "Or if not that one then another. There has to be more we can find out about mages from that religion."

"I agree," said Carina. "We should ask to see the most ancient artifacts and records. We might even find some things that are contemporary to the time of the conflict between the mages and the newcomers. It would make sense that the oldest artifacts are held in a special place, maybe a main temple. As soon as we're within distance we'll search their archives. I doubt the security will be tight. The information isn't significant to the Ostillonians except in a spiritual sense."

"Okay," said Bryce. "Good. We have our first step."

"The *Duchess* has a shuttle we can take down," Carina continued. "If Darius Cloaks both ships the Dirksens won't know we're there."

"I can do that easy!" the little boy exclaimed.

"Assuming they're still on Ostillon," said Oriana.

"They are," Castiel said, smugly, from the corner.

"How do *you* know?" asked Ferne.

"Because I was with them when they talked about it, wasn't I? Idiot."

"Ha!" Ferne scoffed. "You were the one hanging out with the Dirksens but *I'm* the idiot."

"Shuttup." Castiel rose to his feet, clenching his fists.

"Stop it, both of you!" yelled Carina. The children froze, only their eyes moving as they glanced at each other. "Castiel, what makes you think the Dirksens haven't abandoned Ostillon yet?" she asked in the silence.

"I overheard Sable Dirksen talking to her lapdog, Commander Kee, saying something about securing provisions for the troops now that supplies were running low." He sat down and glared at Ferne.

"Huh," Carina said, "so they're keeping the food to themselves while the Ostillonians starve. Figures."

"Where is the Dirksen headquarters, Castiel?" Parthenia asked. "It would be wise for us to avoid it if we can."

"It's in a mountain range a few hours' flight from Langley Dirksen's estate. I don't know the coordinates but I know the way there from the city. It's very well hidden. You can't see it at all from the outside. There's some kind of optical illusion that disguises the entrance. It looks like you're flying into the mountainside but then you pass through it and find you're in a docking bay."

"The Dirksens do love their tech," Carina said.

"No, the entrance isn't Dirksen tech," said Castiel. "Sable told me it was there when they arrived. One of the local dignitaries told her about this ancient, forgotten, mysterious mountain castle to try to gain favor. After he'd shown her the location she had him killed. She said there were a lot of superstitions surrounding the place. I don't think she really liked it, though. It was always cold. It didn't matter what the Dirksens did, they could never heat it."

"I love the idea of Sable Dirksen freezing her behind off," Oriana said. "What's she like?"

"No, wait," said Carina, throwing Bryce a glance. "Tell us more about the Dirksen headquarters."

A mountain hideout with a secret entrance sounded like something mages would build, and Castiel had said it was very old too.

He went on to describe a large complex carved out from the interior of a mountain, a place of many floors yet, perversely, no elevators before the Dirksens moved in. Each bedroom of the original section of the mountain castle held a fireplace and a faucet—fire and water on hand for every inhabitant.

The more she heard, the more Carina became convinced the Dirksens had unwittingly taken over the dwelling of Ostillon's first settlers, a fortress they had constructed as a hideaway when the newcomers turned on them.

If Ostillon held the key to finding Earth, it was there, in the heart of enemy territory.

22

Lomang had requested a parley. Atoi thought this was hilarious. The large, muscly woman had been hanging out on the bridge when the request came through the ship's comm to Carina, courtesy of one of the man's guards.

"Parley?!" Atoi exclaimed. "Who the hell does he think he is? You'd think the weeks locked in his cabin would give him the clue he's a prisoner, not an adversary."

The scarred man, whose name Carina had learned was Chandu, was also present. He scoffed, saying, "Maybe he wants to discuss his method of execution. I don't know why he's still alive, to be frank." His eyes were hard as he directed his gaze Carina.

"Got anything else you want to say?" she asked.

"Yeah, I do. Lomang and his crew are a liability. We should have spaced them all the minute we got them under control. Keeping them alive is dumb."

"Well it was my decision not to murder them in cold blood," Carina said. "So you're saying I'm dumb?" She held Chandu's gaze, unblinking.

"No, he didn't mean it like that," Atoi said, suddenly serious.

Chandu muttered something Carina didn't catch.

"What was that?" she asked, maintaining eye contact with the man.

"Nothing," Chandu said. He strode off the bridge.

"Don't worry about him," Atoi said. "He's always got something to complain about but he's all words and no action. He's just blowing off steam."

"I'm not worried about him," said Carina, "but he should worry about me if carries on like that. The ones who mouth off all the time are the worst. They don't do anything because at heart they're cowards, but they ruin morale, which is worse. I'm going to talk to Cadwallader about him."

"A coward who joined a merc band?" asked Atoi. "That doesn't make a lot of sense."

"He has big strong girls like you to hide behind, don't forget," said Carina.

"Now *that*, I understand. What are you going to do about Lomang?"

"Give him his parley, I guess."

Carina still hadn't come up with an answer to the problem of the smuggler and his men. She wasn't a murderer, and by every measure she could think of, she was the one in the wrong. It didn't matter how many crimes Lomang had committed, that didn't make it okay for her to be a thief.

Though her grandmother was long dead, Carina could feel the old lady's disapproval whenever she thought about stealing the *Zenobia* and its illegal cargo.

Sorry, Nai Nai.

She hoped that returning to the birthplace of mages would excuse her sins.

~

Carina invited Cadwallader along to the face-to-face with Lomang. He was more experienced at that kind of thing and she trusted his judgment.

Lomang had lost weight while he'd been in captivity. The folds of rich fabric that made up his expensive clothes hung loosely on his shrunken frame. Even his favorite blue hat, which he'd seemingly put on especially for the occasion, now looked a little too big for his round head.

"First," he said, holding up a finger as he sat opposite Carina in his cabin, "you must promise not to do that thing you do."

"What thing is that?" She asked, cocking an eyebrow at him.

"Don't play with me." Lomang waved his hands. "*That* thing."

She chuckled. When she or any other mage Cast they didn't wave their hands about, yet the allusion to a stage magician performing a trick seemed impossible to avoid.

"You lock me inside my mind and I cannot control what I do or say," said Lomang. "It is very annoying and uncomfortable, and there is no point to this parley if I can't state my own opinion."

"There's no point to this parley at all," Cadwallader said. "You have no bargaining power. It's only due to Lin's kindness that we're here to listen to you before we refuse your 'offer'." He rested his hands on his spread knees.

Lomang scowled. All his confident bonhomie had evaporated during his incarceration. He looked vicious and vengeful.

Then, suddenly, he smiled and it was like the sun breaking through storm clouds. "I forgive your ignorance. I sometimes forget that I am in another sector and things work differently here. I must work harder to understand your culture and customs."

Cadwallader's eyes flicked to meet Carina's.

"What is it you want to say?" she asked Lomang. "Please don't waste our time with your babble."

"I believe you underestimate what I have to offer you, and how badly things will turn out for you once news of what you've done gets back to my people."

"I have everything you have to offer me secure in the hold of this ship," Carina replied. "And soon the soldiers helping me will have their share of it. As to news of what I've done getting back to your people, you gave up the location of the *Zenobia's* tracker and how to disable it while you were Enthralled. No word of what's happened here will reach your home." She leaned forward. "Be careful what you tell me, Lomang. Don't forget I can put you under and check the truth of your words."

Lomang spread his hands wide in a gesture of defeat, though Carina thought she detected a glint of rage in the man's eyes. "I cannot deny it. You have the upper hand. It is for this reason that I have finally decided to negotiate with you for my freedom and the release of my men."

"You are not in a position to negotiate," Cadwallader said. "If you go free it will be our decision. You have no influence in the matter. Lin, I'm sorry, but I have better things to do than to listen to this puffed-up idiot."

"I want to hear what he has to say," said Carina. "Humor me, please?"

Cadwallader raised his gaze to the ceiling but he remained in his seat and folded his arms over his chest.

"Make it quick, Lomang," Carina said.

"Before I can make my offer, it would be helpful to know what you need." Lomang flashed a tooth-filled grin. "You've seen what's in the *Zenobia's* hold. You've seen the type and range of goods I can acquire. I have contacts on many worlds in this sector and my own. Whatever is your heart's desire, I am confident I can get it for you—at no cost!"

Carina burst into laughter. "You think you could make me

pay for this mythical object you think I want so badly. You might know all about contraband, what you can buy in one place and sell in another at a huge profit, but you don't know me. There's nothing you can get me that I want."

"But you must want something," Lomang said. "*Everyone* wants something. To desire, to strive, to achieve a goal, these are very human traits. And though you are strange and have strange powers, you still seem human to me. What is it you need? What is pushing you on every day? You stole my ship on Pirine. Why?"

"I needed to get off the planet," she said. "I had no intention of taking anything from your hold. What we found in there was a complete surprise."

Lomang squinted at her. "It is true that nothing was missing. Before your brother betrayed me, he said he didn't know why you had gone to Ostillon. He said the place was dangerous for you, that the Dirksens were your enemies. What is the reason you wanted to go there? Is that where we're going now?"

"My motivations are no business of yours," Carina said, irritably.

"Ah, but they are," Lomang said. "They may be vital to my survival. Tell me what is at Ostillon that you want. My men picked you up in a temple. Is it religious salvation you crave?"

"No, I'm not looking for salvation." Carina paused.

Was it possible that Lomang could help in her search for information about mages and Earth?

"You said you aren't from this sector," she resumed. "Where are you from?"

Lomang's features broke into an expression of great relief. Carina guessed he thought he was finally making headway in his effort to save his life. He didn't know she had no intention of killing him.

"I believe here it's referred to as the Geriel Sector," he said, "though of course we give it a different name. Perhaps what you seek may be there? I would be willing to take you to my home planet, where you can search our archives to your heart's content."

"Lomang, if I were to set foot on your planet my life would be forfeit," said Carina, "so let's not pretend that's an option."

"Geriel Sector?" Cadwallader said. "That's a long way from here, and your ship isn't carrying Deep Sleep capsules."

"I purchased the *Zenobia* in this sector," Lomang said nervously.

"So you have another, bigger ship somewhere waiting for you when you want to go home," Cadwallader surmised.

A ship that carried Deep Sleep capsules would be very useful to Carina once she found out how to get to Earth, as well as a major prize in itself.

She and Cadwallader exchanged a look.

Lomang's face fell.

Carina said, "Ever since my family and I took over your ship, I've been defending you and your crew from those who want to space you. You seem like a practical man. You know that killing you all would be the simplest and safest option in this situation. However, as a gesture of mercy, I will guarantee your safety in exchange for the vessel that can travel between sectors. Give me the coordinates and any security or other intel I will need to take the ship."

Lomang wriggled uncomfortably in his seat.

"Remember," she went on, "I will check the truth of what you tell me with my..." she waved her hands. "...special powers."

23

Atoi had invited Carina to eat dinner with the mercs and she was happy to go along. As the days passed aboard the *Zenobia* and Carina spent time with her old buddies, reminiscing about assignments they'd carried out and soldiers who had died or retired, her attitude to merc life had changed. Her old friend and savior Captain Speidel had advised her to get away from it, telling her she wasn't like the others, but that wasn't true. For a time, she'd been very at home with being a merc, despite the violence and danger—perhaps even because of it. Spending years on the streets had accustomed her to a rough and ready way of life.

Living among the Black Dogs again had made her realize how domestic and stifling her life with Bryce and the children had become. She loved her little family but she was too young to be their mother. She felt ill-equipped to provide a childhood for her siblings when she hadn't had much of a one herself.

The passenger dining room was too small to accommodate the Black Dogs who ate aboard the *Zenobia* after coming off guard duty: the crew's mess room on the deck above was used instead. Carina sat with Atoi, Cadwallader, and Stevenson, around one end of a table. Atoi invited Halliday, Brown, and Jackson to sit with them too, for old time's sake.

"So the Sherrerr boy we rescued turned out to be your brother?" Atoi said, scraping the last of her dinner from her plate. "What a coincidence." She'd been eating yam mash and reconstituted meat.

The food was something Carina had never gotten used to in her two years as a merc, though some, like Atoi, seemed to love the slops. Most of the others had finished and were leaving the mess.

"Yeah," Carina replied, "though I didn't find out for a long time."

"Cute kid," said Atoi.

"I keep telling you," Stevenson said. "It's fate."

Carina couldn't tell if he was joking. The pilot didn't seem the type to believe in the supernatural.

"Fate or not," said Cadwallader, "that assignment certainly turned your life upside down, Lin."

"Yeah," Atoi said, "from blood-thirsty soldier to mother hen, all in the blink of an eye." She grabbed her drink and downed it all.

Jackson slammed down his glass. "I remember Orrana now! Shithole of a place."

"If you hadn't lobbed grenades into the refinery stacks we would have had it," said Halliday.

"Didn't save Carver," Jackson said, staring into his drink.

"Or Lee," Atoi added.

"Good soldiers," said Cadwallader. "Both of them."

"I'll drink to that," Jackson said, "but not this piss. This ship of yours got any beer aboard, Lin? Or are you keeping it all to yourself?"

Carina looked at Cadwallader. "In honor of the soldiers who gave their lives to rescue my brother?" she asked. The lieutenant colonel thought a moment then gave a slight nod.

Carina stood up. "I'll be right back."

Atoi and the others cheered.

On her way to the passenger level galley, Carina bumped into Bryce.

"Sorry, I can't stop," she said. "I'm on a mission."

"The kids missed you at dinner," said Bryce. "They were wondering where you'd gone."

"Didn't you get my message?"

"Yes, I got your message."

"Then why didn't you tell them I was eating with the mercs?"

"I did," Bryce replied, an edge to his tone. "My point is, why didn't *you* tell them? Why did you leave it to me to explain?"

"You mean I should send a note to six kids explaining my absence for one meal?" Carina rolled her eyes. "Okay, remind me to do that next time." She tried to step around Bryce but he moved to block her way.

"Is that it?" he asked. "Conversation over?"

Carina put her hands on her hips. "What else is there to discuss? I'm having dinner with some old friends. Since when did I need your permission to do that?"

"Old friends?" Bryce sneered. "Let me guess. The pilot's there, right?"

"So what if he is? What's wrong with you?"

"What's wrong with *you*, Carina? Ever since those mercenaries came aboard you've been acting weird. I want to know what's going on."

"Acting weird? What kind of weird?"

"You've changed," Bryce said. "You've gotten tough, short-tempered, dismissive. It's like you're a different person. Even the kids have noticed."

"Oh they have, have they?" said Carina. "I guess you were all discussing me at dinner."

"As a matter of fact, we were."

"That must have been a lot of fun for you all. Now get out of my way."

Bryce stepped to the side.

"We were talking about you because we're worried about you," he said as Carina passed him. "Because we care," he said to her back.

Carina stomped into the passenger galley. How dare they all discuss her behind her back like she was a conversation piece. After all she'd done for them, not one of those ungrateful brats could tell her to her face how much she was disappointing them all. At least they had the excuse they were kids. The same didn't apply to Bryce. His baseless jealousy was making him nutty.

She found the beer keg. It was only half empty. It appeared Lomang didn't have much of a taste for the brew, and neither she nor Bryce had been interested in drinking it with the kids around. She filled two pitchers and carried them out. By the time she returned to the mess, only Cadwallader, Atoi, Halliday, Stevenson, and Jackson remained. It was just as well. If the other mercs had seen the beer it would have made them envious and caused bad feelings, though doubtless Cadwallader was more than capable of putting any loudmouths in their place.

"Now that's a sight for sore eyes," Halliday said. "How long's it been since we had a drink?" He drained his glass and held it out.

"Too damned long," said Jackson. "Our CO keeps us on a tight leash, that's for sure." His gaze slid sideways to Cadwallader and he smirked.

"Not tight enough, it seems," the leader said, straight-faced as Carina poured his beer.

"Only kidding, sir," Jackson said. "Seriously, if I didn't have someone keeping booze out of my hands I'd be dead by now."

"Are you sure you should have some?" Carina asked.

"There she goes," said Atoi. She made clucking noises and flapped her elbows. "You channeling Jackson's mom, Car?"

"Geez, don't say that," said Jackson, looking genuinely frightened by the idea. "Anyway, my mom's still alive, last I heard."

"Yeah, she is," Halliday said. "She was telling me she gave up having kids after taking one look at you."

Stevenson lifted his beer into the air. "I propose a toast." He waited for everyone to lift their glasses. "Old times!"

"Old times," they all repeated.

Stevenson gave Carina a wink over the edge of his glass as he drank.

The conversation split into two groups. Atoi, Halliday, and Jackson compared their respective parents' disciplinary methods, which included beating them with the back of a spoon, locking them in a cellar, making them clean the bathroom with a toothbrush, forcing them to take ice-cold showers, and threatening to let the Regians take them.

Meanwhile, Cadwallader, Stevenson, and Carina talked about the war between the Sherrerrs and the Dirksens. The two men were interested to hear the inside story on what had been going on.

"We were approached by the Sherrerrs not long ago," Cadwallader said. "Something about a raid on a moon. I didn't like the sound of it and turned them down."

"That might have been Banner's Moon," said Carina. "I took part in that. We stole a prototype of a new weapon the Dirksens had developed."

"Really?" Stevenson said. "What does it do?"

"It sends out a subliminal signal that affects brain function," she replied.

"What, it impairs motor control?" asked Cadwallader.

"No. It affects the emotional state, inducing absolute terror, as I understand it. The soldiers were incapable of any action while under its influence."

"The soldiers?" Cadwallader said. "So you didn't experience the effects?"

"It didn't seem to work on me," said Carina. She shrugged. The conversation was moving in the direction of her magehood and making her uncomfortable. She wished she hadn't mentioned the raid on Banner's Moon.

She shifted in her seat. "I managed to get away from the Sherrerrs not long after that, bringing my half-brothers and sisters with me."

"Did you hear about their flagship, *Nightfall*?" asked Stevenson.

"Hear about it? I was aboard it."

"You were?" Stevenson whistled. "That was one big ship. Did you...?" He paused as his gaze focused on something behind Carina's back. He gave a small cough.

Carina turned. Bryce was standing in the doorway, glaring at her.

She was tempted to just ignore him, but Atoi, Halliday, and Jackson had noticed his arrival too. Now all her merc friends were looking at her, expecting her to do something.

She got up and strode toward him then walked past him and into the corridor.

"Do you want something?" she asked.

"Darius is asking for you," Bryce said. "He wants you to tell him a story before he goes to sleep."

"Can't you do it?"

"He wants you."

"He's seven! He doesn't know what he wants. Would it hurt you to say I'll tell him a story tomorrow? And why did you come all the way up here? It's embarrassing for you to come to the door to collect me like you're my dad."

"I tried to comm," Bryce said. "Your button's off."

"No, it…Oh." Carina didn't remember turning it off but she must have at some point. She turned it back on. "I'm going to be here for a while. Tell Darius I promise I'll tell him a story tomorrow. A long one to make up for missing one tonight."

Bryce didn't acknowledge her reply, only looked at her stonily. "I see your pilot friend *is* here."

"Fantastic observation skills you have," said Carina. "Is that it?"

"Are you going to spend the night with him?"

"What?!"

"You looked like you were pretty close with him just now, and that other guy, Cadwallader. Maybe it's him you're after, not the pilot?"

Carina stepped close to Bryce and poked him in the chest. "Firstly, Cadwallader isn't into women. Secondly, what the hell are you on? Have you been trying out the potions in Lomang's pharmacy in the hold? What makes you think I won't be coming back to our cabin tonight? I'm with you, aren't I?"

"I don't know. Are you?"

"Stars," Carina said, "if you have to ask…Maybe we shouldn't be together. Maybe we aren't right for each other after all. I'm seeing a side of you I never saw before."

"Ditto." Bryce gave Carina a sullen look and then walked away.

She returned to the mess, where the conversation had resumed in her absence. She tried to regain the spirit of the evening but she felt drained. Maybe reconnecting with the Black Dogs had changed her a little, bringing out aspects of her personality that hadn't shown while she was with Bryce and the kids, but so what? It was no excuse for Bryce to turn into a caricature of a jealous boyfriend. She wasn't going to apologize for having a romantic past that didn't include him, and she'd done nothing to justify his suspicions.

Carina sipped her beer and brooded as the others talked.

24

"So you really want to attack probably the most heavily defended place on all Ostillon?" Cadwallader asked, rubbing his jaw.

He and Carina were looking at a holo of the world. The globe turned as they watched it.

"We don't have to attack," Carina replied. "But I do want to get inside."

"And once you're inside?"

"I want to search it. I think there may be information there that's useful to me."

"From what I understand, this place is very large. Searching it thoroughly will take a long time and it doesn't sound like you know exactly what you're looking for."

Carina didn't have a good answer for the lieutenant colonel. She reached out and stopped the globe. "According to what my brother remembers, the Dirksen headquarters must be somewhere in this mountain range." She pointed at the place in the landscape. "He says he'll recognize the route if he goes there again."

"So we have to approach during daylight," said Cadwallader. His expression was doubtful.

Carina hoped he wasn't going to back out. The protocol for accepting work had changed since she'd left the Black Dogs: no more suicide missions, no matter what the payment. Her history with the band wouldn't have any influence. She knew if Cadwallader thought the assignment too dangerous he would refuse it, and the men and women would follow his decision regardless of any friendship with her.

"We won't be relying entirely on your support," she said. "Don't forget we have unusual capabilities ourselves."

"Hmm, yes," said Cadwallader, "your 'special powers'." His tone was skeptical.

They were alone in the mission room. Carina looked around for something she could use for a demonstration. She didn't like the idea of Casting just to prove a point, but she needed Cadwallader to believe her if they were to factor the mages' abilities into their planning.

As her gaze roved the room, a lump suddenly came to her throat and her vision blurred.

"Is something wrong, Carina?" asked Cadwallader.

He'd never called her by her first name before. It made her feel worse.

She rubbed her eyes with the heels of her hands. "The last person I had this conversation with was Captain Speidel."

"You told John about these powers too?" Cadwallader's usually deadpan expression broke. He looked taken aback.

"I made him swear never to tell anyone," said Carina. "I said my life depended on it." She'd guessed that Cadwallader and Speidel might have been more than fellow officers.

She swallowed and continued, "It was how I knew exactly where Darius was when we went to rescue him. I had the tracker the Dirksens had cut out of him. I used it to Cast Locate to find him. But I had to tell Speidel how I knew the location of the child or he would never have authorized the mission."

"I remember," Cadwallader said softly. "He was hazy about the intel, which wasn't like him. I trusted that he knew what he was doing."

Carina hung her head. "I'm so sorry he died."

A silence followed, an informal moment of remembrance.

"John was no fool," Cadwallader said. He sighed and then appeared to draw himself together. "I'm prepared to be impressed. When you're ready, Lin." He spoke briskly. The wall was up again.

Carina had seen an interface screen that she could Transport, but then she had an idea for something more impressive. It would make Cadwallader realize how useful the mage children could be during the infiltration of the mountain castle. She comm'd Darius.

"Hi, Carina," he piped in reply.

"Could you come to the mission room?"

"Sure!"

"I want him to show you something special," Carina said to Cadwallader. "You might be surprised to hear it, but Darius is the most powerful mage among us—probably the most powerful mage in this sector."

"Darius is the little boy who was kidnapped?"

"That's right."

"That is surprising. So this ability is nothing to do age or training?"

"It does require training, but basically you're born a mage or not. My youngest sister, Nahla, has no ability at all. Most of the rest of them are like me—we needed to learn and practice our skills. Darius is naturally gifted. He can even invent his own Casts, something I'd never even heard of.

"I guess this is a good time to tell you about Castiel too. For a long time, everyone thought he was like Nahla, entirely without any mage powers. But when he hit puberty his ability suddenly developed. It was a bad sign. I don't know a lot about it, but from what I understand that usually happens if the person is a Dark Mage."

"That doesn't sound good."

"It's not. For a long time, Castiel has lived up to the image. He's done some terrible things. Now he *says* he's come over to our side and wants to be a part of the family again... but I don't believe him. It's pure expediency to get what he wants."

"And what's that?" Cadwallader asked.

"I honestly don't know. All I know is we mustn't ever trust him. He could turn on us any minute. Of all the kids, he's the most like his father, and his father was a monster."

"Okay, noted." Cadwallader turned his attention to the mountain range on the holo of Ostillon as they waited for Carina's youngest sibling.

A few moments later, Darius arrived.

"Hey, Carina," he said as the mission room door drew back. He ran up to her and gave her a hug, though it had only been a couple of hours since they'd seen each other at breakfast.

"Hey, sweetie," she replied. "Could show the lieutenant colonel one of your Casts?"

"Okay! Which one do you want me to do?"

"I was wondering if you could Cast Guise again."

"Of course I can. Who should I Cast it on? You?"

"I thought maybe you could do it on him."

Cadwallader looked concerned. "Um...What does this entail exactly?"

"You don't have to do anything," said Carina. "And, don't worry, it won't hurt."

"I hadn't imagined it might hurt until you said that." Cadwallader seemed to be joking.

Darius was studying the man carefully. He wasn't as familiar with the mercs as he was with Bryce, Carina supposed, so he needed time to take in his appearance. It was something worth remembering if she wanted Darius to impersonate someone during the attempt to infiltrate the Dirksen headquarters.

Her little brother took his elixir canister from his belt and drank some of the liquid.

"I wondered why you all carried those flasks," Cadwallader said.

Darius's eyes closed. Then he became Cadwallader.

The real one swore and stepped backward, stumbling over his own feet. He turned so white Carina thought he might faint or vomit.

"It's only an illusion," she said. "Nothing more."

Cadwallader tried to regain some composure, straightening his jacket, but he continued to stare at Darius/Cadwallader. Carina wondered if she'd gone too far. She hadn't intended to frighten the officer. She guessed she'd forgotten he'd never seen even the simplest Cast before, let alone one of Darius's off-the-wall extravaganzas.

"Remarkable" Cadwallader said finally. "I presume he can change back? Having two of us around might be confusing."

"Casts are temporary," said Carina. "He can't change back at will—or I think you can't, can you, Darius?"

The copy of Cadwallader shook his head.

"But the Cast will fade soon," she continued, "and then he'll be back to normal."

"I can't deny it's extremely convincing," said Cadwallader. "Can I touch you, Darius?"

"Sure," he replied. "I don't mind."

The merc approached Darius, reaching out a hand. He touched 'his' chest, and his hand disappeared. "There's nothing there. I can't feel a thing." His tone was wondrous.

His arm moved downward.

"That's my head!" Darius exclaimed.

Cadwallader chuckled. "Extraordinary." He turned to Carina, withdrawing his arm from his fake twin. "He appears to be altering light somehow, creating an illusion."

"It seems to be a fundamental law of Casting that we can't create something from nothing. We can only alter or move what's already there."

"Is this what helped you to be a good soldier?" asked Cadwallader.

"No," Carina replied. "I hardly ever Cast while I was on duty. It was too dangerous for me. I didn't want to get found out. Once people know what you can do, it just brings a whole world of trouble, believe me. That's why I'd appreciate it if you and the rest of the Black Dogs never tell anyone else about us."

Cadwallader nodded.

Carina was relieved she didn't have to go to the effort of trying to convince him of the truth of her words.

"You understand I can't guarantee that, however?" he said. "Soldiers get injured and retire or they simply leave. I can't police what they do when they're no longer under my authority."

"I know. If I find what I need on Ostillon, me and my family will hopefully be far away before word gets out."

Suddenly, Cadwallader's mouth dropped open. "The defense of the embassy! The enemy soldiers disappearing. That was real. It was you!"

"I didn't have a choice," Carina said. "We would all have died if I hadn't done something."

"Huh! I didn't believe it for a minute. I thought it was battle stress making the troops hallucinate."

"We were stressed, but it was real."

The second Cadwallader disappeared and Darius stood in his place, looking pleased with himself. The original squatted to get down to his eye level and ruffled the boy's dark brown mop of hair. "You're a smart boy, aren't you? Your sister's proud of you. She doesn't say it, but I can tell. And so she should be. You're going to be a big help when we pay the Dirksens a visit."

Cadwallader stood up. "It's time your siblings received some basic training if you intend for them to take part in this mission. They'll need weapons as well as their powers if they're to defend themselves against armed soldiers. Unless you have a Cast that stops pulse fire?"

"No. Not even Darius can do that. But I've already given my siblings some weapons training. And Bryce went through Basic with the Sherrerrs."

"Good. Then all we need to do is get them working as a team with the troops."

"Oh, I didn't think that would be necessary."

"You didn't?" Cadwallader asked. "Then what was your plan? You haven't detailed anything."

Carina sighed. "That's because I don't have one."

"The powers you and your family possesses are impressive, but they aren't all you need more than that to get inside the Dirksens' mountain castle and keep you safe while you search it. Otherwise you wouldn't be paying for our services. I've noticed you seem to be going to some effort to keep your siblings and the Black Dogs apart, but the only way you're going to succeed in your endeavor is if both parties work together."

"That's what I was afraid of," Carina said.

25

Telling the Black Dogs about the mages' abilities had been unavoidable. Carina had realized that before she made contact with them. Working in proximity, it was inevitable that the mercs would see the mages Casting. She'd gotten the information out in the open right from the start, but the act had weighed heavily on her. Nai Nai had conditioned her to deeply fear exposure, and for good reason: the old woman had lost her son and daughter-in-law to a trap laid by Stefan Sherrerr.

In the end, Carina had decided that the risk was worth it if it meant they could discover the information they needed to find Earth. If they had that they could leave the sector forever, hopefully before the mercs could turn on them.

It was the period between the telling and the leaving that worried her. Bryce had shown her that not all non-mages were out to exploit and enslave her, and she trusted certain members of the Black Dogs, like Stevenson, Cadwallader, and Atoi. However, to many of them she was nothing more than an ex-merc. They had no history with her, no comradeship or sense of obligation. She couldn't predict what they might do once they had thought through the possibilities. Others, like Chandu, she didn't trust at all.

So it wasn't only Bryce's concern about Parthenia's vulnerability that had motivated Carina to keep her siblings away from the mercs, it was also a fear of familiarity between the two groups. She didn't want her brothers or sisters to feel comfortable and relax their guard around the military men and women.

But Cadwallader's logic was faultless: she couldn't expect to get into the Dirksen headquarters without a coordinated plan including the mages and the mercs. They would have to try out plans and rehearse the steps together.

The problem was, they had nowhere to practice. Neither the *Duchess* nor the *Zenobia* had facilities for military training. When Carina had been with the Black Dogs they had trained in uninhabited regions of sparsely populated planets. But as far as she knew, no such places existed between them and Ostillon, and she didn't want to waste time with a diversion. Each day that passed ate through the value of the goods in the hold.

Several days after their first discussion about the assignment Cadwallader asked Carina to join him again in the mission room.

"I asked Stevenson to keep an eye on the scan data for a place we could use for a rehearsal," he said as she entered the room. "He found this." Ostillon had been replaced on the holo display by another world she didn't recognize. "We're three cycles out from it. With the opportunity to train it allows the diversion will be worth the extra time, I believe."

"I don't think it's safe to set down on an inhabited planet," she said. "I don't want to take the risk."

"It isn't inhabited," said Cadwallader. "It's a rogue planet."

"No kidding." She stepped closer to the spinning sphere. "What liquid is making up those oceans?"

"It's water. Geothermal energy is keeping the place above

zero degrees. It even has a magnetosphere and it's retained a hydrogen and helium atmosphere. We would have to adapt some EVA suits for the children."

"You can't Cast in an EVA suit," Carina said, tapping her elixir canister.

"I don't see why not," said Cadwallader. "A water supply can be fitted inside for long assignments. That stuff you drink is just another liquid."

"Hmm. Good point. I guess I'd never thought about it. What's the planet's gravity?"

"That's the catch. It's one point six standard."

Carina grimaced. The children were entirely unused to moving about while weighing more than fifty percent heavier than their regular weight. And the argument that training in high-grav made you fitter for fighting at lower gravities didn't apply to this situation. You didn't need to be fit to Cast.

"The troops have to rehearse somewhere," said Cadwallader. "They've never worked with mages before, and probably won't ever again, though that's beside the point. You know the drill. It's usually us versus combatants. But this time around there's going to be a bunch of kids performing magic tricks, getting in the way most likely, and strange stuff will be happening that's going to throw the soldiers off their game. They need to know what to expect. And do you want your brothers and sisters to be around a firefight without any idea of what's going on? I don't need to tell you how dangerous that is. It isn't only the Black Dogs who need these rehearsals, it's the mages too."

"I know, I know," Carina said. She took a breath. "Okay. We're three days out, you say? That should be enough time to modify some suits."

"Right. I suggest this area for the rehearsal." Cadwallader pointed to a mountainous area on one of the globe's continents.

The data indicated there should be plenty of caves. "Maybe we can find a cavern to represent the mountain castle."

THE YOUNGER CHILDREN became alive with excitement when they heard the news. Carina had brought them into her and Bryce's cabin to tell them.

"Do we get to fire weapons?" Oriana asked, her eyes shining.

"Probably not," replied Carina. "Your role is to Cast, remember?"

Oriana's mouth turned down in a pout. "But we will be armed, right?"

"Yes, you'll be armed because you'll be armed for the real thing since you need a weapon to defend yourself. But the aim of the exercise is to practice working with the mercs. They're the ones who'll be doing most of the shooting."

"Cool!" Ferne exclaimed.

"Am I coming too?" Nahla asked.

There was an awkward pause. Nahla couldn't Cast, and as a child she certainly couldn't fight. There was nothing she could do except get in the way, and while the last thing Carina wanted to do was hurt her little sister's feelings, she couldn't afford to spare them when her presence could put others at risk.

"Not this time," she said. "But when you're a bit bigger I'll teach you everything I know about fighting."

Sweet-natured Nahla seemed satisfied with this response.

Then Castiel said, "You can't join in because you aren't good enough. You'll just get in the way."

Nahla's eyes grew shiny and her chin trembled.

"Castiel," said Carina through clenched teeth, "I swear, one more comment like that and you'll be back in the brig, sharing a cell with that mutant in Lomang's crew. I bet he hasn't forgotten how you betrayed them."

"You wouldn't dare," Castiel said. "You need me."

"No, we don't," said Parthenia. "We can manage perfectly well without you."

"Try me," Carina added. "Have you ever known me not to follow through on a threat?"

Castiel glared at her but he said nothing.

"So what's the plan?" Bryce asked.

Things between him and Carina had been at a stalemate since their most recent spat. They were civil but nothing more. Carina didn't know if Bryce had stopped bothering her because he'd realized he was being an idiot or because he'd decided he didn't want to be with her but was waiting for a good moment to tell her.

She still felt the same about him and would be heartbroken if he wanted to split up, but she knew she'd done nothing wrong and had nothing to apologize for. If anyone needed to apologize it was Bryce, for his unfounded, ridiculous, and shaming accusations and for embarrassing her in front of her friends.

"I'm still working on the details with Cadwallader," Carina replied. "When it comes to the actual thing, we decided the best approach is to fly the shuttle into the range during daylight so Castiel can direct us to the hidden entrance. Darius will Cloak the shuttle so we won't be seen."

"Yes!" the little boy interjected, punching the air.

"After Stevenson drops us off he'll return to the ship. It's unlikely there's going to be anywhere to set down out there, and even if there was we wouldn't be able to hide the evidence that a vessel has landed. Then we'll wait until dark to approach the castle. But for the rehearsals we don't have to worry about most of that, only the approach over mountain terrain. What we'll be practicing is infiltrating the castle, taking out the guards, and searching the place for information about mages."

"Do you think they will have left anything behind for us to find?" Parthenia asked. "I mean, why would they?"

"I agree it's possible there's nothing there," Carina admitted. "If so, we'll be back to square one. But there's still the religious artifacts on Ostillon. They might hold some clues. Maybe we can steal the originals and see if we can glean some information that way."

"I thought mages weren't supposed to steal?" Darius asked.

"Huh," Castiel said. "Carina's stolen the *Zenobia's* entire hold of contraband. How do you think she's paying the Black Dogs?"

"Is that true, Carina?" Darius asked, his large, deep brown eyes wide and fixed on her.

"Er," she said. She couldn't deny it.

Castiel was smirking as he waited for her answer.

"We are giving the things Lomang was smuggling to the Black Dogs," said Carina finally. "But they're things that should never be bought or sold anyway, and Lomang was going to enslave us."

"And what about the religious artifacts?" Castiel asked, folding his arms. "I'm sure they have deep spiritual significance to the people of Ostillon."

"Yeah, people who invaded an occupied planet and drove the mages into hiding," said Bryce.

Carina said, "Darius, I don't have a good reason to justify what we're doing. Two wrongs don't make a right, and if we weren't in the position we're in I wouldn't even contemplate what I'm proposing. But mages have been pushed into a corner for no fault of their own, just for living their lives the best way they can. It's long past the time we made a stand and took back what should be ours: the right to live free of the fear of persecution and enslavement. And if I have to break a few rules to achieve that, so be it."

"I don't mind breaking any rules," said Ferne.

Oriana punched his shoulder.

26

Carina lowered Darius's visor and stepped back. Her brother looked incredibly cute in his little EVA suit. They were in the *Duchess's* shuttle bay with the other mages, gearing up for the rehearsal.

"Take a small sip of elixir to check the feed is working," she said.

"I can hear you inside my helmet!" Darius exclaimed.

"Yes, we'll all be able to hear each other when the rehearsal starts, so you have to be careful not to talk unless it's about something important. If you want to talk to anyone one-on-one you have to give a voice command. Don't worry about that for now. Just try to sip some elixir."

He closed his lips around the end of the straw that protruded near his mouth, then gave Carina a thumbs-up.

"Great," she said.

The other kids had finished putting on their suits.

"All the weapons are in training mode," she told them. "Don't adjust the settings or you could hurt someone. If you get hit an alarm will sound, once for a non-lethal injury and twice for a fatal wound—though in reality any hit would probably be lethal because it would breach your suit and you'd suffocate."

"Now then, Carina," Bryce said dryly. "Don't candy-coat it just because they're kids. Tell it like it really is."

"If you receive a non-lethal hit," said Carina, ignoring him, "you can move for...Let's say three minutes, slowly. If you hear the alarm sound twice, lie down. You're dead."

"I'm gonna shoot you all," Castiel said, moving to draw his pulse gun from its holster under his arm.

Carina was on him in a flash. She snatched the weapon from his hand.

"No gun for you this time around," she said.

"Hey!" Castiel protested. "I was only kidding."

Carina leaned into the boy so their visors were touching. "You never play around with weapons. Not ever. I don't care if you're still a kid. These are not toys. And if you can't understand that basic fact, you stay behind when we go to Ostillon. Maybe you stay behind forever."

"I won't let you leave me there!" Castiel exclaimed. "I won't allow it. I'll take Nahla again!"

"That's it," said Carina. "Take off your suit. You're going back to the *Zenobia*."

"No, I didn't mean it! Honestly, I didn't!"

"You're done. You had your chance and you messed up. This rehearsal is too important to waste any more time on your nonsense. Go back to the ship."

"Please," said Castiel. "I...I'm sorry. I promise I won't do anything else. I don't even want the gun back. I know I was stupid and I'm sorry."

"No," Carina said. She turned to her other siblings. "The rest of you get in the shuttle. The mercs will be along in a minute."

Castiel's shoulders sagged. He looked regretful and forlorn, but Carina didn't believe he was genuine. Even if the boy really had decided to try to reform, he clearly remained full of bitterness and spite. She wasn't confident he could ever overcome it, and she wasn't going to sacrifice the other kids' safety to make him feel better about himself.

"Maybe you should let him come," Parthenia said. "He did apologize."

"Yeah," said Ferne. "He was only messing around. I'd hate to be left behind. Nahla's coming along even though she won't be taking part."

Nahla was going to remain on the shuttle with Stevenson while the rest of them carried out the rehearsal.

Ferne's input surprised Carina. Of all the siblings he seemed to dislike Castiel the most.

"What do you think, Bryce?" she asked.

He shrugged. "Up to you."

Thanks for the support, she thought. "Okay, Castiel. You can come, but step one foot out of line and you're going straight back to the shuttle."

Castiel mumbled something that sounded like "Thanks," and for once his tone wasn't sarcastic.

Carina still didn't trust him.

THE RIDE DOWN to the unnamed, uncharted rogue planet brought back memories of Carina's merc days. The bare metal interior and cramped confines of the shuttle's cabin were exactly as she remembered. Their EVA suits supplied their air so they couldn't smell the cabin's air, but the place probably stunk. There was no real reason for cleaning it.

After leaving the *Duchess's* a-grav, they all bobbed against their harnesses, two long rows of mercs and mages, facing each other, no one speaking. Cadwallader sat in the place Captain Speidel had occupied on many of their shorter missions.

Carina recalled Smitz chewing that foul herb he loved so much and her trying to avoid the gobs of spit he would send out, and that time he'd tried to take her elixir, thinking it was water. She also recalled the merc bodies they had stowed in the well along the floor between the facing rows, as they took them back to the *Duchess* for formal burial.

The rogue planet's gravitational force increased, and everyone sank onto the benches. Carina had warned the children they would feel much heavier while they were on the planet. Would they be able to cope? Perhaps not, after the initial novelty wore off.

Suddenly, the shuttle dropped, causing some of the kids to scream, though Carina thought they sounded more excited than scared. She mentally sighed. The rehearsal wasn't supposed to be a fun exercise. She didn't know how to make her siblings appreciate the real danger they would be facing when they attempted to penetrate the Dirksen defenses on Ostillon.

The shuttle dropped again, then juddered.

"Just a little turbulence," Stevenson said over the comm. "Nothing to worry about."

He'd suggested that Nahla ride up front with him in the copilot's seat. Carina doubted anyone had ever shown the little girl so much attention. She was probably having the time of her life.

As they drew closer to the gravity well of their destination, everyone settled down on their benches. It wouldn't be long until they landed, then the 'enemy' would take their positions.

Half the mercs taking part in the rehearsal wore bands that designated them as Dirksen troops and they would be identified as such on the visor HUDs. Carina and the other mages were playing themselves, and Bryce would be fighting alongside the friendly mercs. The aim was to attempt to enter a cavern that the enemy mercs would defend, using dummy arms fire and Casting.

After discussion with Cadwallader, Carina had suggested Casts the mages might use, primarily Transport, Fire (as a diversionary tactic), and Enthrall. Carina had contemplated using Darius's new Guise Cast, but he was the only one who could do it and he didn't know exactly when it would fade. She wanted to avoid exposing the little boy to excessive risk. She was uncomfortable enough with taking him along but she also knew his powers would be invaluable in a crisis.

Cadwallader had asked the inevitable question: could mages kill?

A gun is faster, she had replied. It was her standard, non-committal response. She wasn't about to ask her siblings to kill anyone. If they had to, under threat of losing their own life, they knew how. After seeing their father die, they didn't need reminding of the appropriate Cast. Cadwallader hadn't pushed the issue.

"Touchdown in three minutes," said Stevenson.

The gravitational pull had been steadily increasing as they descended. The mercs didn't remark upon it as they were used to non-standard gravities.

"I'm getting squashed!" Darius exclaimed. He lifted an arm. "My arm is heavy."

"It's going to be harder for you all to move around," Carina reminded the kids. "If it gets to be too much, let me know then go back to the shuttle and rest. I don't want you to fall down or have some other kind of accident while we're here. The EVA suits are tough but they aren't impregnable."

A short while later, the shuttle gave a brief shudder as it landed. The exit portal swung up.

"I didn't think it would be dark," Oriana said.

The landscape outside was nearly indiscernible. Black humps stood out against the brilliant stars of the background.

“What did you expect?” asked Ferne. “There’s no sun.”

“Your helmet lights will come on when you step outside,” Carina said. “It’s better this way. Our attempt to enter the Dirksen mountain castle will take place at night too.”

“Let’s go!” Darius unfastened his safety harness.

“Wait,” said Carina. “Our enemies have to take their positions.”

Cadwallader had already ordered the mercs who were playing the adversaries to exit the vessel. The ‘friendly’ team left next. Finally, it was the mages’ turn to walk down the ramp that led outside.

Carina followed the kids, her HUD displaying a rapidly dropping temperature and adjusting atmospheric gas levels. The temperature stabilized at one degree C. The atmosphere was composed almost entirely of hydrogen.

Like a line of extremely disciplined fireflies, the lights of the ‘enemy’ mercs were already departing across the landscape. Cadwallader was going with them. Atoi was to be the CO for the friendly mercs. The imbalance in experience between the two commanding officers was probably deliberate on Cadwallader’s part. He wanted to make the task as difficult for the attackers as possible.

With the mages’ scant exposure to combat, that wouldn’t be hard.

27

Atoi was leading them toward a high ridge that overlooked the cavern entrance, probably guessing that Cadwallader would have posted lookouts along the easiest, most obvious routes. To avoid detection by the enemy, she'd ordered them to turn off their helmet lights, so they were traveling on night vision. Starlight glimmered brightly on the EVA suits and visors. Ahead of Carina a line of figures snaked across the dull black mountainside.

She was bringing up the rear, last of the mages. They'd been going for half an hour or so, and she was breathing heavily in the one-point-six *g*. She hadn't realized she'd gotten so out of shape. All the mages were beginning to lag behind the mercs.

She opened a channel to only her siblings. "Hurry up. This is a team effort, remember? Don't let your fellow soldiers down."

Oriana was the only one to reply. "I'm so heavy. I'm never eating flannock fishcakes again."

"You don't even like flannock fishcakes," said Ferne.

The aim of the rehearsal was to penetrate all the enemy's

defenses. As a practice for the real thing it was barely adequate but they didn't know what they would be looking for or where to find it if they *did* manage to get inside the mountain castle, so they had to improvise as best they could. At least the mages would have the opportunity to become accustomed to operating in a battle situation.

"Halt," said Atoi.

They had to be near the cavern. Carina peered over the edge of the ledge but at first all she could see was the rough side of the mountain. Then a ragged mouth seemed to open in the mountain's face. Two figures stood just inside the entrance. Easy targets.

"Captain, do you want the mages to take those two guards out?" Carina asked Atoi.

"You read my mind," the other woman replied. "And if you can do it without alerting any of the others, the kids get to play with Jackson's prosthesis."

"Hey!" came Jackson's protest over the comm.

"I'll do it!" yelled Ferne.

"Shh," said Carina. "Wait for the order. Do you see who we mean?"

"Uh huh," Ferne replied. "I'll Enthrall the one on the left and Oriana can do the other."

A few moments later, he said, "Done."

"Mine too," said Oriana.

"Is that it?" Atoi asked. "They don't look any different."

"That's what you wanted, isn't it?" Carina asked. "When they see us appear they won't react, and they'll do whatever you tell them for the next ten minutes to an hour."

"I guess we have to trust you," Atoi said. "Okay, troops, rappel down to the entrance and storm the place. Kill those two at the entrance first."

"Kill them?" said Parthenia in a horrified tone. "But they aren't dangerous now they're Enthralled."

"They aren't dangerous *yet*," Atoi corrected.

"You don't need to rappel down," Carina said. "I can Cast to move you all faster. Just tell me where."

"Uh, okay," She related the positions she wanted the troops, which were basically just out of sight of the entrance.

Carina had moved more soldiers and further at the disastrous defense of the embassy. This time they were all in sight, which made the task easier. "Right, get ready," she told them. "And don't panic. I don't want you falling over when you hit the ground in this high-g and breaking a leg." She sucked elixir through her helmet tube and sent out the Cast.

Exclamations of surprise and colorful cursing came over the comm as the mercs found themselves floating through the atmosphere and down the cliff face.

The children giggled.

Carina set them down gently. "Now it's our turn," she said to the kids.

As the mercs set off at a run toward the cavern entrance, she and the children lowered themselves to the spot the mercs had just left.

"C'mon," she said as soon as they landed. "Let's go."

"I can't run," Oriana complained. "I can barely walk."

Despite her complaints the young girl picked up her pace. Up ahead, the battle's pulse fire flashed from the cavern entrance.

"It would make more sense for us to lead the attack," Parthenia puffed. "If we Enthralled or Transported everyone we saw, no one would get hurt."

"Don't be stupid," said Castiel. "They're soldiers. They're paid to die."

"All of you, be quiet," Carina barked. "We go in second this time. That's the plan."

They would try it the other way around next time, with additional strategies from Cadwallader to rehearse.

Atoi comm'd that the cavern entrance was clear.

"Darius, behind me," Carina directed. "The rest of you, flank me as I told you earlier."

Every mage except Darius carried a weapon. Carina didn't trust any seven-year-old not to shoot someone or themselves by accident, and though all the weapons were set to practice mode, she didn't want Darius to become accustomed to having one. She would protect him—with her life if necessary.

Parthenia and Castiel took the two positions farthest from Carina, and Oriana and Ferne walked nearest to her. The ability to sip elixir and keep their hands free was an advantage that Carina had never appreciated before. But then, mages usually had no cause to be toting a gun and Casting simultaneously.

The two guards Oriana and Ferne had Enthralled were sitting outside the entrance, 'killed' by Atoi's troops. As they walked inside, Carina saw two more pairs of boots behind rocks, which her HUD also marked as 'dead'. Cadwallader's battle strategy didn't seem to be working too well, but Carina guessed there was more to what he was doing than met the eye.

Flashes from the opening at the back of the cavern spoke of a second encounter. Atoi's advance had met resistance.

"Slow down," Carina said as the mages approached the rear of the cave. She comm'd Atoi for an update.

It was several moments before her old friend replied. "Shit, it's not good, Car. They've got us pinned down. Cadwallader laid an ambush, the son-of-a-bitch."

The fizz and hiss of pulse fire sounded over the comm.

"Roger," Carina said. "Coming in."

"No," said Atoi. "Wait there. We don't need rescuing by a bunch of kids."

"We can help."

"Negative," Atoi said. "I repeat, negative. Do not advance. The area is not secure."

"Yeah," said Carina. "I'm not a Black Dog anymore." She closed the comm and opened another to the mages. "We need to go in and rescue our troops."

"Yes!" Oriana exclaimed. "Let's do it."

The six mages walked through the aperture at the back of the cave, where the floor sloped sharply downward. Carina went first into the gap. She crouched down and signaled to the others to do the same. They advanced more slowly.

The EVA suits gave out next to no heat and here, where the natural light levels were very low, they would reflect little light for the night vision to pick up. The enemy troops—and they themselves—would be hard to see.

Though there was little natural light, occasional bursts of pulse fire had radiated up the—

She'd seen something! For an instant, the flash of a pulse in the distance had bounced off a small, domed surface just beyond a rocky protrusion into the passage. The dome was too smooth and regular to be natural. It had to be the helmet of a merc Cadwallader had stationed there to wait for them.

Carina lifted her weapon to her shoulder. She could Cast Enthrall in the vicinity she'd seen the helmet but without a clear line of sight she couldn't be completely confident it would work, and the only way to find out would be to expose one of them to attack.

She aimed in roughly the right direction, and waited.

Another flash came.

She fired.

Had she hit the waiting merc?

"Why are you shooting?" asked Castiel. "We're the mages. We should be Casting."

Ignoring him, she said, "I'm going forward. Stay back until I tell you it's okay to join me. If I get killed, retreat." Maintaining her crouch, she went deeper into the tunnel. Behind the protrusion, she found the merc she'd shot. He gave a wave.

Carina comm'd the mages. "Okay, advance."

Cadwallader's response to the signal from the EVA suit of the downed merc was immediate. Troops came running up the tunnel to meet them. Carina shot one but missed the other, who carried on firing.

"I'm wounded!" yelled Ferne.

Suddenly, the remaining merc stopped dead and dropped her weapon.

"I Enthralled her," Parthenia said.

"So did I," said Oriana.

"And me," added Castiel.

The poor soldier had been hit with three Enthrall Casts at once. Carina gently moved her to the side of the tunnel and made a mental note to make sure she would be guided back to the shuttle and not left behind. She would probably be out for a while.

Five of the enemy lay dead behind them, one in front of them, and one more had been incapacitated. Cadwallader was getting low on troops. He probably barely had enough to keep Atoi's group locked down.

Carina realized he wouldn't have received a signal from the Enthralled merc's suit. Physically, she was absolutely fine, and no pulse rounds had hit her as far as Carina knew. Cadwallader might think the tunnel remained defended.

The mages continued to slowly walk down the pitch-dark tunnel. Even with night vision it was hard to distinguish the way ahead. The craggy walls were drawing in, and soon they were down to single file, with Carina in front.

A stony dead end confronted them, but the flashes from the battle ahead revealed a crack in the wall to the right. Carina told the others to halt. She approached the crack and peeked in. Another blank wall of stone stood only a meter or so away. From the intensity of the flashes of light, the battle seemed to be going on just beyond it around a sharp turn.

Carina guessed that as soon as the mages emerged from the second turn they would be revealed. Yet if they were to be of any use to Atoi's team, they had to see the opposing troops.

She wished there was a Cast called Seeing Around Corners. She would have to ask Darius if he could invent it. For now, however, there appeared to be only one course of action.

She quickly explained her plan to the mages.

"Stick to my behind like glue," she said to Darius, who giggled.

"Ready?" she asked.

Five helmets nodded.

"*Go*!"

Carina ran into the gap in the wall and turned hard right. A wider space opened up. She ran into it, firing. Cadwallader's troops ranged around the edges, focused on a spot in the corner.

She got off four or five rounds before any of the enemy knew what was happening. She wasn't sure how many she'd hit. They were turning, but there was no cover, except in the corner where Atoi's team had to be. She ran toward it, continuing to fire.

WOUNDED RIGHT LEG appeared on her HUD.

The dark space was lit with flashes. Carina didn't have time to look back at what the kids were doing. Enemy troops in front of her were freezing. Others disappeared entirely.

She was at the corner, running between a gap in the low rocks.

More enemy mercs appeared from the other side. Atoi's team fired on them.

Where's Darius?

Carina found her brother beside her, eyes closed.

Two more mages made it to the corner. Two lay on the cavern floor.

"Cease fire," came Cadwallader's command over the comm.

Next to Carina, a mage raised their weapon. She recognized Oriana. Reaching out, Carina pushed her sister's muzzle down.

The mercs who had been pinned down relaxed. The enemy soldiers were all either dead, wounded, not responding because they were Enthralled, or simply gone.

Atoi stood up. "Shit, Car, I thought I told you to stay back."

"What did you expect me to do? Leave you all to die?"

"I expected you to follow orders," Atoi said. "If we don't work as a team we'll fail. Why do I even have to remind you of that? And they're kids." She pointed at the two mages who had been fatalities in the battle. "We don't expect them to die for us."

Ferne and Parthenia were rising to their feet.

"They have to learn that it's a real risk," said Carina. "They have to learn caution, and maybe we have to work on some better tactics. That's the point of the rehearsal."

A heavy hand clapped her on her shoulder. "Lin, Atoi," said Cadwallader. "Debriefing back on the *Duchess*."

One of Atoi's team pushed roughly past Carina and stomped away.

Her HUD told her it was Bryce.

28

As Carina got ready for bed that evening, Bryce was cold and silent. He'd said very little since the rehearsal and even then it had been mostly to the kids. Predictably, Darius was quiet too, picking up on Bryce's mood.

Carina decided to try to break the tension while the little boy was showering, if only for her brother's sake. There wasn't a lot she could do about him being a sponge for the emotions of those around him, but what she could do, she would.

"What's up with you, Bryce?" she asked, in as neutral a tone as she could manage. He'd been a PITA lately with his irrational jealousy. The future she'd imagined for them both was looking increasingly hazy. She found it hard to be around him without feeling resentful and angry.

He was sitting on the edge of the bed, facing away from her, resting his elbows on his knees. He turned his head, and the look on his face cooled the fire of her annoyance like the fall rain cooled the heat of summer on her home world. He wasn't pissed at her, he was sad.

"Where did Carina go?" he asked. "'Cause I don't know who the hell *you* are."

"What do you mean?"

He didn't answer, only stood up and pulled his shirt off over his head.

"Bryce, answer me," Carina pressed. "What do you mean, you don't know who I am? I'm the same person I've always been. If anyone's changed, it's you."

He walked into the closet.

"Dammit, don't walk away from me when I'm trying to talk to you!" she shouted.

"Stars," he replied, "I'm getting a clean shirt." He walked out into the bedroom. "This is *exactly* what I mean. What's wrong with you? Ever since those mercs came aboard you've been cranky and distant. It's like you're drawing away from me and the kids."

"Not this again," Carina said. "I can't help it that I knew some of the Black Dogs before I met you, and, yes, some of them are men, and, yes, I do have a 'history', as you like to put it, that doesn't include you. Just like you have a history that doesn't include me. If you want us to stay together you're going to have to get over it. I'm not going to act like a stranger to people I know and like just to spare your overly sensitive feelings."

"I'm not talking about that," said Bryce. "I'm talking about the way you act, the way you treat the kids. You don't spend time with them like you used to, and—"

"In case you haven't noticed, I am trying to plan a raid on the headquarters of one of the most dangerous clans in the sector."

"And when you do talk to them," he carried on, "it's like you don't care about them."

"What? Of *course* I care about them. You know what I've

been through, the risks I've taken, to save them and protect them."

His remark had hit her core. Angry tears threatened but she swallowed them down, refusing to show any weakness.

"That was in the past. Things are different now. Sure, Darius still has your attention but the others don't. Look at what happened today. You acted like your brothers and sisters were mercs. They aren't. They're just kids, and spoilt, rich kids at that."

"I realize that. That's why I've been trying to keep them and the mercs apart, but if we're to stand a chance of getting into the mountain castle—"

"Parthenia and Ferne *died*."

"It was a rehearsal!"

"It was a rehearsal for the real thing," he shouted back. "Is the information you want worth sacrificing those kids' lives for?"

"Do you have any *kind* of idea what their lives will be like if we don't get out of this sector?" asked Carina. "If I don't find them somewhere safe to live they'll end up like Ma, or like me, in the gutter and then killing for a living."

"Oh, please don't try to tell me how hard you had it," Bryce said bitterly. "You're forgetting what my life was like when we met, when I didn't know if the next day would be my last. Remember who you're talking to, Carina. But I don't go belly-aching about it."

"You're not a mage! No one is hunting you down for what you can do. Your life is your own. If you want to go back to your family, you can. Mine is gone. Even the mage clan is gone, scattered to the stars. I have to find us a new beginning. If you don't want to help me, that's fine. I'm sure your family would love to have you back."

"Maybe I should go back to them then."

"Maybe you should."

Darius walked out of the bathroom in his pajamas, done with his shower. He halted and swayed backward a fraction, as if an invisible wave had washed over him. His eyes widened and he looked from Carina to Bryce. Not a word needed to be said. He'd felt their mutual anger as if it were palpable.

Carina covered her eyes with one hand. Hurting her little brother was the last thing she wanted to do. "Darius, maybe you should stay in Parthenia and Nahla's room tonight," she suggested.

"But, I…" Darius's protest petered out. Even he seemed to think it was a good idea in the circumstances.

"Yeah," said Bryce. "I'll take you."

"No," Carina said firmly. "I'll do it."

She took Darius's hand and walked with him to the cabin next door, where Parthenia and Nahla were already in bed and reading, tired after the day's excitement. Parthenia made room for Darius in her bed and Carina kissed him goodnight before leaving.

When she got back to her cabin, Bryce was in bed, lying on his side.

She turned off the light and joined him. They lay facing away from each other and didn't say another word.

It was some time before Carina slept.

29

The second rehearsal took place the next day. This time, it was the mages' turn to lead the attack, if 'attack' was the right word to describe what was proposed.

The children didn't stand a chance of succeeding in a full frontal assault so they were going to try to get past all of Cadwallader's troops without raising an alarm. If this proved unsuccessful, Atoi's mercs would try to save them and get them out. As far as Carina could work it out from what Castiel had said about the mountain castle, the backup scenario was a possibility.

The alternative possibility that Castiel was feeding them bullshit was also never far from her mind.

In the initial discussions with Cadwallader about the practice sessions, he'd proposed that the defending troops should behave as if they were unaware of mages and Casting. But Carina had pointed out that Castiel had spent time with the Dirksens, and that their leader, Sable Dirksen, was in all likelihood fully briefed on what mages can do. Carina had insisted that Cadwallader prepare his troops accordingly. She'd also told her siblings they should not expect to surprise anyone with their powers. The only advantage they had was that Sable Dirksen was unlikely to be expecting them to walk right into her headquarters.

Carina and the mages were approaching the cavern, taking an easier route this time, where the slopes were less steep and the loose shale was sparse.

"Darius," Carina said, "Cloak us."

Providing they stuck together they would not be seen by Cadwallader's soldiers for as long as the Cast lasted. In theory, they would be able to explore the entire mountain castle in this manner, but there were several flaws to this plan.

Some days prior, Carina had asked Darius to Cloak himself several times in order to measure how long the Cast lasted. She'd discovered that, unfortunately, the period varied between two and fifteen minutes. Even worse, the Cloaked would not be able to tell when the Cast wore off. The first indication they would have that they were no longer visible might be pulse rounds in their backs. To have any certainty of avoiding detection, Darius would have to Cast Cloak every two minutes. Even for a mage of his powers the exercise would be utterly exhausting if not impossible.

"Car," came Atoi's voice over Carina's comm. "Sitrep."

"Two minutes from the entrance," she replied. "No sign of any guards yet. Cloaking up."

The woman's request irritated Carina. Did she expect the mages to fail so easily? Carina and her siblings had saved Atoi's ass only yesterday.

Cadwallader had posted two guards at the entrance, the same as in the previous rehearsal. Carina reasoned that slipping in between them shouldn't be too hard, Carina reasoned. She didn't want to Enthrall them if she didn't have to. Castiel had said Sable Dirksen knew about Enthralling and perhaps she'd informed her military of the signs so they would know when one of their number had been compromised.

As before, Carina took the lead. The rest of the mages formed a tight diamond with Darius at its center. Parthenia took the rear point.

The dark entrance to the cavern gaped in the mountain face. Cadwallader's two mercs stood on either side, silent, stock-still sentinels.

The mages drew closer, and closer still. Carina was navigating a path that ran exactly between the two soldiers, who stood about fifteen meters apart.

"'Kay, stick tight together," she comm'd. "We're nearly there."

The mages walked slowly onward. Cadwallader had set no time limit on the rehearsal and Carina didn't want to rush and make mistakes.

Before they even reached the entrance, however, they were discovered.

"Halt," barked a guard over his external comm. "Who goes there?" He raised his weapon and pointed it almost directly at the group of mages.

"Shit," said Carina. "Stop. Get down low. Ferne, Oriana, Enthrall them both."

"How does he know we're here?" Darius asked.

The other guard had caught on and was also aiming at them.

"He heard us," Carina replied. Though they were wearing EVA suits, the rogue planet had an atmosphere. The guard must have heard the sound of their footfalls in the silence of the barren world. He'd also clearly been briefed about the Cloak Cast.

The first guard fired. The pulse narrowly missed Carina's helmet.

"Ferne, Oriana?" she said.

"I did him," said Ferne.

The guard didn't fire again. And after Oriana's Cast, the other looked uncertain about why she was holding a weapon.

"Right," said Carina. "Let's go. Quiet as you can."

The mages passed between the two Enthralled guards. They were inside the cavern but already things weren't going to plan. The first guard had had time to inform Cadwallader about the suspicious sounds outside. The lieutenant colonel would probably already be checking to see if the entrance guards had been Enthralled. A couple of questions would be all it took.

"We have to hurry," Carina said. "We—"

"Watch out!" shouted Castiel.

Four mercs had popped up from behind rocks inside the cavern to take random shots.

"I'm gonna fire back," Castiel said.

"No," Carina replied. "Then they'll know exactly where we are. All of you, pick the one closest to you and Cast Enthrall."

A pulse round came perilously close.

"I've been hit!" Oriana exclaimed.

Carina closed her eyes to Cast. Maintaining concentration in the circumstances was hard. She split the Enthrall character and sent it to two of the mercs for good measure.

A beat later, the shooting stopped.

"Oriana," she said, "how badly are you hurt?"

"My visor says I'm incapacitated."

"Damn. We'll have to leave you here."

"But outside of Darius's Cloak they'll see her," Parthenia protested. "What happens when the Enthrall Casts start to wear off?"

"It's either that or she tries to leave," Carina said. "But leaving the hideout without the protection of a Cloak would be more dangerous. We'll have to assume we would find her somewhere to hide."

"I'll go behind that rock," said Oriana. "The guards won't notice me while they're Enthralled."

"We have to hurry," said Ferne. "We have to get down that tunnel before reinforcements arrive."

Oriana left.

"Okay," said Carina. "Let's move forward, fast."

The group advanced. Carina asked Darius to Cast Cloak again to keep them covered for the next encounter.

They cautiously passed through the aperture at the back of the cave.

Suddenly, mercs burst from the crack at the end of the tunnel that led to the second cavern.

"Get back!" Carina yelled to her siblings.

If they were Cloaked and they pressed against the tunnel wall, the soldiers might pass them by. She was surprised that Cadwallader had discovered their entry so quickly, or maybe he was guessing based on timing.

"Evacuate!" Cadwallader shouted over Carina's comm. "Evacuate immediately! Everyone back to the shuttle. Run!"

"Huh?" said Ferne.

"What's going on?" Parthenia asked. The mercs had reached them and run directly past.

"I don't know," Carina replied. "But something's up. We'd better do what he says."

They ran out of the tunnel and into the entrance cavern. The Enthralled soldiers were following Cadwallader's command and leaving.

Carina ran back across the mountainside toward the shuttle, checking her siblings kept up. It was hard going in the one-point-six *g*. The way back was uphill, and she was soon sweating and panting as she made her way up the slope.

She stopped and looked back. The kids were having an even harder time of it. Castiel and Parthenia were several meters behind her and the two shorter figures of Ferne and Oriana were farther back still.

Darius! Where was Darius?

Carina realized the others had moved out of the vicinity of his Cloak so she could see them, but he was still affected by it. She couldn't see him anywhere.

"Darius," she said over comm. "Where are you?"

"I'm here," came the little boy's reply.

In any other circumstances his typical seven-year-old's response would have been funny, but at the moment icy panic clutched at Carina's heart.

"You're Cloaked, remember?" she said. "I can't see you. Can you see me?"

"Er..."

The icy hand clutched tighter.

"No," said Darius. "I can't see anyone."

30

"Where are you, Lin?" Cadwallader asked over Carina's comm.

"I'm looking for my little brother," she replied. "Whoever modified his suit accidentally removed the tracker. He isn't on the system."

The rest of her siblings had told her they'd made it to the shuttle, but Darius remained somewhere on the rocky mountain slope.

"The *Duchess* is about to be attacked," said Cadwallader. "Return to the shuttle now."

"I can't leave him here!" Carina exclaimed.

"We can get him later."

"No," she said, fear and concern raising her pitch. "He'll be terrified if we leave him here alone."

A pause.

"You have two minutes, then the shuttle's leaving, with or without you." Cadwallader closed the comm.

"Darius!" Carina said. "Tell me what you can see."

"I can see a bunch of rocks."

The dark, rocky, sloping landscape spread out in front of her, bereft of movement. Carina could hear nothing over her external comm except the hydrogenous atmosphere sighing over the stones. Somehow, Darius appeared to have run in another direction after leaving the cavern.

Carina blamed herself for leaving him behind in her haste. If she couldn't find him in time, Cadwallader would just have to leave without them both.

"What are the rocks like?" she asked.

"One of them looks kinda like Parthenia's tarsul," Darius replied.

Carina had no idea what a tarsul looked like. "Are they big rocks?"

"Yeah."

"How big? Bigger than me?"

"Yeah. Much bigger than you."

Carina swung around in a circle, trying to see what area of the mountain Darius might be looking at. To her surprise, she saw a merc running toward her from the direction of the shuttle.

It was Bryce.

"Go back," she said to him. "You can't get left behind too."

"Shut up," Bryce said. "You're wasting time. Where was the last place you saw him?"

"In the cavern. He took a wrong turn somewhere on the way back." As she spoke, Carina spotted a patch of large rocks over Bryce's shoulder. "I think he might be up there." She began to run up the slope. "Darius, look down the slope. Look for me and Bryce."

"One minute, Lin," said Cadwallader.

"It's okay, we've found him," Carina lied. "We're going to make it."

Forcing her leg muscles hard against the gravity, she sped up the slope. Loosened shale slithered past her in an avalanche of stones. She slipped, fell to her knees, got up, and ran.

"I can see you!" said Darius. "I can see you and Bryce, Carina!"

"Great," she huffed, barely able to speak. "Run to us, Darius. Remember we can't see you. But be careful. It's easy to slip."

She continued to struggle up the slope. The shuttle was more than a minute's run away even in standard gravity. They were never going to make it.

Something impacted her. Carina looked down and saw Darius clinging to her middle. She'd come within the influence of his Cloak.

"Whoa," said Bryce. "Where did you go?"

"I've found him," Carina said. "He's here."

Bryce was only a couple of meters away, turning around as he scanned the view. He stopped, his helmet's visor pointing directly at them. "There you are."

The Cast had finally worn off.

"Darius," said Bryce. "Jump on my back."

The three set off for the shuttle. The two minutes Cadwallader had given her were up, Carina had no doubt. Relying on his kindheartedness to wait for them was probably useless. He would not risk the safety of all his mercs for the sake of three people, even if one of them was only a kid.

They rounded a ridge. The *Duchess's* shuttle stood on roughly level ground in the distance, squat on its eight feet like a black bug. As she ran toward the vessel, her muscles screaming with the effort, the ramp rose and the hatch shut.

"Shit," she said. She opened a comm. "Cadwallader, wait. We're nearly there."

The hatch remained closed. Carina fully expected to see the shuttle's engine fire.

She noticed Bryce was no longer beside her. He'd dropped behind.

She ran to him. "Darius, get on me."

Bryce didn't protest.

Darius, usually easy to carry, felt heavy as he wrapped his legs around her waist and his arms around her neck.

The shuttle still hadn't taken off. It was less than a hundred meters away. If its engine fired when they got closer they would be seared by the heat, their EVA suits offering little protection.

Then, while Carina's gaze was glued to the vessel, the ramp lowered. She thanked the stars mentally. She had no breath for words. Cadwallader was kinder than she thought.

Seconds later, they ran up the ramp. It closed as they were on it, sending them tumbling into the ship and through the airlock until they ended up sprawling on the floor of the cabin, between the feet of the mercs and mages. Carina felt the harsh shudder of the shuttle's engine starting up. Next, she was forced into the floor by the acceleration force as the vessel tore itself out of the planet's heavy gravity.

She couldn't speak. She couldn't move. All she could see was EVA suit boots and Darius's small form, lying on his back with his arms and legs spread out. Even in the extreme circumstances, he was starfishing.

"I'm so glad you made it," said Parthenia.

"What's going on?" asked Bryce. "Has anyone said why we had to evacuate?"

"There's a warship bearing down on the *Duchess* and *Zenobia*," Ferne said. "It isn't answering any hails. Cadwallader thinks it's going to attack."

"We really thought he was going to leave you all behind," said Parthenia.

"He *was* going to leave them behind," Castiel said. "Didn't you hear him arguing with the pilot?"

Carina's lungs continued to work overtime, her chest rising and falling heavily as she recovered from her desperate run.

"What?" she gasped. "Cadwallader was arguing with Stevenson?"

"Yes," said Castiel. "The pilot refused to leave without you. Cadwallader told him the next planet we get to, he's out of a job."

"Thank the stars for old flames, huh, Carina?" said Bryce dryly.

31

Aboard the *Duchess,* everything seemed in chaos.

Before the shuttle's ramp had lowered the mercs had crowded at the exit hatch, and as soon as it was down they sprinted out into the ship, not wasting time to take off their EVA suits. After the mercs had exited, Carina, Bryce and the children walked out into the shuttle bay. Nahla joined them.

Carina lifted her visor.

Mercs were running everywhere. Even Stevenson didn't stop to say a word before dashing out of the shuttle bay. Carina quickly lost sight of Cadwallader as he merged with the soldiers preparing for an attack.

"What should we do?" Ferne asked.

"Stay the hell out of the way for now," replied Carina.

She knew that what appeared to be pandemonium was only the mercs getting to their stations, whether that was to man the ship's weapons, prepare to repel boarders, or some other defensive task. She had played that role herself more than once, but now she had no role except to keep the children safe.

"Maybe we should return to the *Zenobia*," said Bryce.

"No," she said. "If we do come under attack we're safer here than aboard a passenger vessel."

All of a sudden, the floor lifted and turned, throwing everyone down.

"Get back into the shuttle," Carina said. It was all she could think to do. They couldn't help the mercs in a space battle. Starships moved too fast for Casts to work. But the shuttle was firmly clamped into the bay and the children could wear the safety harnesses inside.

The *Duchess* bumped and lifted again. Stevenson was probably making evasive maneuvers to avoid a long-range attack. But the mercs' ship was attached to the *Zenobia*, which would make everything more difficult. A few of Cadwallader's troops still remained aboard the smuggler's vessel, guarding the prisoners.

While the children were strapping themselves in, Carina ran along the side of the well between the rows of seating and into the empty pilot's cabin. Sitting in Stevenson's seat, she activated the controls. Bryce sat next to her in the co-pilot's position.

"What are you doing?" he asked. "Are you planning on flying us out of here?"

"That would be insane," she replied. "I want to find out what's going on."

The shuttle's console displayed the feed from the main ship. It took Carina a moment to figure out what she was seeing. Then she spotted it: a ship the size of a destroyer was approaching. The scan data indicated four pulse cannons, a single particle lance, and a smattering of smaller weapons, probably kinetic for close-range combat.

"Why the hell is that coming at us?" asked Bryce.

"I have no idea. *Whoa*." The *Duchess* had swung violently

around. Carina grabbed the console, her stomach feeling like it was taking its time to catch up with the rest of her body.

The *Duchess's* pulse cannons fired.

"Isn't that premature?" Bryce asked.

"I don't think so," Carina replied. "From the ship's maneuvers I think we've already been fired upon."

A sudden acceleration flung her back in her seat. The force pinned her in place and she looked down her nose at the display.

"I guess we're trying to get away," said Bryce.

"No. We're heading straight at them. Cadwallader's trying to scare them off."

The enemy ship fired all four pulse cannons at once.

"Shit," Carina said. She activated the shuttle's comm. "Brace yourselves, kids."

The *Duchess* returned fire, blasting three of the enemy's pulses to pieces, scattering their subatomic particles across space. But the fourth one made it through. The *Duchess* shuddered at its impact.

"Carina," said Darius over the passenger comm. "I think I'm going to be sick."

She heard Parthenia say something to him before the comm cut out.

"I don't know what Cadwallader's thinking," Carina said. "That particle lance could cut the *Duchess* in two if we get too close."

The lieutenant colonel's tactic of going on the offense didn't seem to be working. The enemy ship wasn't backing off or even slowing down. The two ships were flying at each other at top speed. Carina wondered what Lomang and his men were thinking, trapped in the brig and their cabins. They would have no idea what was happening.

"I still can't understand why that ship's attacking," Bryce said. "How did it even happen to be passing in this region of space? We aren't on a trade route. We're in the middle of nowhere."

"Your guess is as good as..." She paused.

Bryce had made a good point. It was too much of a coincidence that another starship was within distance to pick up their trace, and the ship was a destroyer that wanted to attack them. The chances were so remote as to be nearly impossible.

"Does someone have a vendetta with Cadwallader or the Black Dogs?" Bryce asked.

"It's possible. Merc bands tend to make plenty of enemies along the way. But something tells me that isn't it."

Fire flashed from the destroyer and four pulses of pure energy flew toward the *Duchess*. Carina cursed under her breath. The merc ship could only take so much battering. Cadwallader's strategy of aggression seemed desperate, as if he knew they couldn't outrun their attacker. Yet neither could the ship withstand a close encounter with the particle lance.

This time, two of the pulses made it through. The judder the *Duchess* gave seemed about to tear her apart.

"This is it," said Bryce. "We aren't going to make it."

She had to agree. The *Duchess* wouldn't survive another hit like that. The enemy didn't even seem to want to preserve the mercs' ship for boarding. It was intent on blowing it to pieces.

They were going to die, and no one knew why.

Carina gasped. The scanners were picking up energy building in the particle beam. The enemy was preparing to strike its final blow.

She turned to Bryce. He read the look on her face and his own paled.

Carina reached out for his hand.

"Bryce, I'm sorry—"

"No," he said. "I am. I've been a—"

"No, it was my fault."

There were no more words to be said. Carina gripped Bryce's hand tightly.

The scan readings were going off the scale. White-hot brilliance shone out from the destroyer. A blade bright as starlight leapt across space, bridging the gap between the *Duchess* and its vanquisher.

Carina tensed, wanting to scream, but no sound came out.

Then it was over.

32

The blade had vanished and they were still alive, but something was very, very wrong. The emergency lights were flashing and the reverberating, repetitive alarm wailed.

From outside the shuttle came a terrible roar and a cacophony of objects clashing and banging. The shuttle shook. Outside the *Duchess* the destroyer continued to bear down on them but its pulse cannons remained inactive and the particle lance was drained of energy.

Perhaps the enemy did intend to board after all.

Carina couldn't figure out what the noise was. It was familiar, yet she couldn't place it. Then it hit her. She'd heard the same sound years before when the *Duchess's* hull had been breached. What she could hear was the rush of escaping air, but highly magnified. This wasn't a small hull breach, it was a massive hole cut in the side of the ship. Maybe the mercs' vessel had been sliced in two as she'd feared.

She comm'd the children. "Close your visors. You'll be breathing your suit's atmosphere from now on. And, whatever you do, do *not* unfasten your safety harnesses."

The bay was empty, the shuttle was clamped to its floor, and in their EVA suits they couldn't feel any of the effects of the breach, only hear the awful toll it was taking on the ship. Carina watched her HUD as it displayed the falling atmospheric gases. Many mercs had probably been sucked out into space, though luckily most of them were also wearing EVA suits and should survive if they were picked up.

Anything not bolted down would be gone and anyone in the way of an exiting object would be injured or killed. If the particle beam had sliced into the *Duchess's* engines the ship would be dead in space, vulnerable to whatever the enemy had in mind for its occupants. Carina hoped that none of the mercs would spill the beans about her family's mage powers, but she had to face the fact that one or two of them almost certainly would, hopeful of buying some clemency from their attackers. The one called Chandu, for instance—he wouldn't hesitate to betray them.

Cadwallader and Atoi would probably be killed. As officers, they presented the greatest threat to the captors as the most likely leaders of escape attempts. On the other hand, the enemy could just kill everyone.

"What's happening, Carina?" Parthenia asked shakily.

"We've been hit. Just sit tight, everyone, until we know more information." She couldn't think what else to say. The thought of the danger her family was in was killing her.

"Is everything going to be okay?" asked Oriana.

"Just sit tight," Carina repeated.

An age seemed to pass. Each second Carina imagined enemy soldiers coming in to search the bay and finding her, Bryce, and her family. They still had the weapons they'd been carrying for the rehearsal. They could fight back, firing and Casting, but what would be the point? They had nowhere to go, no safe haven to retreat to. The *Duchess* was so damaged that even if they managed to take her back and expel the boarders, they couldn't escape in her.

The shuttle's console was not connected to the *Duchess's* diagnostics, and Carina didn't want to distract Cadwallader or Atoi from whatever they were doing to save the ship and the mercs, not even for a second, so she couldn't find out what had happened. They all waited, not speaking, for whatever would happen next.

First, the dreadful clanging stopped. Whatever had been loose aboard the ship had been sucked into space. Then, the roaring faded away. The atmospheric readings on Carina's visor began to rise. The mercs had sealed the breach. Or had it been the enemy, after boarding the ship? No one had entered the bay.

Carina couldn't wait any longer. She unfastened her harness.

"What are you doing?" Bryce asked.

"I'm going to find out what's going on."

She opened the pilot's hatch and climbed down onto the floor of the bay. She could hear voices but they were distant. She lifted her visor. No fighting seemed to be in progress so either the *Duchess* hadn't been boarded or the fight was over.

She stepped over a clamp that held one of the shuttle's feet and crossed the bay to the exit. The portal had been open the entire time, but since all the mercs had left Carina hadn't seen anyone cross it.

She walked out into the passage. Running footsteps echoed from the metal floor and walls. It sounded like just one, heavy person, running in booted feet, getting nearer.

She turned, intending to scoot back into the bay, but she was too late.

A figure appeared, wearing an EVA suit. It was a merc, her visor down. Carina's was up so she had no HUD to tell her who it was. The person didn't slow down or break step as they drew nearer. Carina was about to back into the wall to make room, when the merc grabbed her into a hug, lifting her off of her feet.

Atoi lifted her visor. "You're alive! Stars, I thought you and the kids had been sucked into space."

"We waited in the shuttle," said Carina. "When I saw the attack I told everyone to strap in."

"Good that you did. We've lost half the platoon. It's going to take us forever to retrieve them all."

"So we weren't boarded?"

"No, they don't seem interested in us, whoever the hell they are."

"Huh? They didn't even try?" asked Carina. "Or did we damage their ship after all?"

"Not enough to stop them from trying to board. C'mon. I'll show you what happened."

"Wait," she said. "Is it safe for the kids and Bryce to leave the shuttle?"

"Should be fine. We've sealed the hole pretty tight."

Carina comm'd Bryce with the good news then set off with Atoi.

They didn't have far to go. Atoi took Carina to the *Duchess's* docking port, mechanics brushing past the two women, running to and from the structure.

A breach sheet covered the circular hatchway. Hollows dipped across the entire sheet's surface, outlining thick bars that ran across the farther side.

"We had to weld the bars in place," said Atoi. "But it's pretty tough now. Should hold until we reach a planet or shipyard."

"The enemy cut away the docking port?" asked Carina.

"Cut right through it," said Atoi.

It seemed an odd thing to do. Boarding a ship was hard when atmosphere and miscellaneous objects were flying out of it. Then she remembered. "But...that's what was..."

"Connecting us to the *Zenobia*," Atoi finished, nodding. "It was the *Zenobia* they wanted, not us. As soon as they'd severed the *Duchess* from her they stopped firing. They grappled her."

In one way the enemy's focus on the passenger vessel made sense. The *Zenobia* was carrying plenty of valuable contraband —but that meant the attackers knew about it, and Carina couldn't figure out how. After she'd gotten the information about the ship's tracker from Lomang and sent a message packet to the Black Dogs, she'd been careful to shut the device down. In any case, the point of the tracker was to enable Lomang to locate his ship, not someone else. And they'd traveled for weeks since then. Had the enemy ship trailed them the entire way, following the *Duchess* and *Zenobia's* traces?

Atoi laughed at her expression. "Yeah, we can't figure it out either, Car. But you'd better go and see Cadwallader. You two have to decide what happens next."

Carina realized her new situation with shock and dismay. Now the *Zenobia* was gone, so was her only way of paying the Black Dogs. And if she had nothing to pay the mercs, there would be no attempt to infiltrate the Dirksens' headquarters, no protection from Ostillon's hungry mobs, and no safe passage anywhere in the sector, let alone to Earth. What was more, she hadn't a clue how she would pay Cadwallader for services rendered so far.

She would have to rely on his generosity for food and board until they reached the nearest habitable planet, too. Surviving the enemy's attack had seemed a miracle, but for her personally it had brought a disaster.

"I'll come with you," Atoi offered.

"Thanks," Carina said. "Together, we might pierce the man's flinty heart."

33

Cadwallader was in his office. He'd changed out of his EVA suit, though it was draped over a chair, as if he imagined he might need to put it on again in a hurry.

"I thought I might see you soon," he said as Carina and Atoi walked in. He seemed unsurprised that Carina hadn't been harmed, but she realized he had access to all the EVA suit signal data. He knew she'd been in the shuttle the whole time.

"Sit down, Lin. Atoi, you're dismissed. Go and supervise the repairs or do something else useful."

Atoi raised her eyebrows at Carina as she turned and left.

Carina sat down opposite the lieutenant colonel. She unfastened the front of her EVA suit and removed her helmet. "Sir," she said, out of force of habit. She couldn't sit in that room with that man and in a subordinate position without reverting to the familiar salutation. "Is there any chance at all of getting the *Zenobia* back?"

"Not a single one in all hell's domains," Cadwallader replied. "We're damned lucky to have come out of the engagement with so few casualties. I'm not prepared to risk the *Duchess* for even twice the contents of the *Zenobia's* hold."

"What about Lomang's other ship, the one that can travel between sectors? We could go there and—"

"Impossible. The *Duchess* would never make it that far."

Gloom settled deeper over Carina. "How many lives were lost?"

"Four, so far."

"What happened to the guards you left aboard the *Zenobia*? Are they still there?"

"No, I recalled them when the battle started to turn sour. I was prepared to lose the *Zenobia* to boarders but not the *Duchess*."

"In the end the decision was made for you."

"Yes. The casualties resulted from the massive decompression after the particle lance got us, but we're in contact with most of the troops who were sucked out of the ship. Stevenson's going to take the shuttle out to retrieve them." Cadwallader's jaw muscles flexed as he mentioned the pilot's name.

Carina regretted that he'd been reminded of Stevenson's refusal to follow orders so that she, Bryce, and Darius could get back to the shuttle before it returned to the ship. The delay wouldn't have made a difference to the outcome of the battle, but to Cadwallader, that wasn't the point. She felt bad for Stevenson, who had been flying with the Black Dogs for several years and was well liked.

"Thank the stars they were wearing EVA suits," she said.

"Indeed."

An uncomfortable number of seconds passed.

Cadwallader leaned forward and rested his elbows on his desk. He passed a hand over his face and his shoulders slumped. His adamantine facade crumbled a little and his pale blue eyes became tired and defeated. "Lin, things aren't going too well for the Black Dogs. As time has gone on I've come to understand why Tarsalan agreed to all those suicide missions. It turns out the mercenary business isn't as lucrative as some might imagine. This job you offered us was set to restore the company's financial reserves, which have nearly run dry. The *Duchess* needs extensive repairs, restocking and refueling. This all cost money we don't have. I'm afraid it's the end of the line for us, and with the best will in the galaxy, we won't be able to help you in your undertaking."

"That's okay," Carina replied. "I guessed as much. But, well, now we have nowhere to go, so..."

"For goodness' sake, I'm not planning on marooning you all. You can stay with us until we reach a world where I can sell the *Duchess* and all our equipment. Then I'll split the proceeds and the mercs can disembark."

Carina exhaled. "Thanks."

"It'll be a squeeze," said Cadwallader, "but we'll find berths for you all. Perhaps you can pay for your passage by providing entertainment with your tricks."

Carina's eyes widened.

"Just kidding." Cadwallader cracked a smile. "Ahh..." He stretched his arms and back. "It's been an interesting few years but perhaps it's time to move on to something new."

"Will you sign up for the military again?" Carina asked.

"I don't know. The only options available these days are to work for the Sherrerrs or the Dirksens, and I don't like either of them. Maybe a whole change of pace is what's called for. A new beginning."

"That's what I would like too," said Carina. "For me and my family."

"I wish you luck," Cadwallader said. "You and your bunch of gutsy youngsters."

A light flashed on his desk's console, and he pressed it.

"A shuttle has left the *Zenobia*, sir," said a voice.

"Is it heading our way?" asked Cadwallader.

"No, it appears to be heading into deep space."

The lieutenant colonel frowned. "Deep space? Where the hell is it going?"

"Nowhere, as far as we can tell, sir. Its current trajectory doesn't lead anywhere."

"Is the destroyer firing on it?"

"Not yet, sir."

"Well, is it sending out a distress signal?"

"No. Oh, wait a minute. Yes. It's just started...sir."

"The *Zenobia's* shuttles are tiny," Carina informed him. "They're two-seaters, emergency evac only. I checked them out when we took over the ship. They don't carry much fuel or provisions. Whoever's inside it won't get very far."

Cadwallader seemed to turn over the news in his mind for a moment, then he said. "You know what, I'm interested to find out what this whole thing has been about, even if it means one or two more mouths to feed" He spoke into his comm button. "Stevenson, your first pick up is that shuttle that's just left the *Zenobia*. Tow it into the bay." He closed the comm. "Let's go and see who's so desperate to get away from the smuggler's ship," he said to Carina.

THE *ZENOBIA'S* shuttle was spherical. Four pointed legs stuck out from its base so that it rested securely on a flat surface. Carina and Cadwallader watched it through the window of the closed bay door, waiting for Stevenson to leave on his next trip to begin picking up the stranded mercs and for the outer doors to close.

Carina had passed Bryce and the kids on her way over to the bay. To her relief, her siblings hadn't appeared too shaken up by the attack.

Whoever was inside the tiny ship in the bay had the good sense not to emerge while the transition was going on. When the safety light activated, Cadwallader opened the bay's inner doors and motioned for the pair of mercs he'd asked to accompany him to go inside.

Together, he and Carina walked to the dull gray sphere. A single line traced a rectangle on its surface. The two mercs stood on each side of the rectangle, aiming their weapons at it. As Carina and the lieutenant colonel arrived at the shuttlecraft, the line broke. A rectangular chunk of the shuttle's hull pushed out and lifted up on slim hydraulic cylinders.

When the occupant emerged, for some reason Carina couldn't quite understand, she was not at all surprised to discover it was Lomang.

The smuggler had slimmed down some more since the last time she'd seen him. His weight loss was fortunate: he might not have been able to fit through the hatch otherwise. His iridescent blue, conical hat had returned to its usual position on his head and he smiled ingratiatingly.

A ladder of woven metal had dropped from the shuttle. Lomang climbed down rather clumsily before speaking. He bowed and said, "My humble thanks for rescuing us. Your kindness and mercy will be long remembered in my family."

"Us?" said Cadwallader. "Tell whoever remains in your vessel to come out immediately."

"Naturally," said Lomang. He spoke in another tongue, issuing a command toward the hidden passenger.

This time, Carina *was* surprised at who emerged from the shuttle's interior. It was the giant. The ladder swayed and creaked as the huge man descended it. In truth, he could have probably stepped down from the open hatch directly to the floor without much difficulty.

The giant displayed nothing of his former threatening demeanor. Like Lomang, he appeared grateful and submissive, bending as low as his large frame would allow.

"Please allow me to introduce my twin brother," said

Lomang. "Though I believe you have already met." He looked sheepish.

"Your *twin* brother?" Carina blurted.

Annoyance paid a brief visit to the smuggler's features, then he was all smiles again. "Fraternal, of course."

Cadwallader commanded his soldiers to search the brothers and the shuttle. When no weapons or explosives were found, he ordered them to take the men to the mission room.

After the smuggler and his brother had left, Cadwallader took a look at the interior of the shuttle himself. Appearing to be satisfied with his inspection, he climbed down the ladder.

"What do *you* think this is about, Lin?"

"I can only think that Lomang must have made himself more than one enemy in his time in this sector. He was dealing in illegal goods so it seems inevitable he would rub up against some dangerous people. Maybe he tricked someone and they've hunted him down, though I'm not sure how."

"That would explain why their beef was with him, not us," Cadwallader agreed.

"And how the attacker knew the *Zenobia* was carrying highly valuable cargo."

"The *Duchess* isn't exactly worthless," Cadwallader pointed out, "but it's pretty obviously a harder prize to win. You know this Lomang better than anyone. Would you help me question him?"

"I'd love to." Carina's curiosity was deeply piqued. There was clearly a story behind the recent events, and the slimmest of chances she might learn something that would lift her out of her current mess.

34

As Carina settled in for another interview with Lomang, she considered immediately Enthralling him in order to be confident that what he told her and Cadwallader was the truth, but she dismissed the idea. The problem with interrogating an Enthralled person was that they would only answer the exact question you asked them, and in an emotionless manner. They would give no indication of the sensitivity of the information they were telling you, and hence no clue about when it was appropriate to probe more deeply.

Unless you knew the right questions to ask, you might skirt past a vital fact without even knowing it.

Questioning a subject when they were in full control of themselves and reading their 'tells' would be more effective. Carina would also be able to hear the difference between what Lomang said while not Enthralled and then while he was under, which might reveal something he wanted to hide.

Lomang and his brother sat side by side in the mission room, flanked by two mercs pointing weapons at them. Even so, Carina didn't feel entirely safe in close proximity to the giant.

He looked capable of inflicting considerable damage before pulse rounds would fell him.

"I would like to introduce my brother," Lomang said, noting Carina's gaze on the large man. "His name is Pappu. As I said, we are twins, but I am older by three minutes." Lomang held up three pudgy fingers and grinned. "Such small accidents of fate make all the difference, do they not, brother?"

"They do, brother," said Pappu, folding his arms and gazing at Carina.

The way his muscles bulged and moved under his skin reminded Carina of the animals they had ridden on Pirine when leaving the Matching. Was he remembering she left him in the hold, trapped within the mech's pincers, for hours?

"Tell us everything you know about the people who attacked us," said Cadwallader.

"Ah, where to begin?" Lomang replied. "It is a very long story."

"We have time," Cadwallader said. "However, if I feel you're wasting mine, I'll return you to your hollow ball and send you back into space."

"Then I will tell you the condensed version," said Lomang. "The dear person who so badly wanted the *Zenobia* as to inconvenience yourselves is the illustrious Mezban Kabasli Noran, Procurator of the Majestic Isles, Member of the Encircling Council, and—I am deeply proud to say—my wife."

A profound silence followed this announcement. Then Cadwallader gave a small cough and shifted in his seat. "The person commanding that destroyer is your *wife*?"

Lomang nodded. "She has spirit, does she not?" He smiled proudly.

"Your wife put you and your brother into that tiny shuttle and expelled you into deep space?" Carina asked.

"What can I say?" asked Lomang. "She is disgusted that I allowed my ship to be taken. I and my crew all remained under confinement when she boarded the *Zenobia*, you see. She wishes to dissolve our marriage. Pappu, as my brother, has been similarly rejected by her on the basis of his close association with me."

"Don't you have divorces on your world?" Cadwallader asked. "Setting you adrift in deep space with only enough air to last you a day or two seems... excessive."

"My dearest Mezban sometimes overreacts a little. She may have changed her mind and retrieved our shuttle eventually."

"Or she may not," Pappu said phlegmatically, his voice rumbling in a bass tone.

"Or she may not," Lomang agreed. "Hence our gratitude regarding your kindness. I assume now that we pose no threat to you we may have the freedom of your ship?"

A great bark of laughter erupted from Cadwallader.

Carina said, "I think you have your answer. There's something I don't understand. How did your wife find you?"

"I had sent her a message before you took over the ship with the help of your traitorous brother. My wonderful wife has probably been searching the sector for me ever since she discovered myself absent from our home. After I sent her the message to set up our reconciliation—and what a reconciliation it would have been!—she must have gone to the coordinates I sent her and then, finding my ship gone, followed its trace. When she saw the *Zenobia* had been taken by a military vessel my beloved one came to my rescue."

"She came to your rescue," Carina said, "yet she's disgusted you allowed your ship to be taken and she wants to dissolve your marriage."

Lomang smiled sardonically. He and his brother exchanged a glance.

"I confess there is more to my story that would rather not tell you," said Lomang, "but I know you have the power to extract the information from me whether I like it or not. Unfortunately, certain items Mezban seeks—which I borrowed from her some time ago—were not aboard the ship, and she grew rather angry. Her passions run high in all regards, but especially when it comes to her property. I was going to return the items, naturally. But events took an unexpected turn when you took over my ship. Since then, my wife's goods have been purloined, and my brother and I have been forced to suffer the consequences."

"Your wife's stuff has gone from the ship?" asked Carina. "If it has, none of us has taken it. At least, nothing's been removed from the hold of the *Zenobia* as far as I know. All I and my family took from the ship is the clothes we're wearing. We left everything else behind when we went on the rehearsal."

The last remark was addressed to Cadwallader. She wondered if it was possible a merc had snuck into the hold but it seemed unlikely. She'd fixed the security so that only she or Bryce could enter it, and she couldn't imagine Bryce would take anything without telling her.

"I accept your words," Lomang said. "And yet, those items are missing. They were never located in the hold."

Carina was flummoxed. "What are we talking about here? Maybe someone took some things without understanding their value."

"The items, my dear, are heirlooms my wife inherited from her mother, who inherited them from *her* mother, and so on, back seven or eight generations. They are precious stones, set into jewelry, but the settings are unimportant."

Cadwallader said, "You stole your wife's jewelry and ran away with it, so she came after you with a *destroyer* to get it back?"

"The stones are extremely rare," said Lomang. "They have never been discovered anywhere else in the galaxy except upon my home world, and no new stones have been discovered there for hundreds of years. There is no word for them in your tongue."

Lomang continued, "Expressing my deep apology for my actions and my even deeper, most profound love, I promised I would return her jewelry to her and show her all the goods I had obtained with them. I had used the stones as promised payment for the cargo you discovered in my ship's hold. When the time for exchange came I substituted fakes. Due to the stones' rarity, no inspection device exists to confirm their authenticity. But when I went to the secret hiding place, the jewelry was gone."

"Then she has to believe we have it," said Carina.

"At the moment, the thought doesn't appear to have crossed her mind," said Lomang. "She is in one of her wonderful fits of passion. She is a sight to behold." He paused and his eyes became shiny with tears. "I hope this is not the final time I am privileged to witness her in full flight, so to speak."

Cadwallader stood up and walked a few steps away. He murmured into his comm.

"For some reason," Lomang said, "she thinks I am lying to her about the stones, and that I bargained them away for the cargo in the hold. Why she should believe this, I do not know."

"Perhaps," said Pappu, "it is because you have lied to her many times in the past."

"Yes," Lomang conceded. "That may be the reason."

Carina felt the *Duchess's* engines kick in and the ship begin to move.

"Uh, sir," she said to Cadwallader. "I'm going to go find my little brother. He can Cloak the ship. That way, when Lomang's wife calms down and starts thinking straight, she'll find it hard to follow us."

"That sounds like a very good idea," Cadwallader said.

35

Cadwallader assigned Carina, her family, and Bryce a four-bunk cabin to themselves. It was cramped to say the least. Bryce and Darius were to share one bunk, Carina and Nahla another, Oriana and Ferne the third, and Parthenia had the final bunk to herself. Castiel elected to sleep on the floor. Carina had suggested that Oriana and Parthenia share one bunk and Ferne and Castiel share another, but Castiel had refused, saying he wasn't going to sleep with anyone's stinky feet in his face.

The comparison between the mercs' quarters aboard the *Duchess* and the luxurious passenger cabins of the *Zenobia* was marked, but, as the children took in their new living and sleeping area, Carina was surprised and pleased to hear not one complaint nor even a comment. Her siblings appeared to have gotten used to roughing it and adapting quickly to new situations.

In some ways it was a shame they had to undergo the transformation. She wanted nothing more than for them to lead normal lives where they were free from the threat of persecution and personal danger. On the other hand, if they were to somehow make it to Lomang's inter-sector vessel and then to Earth, adaptability would be a distinct advantage.

After deciding who would sleep where, Carina sent the children to the mess for a meal. It had been hours since any of them had eaten. She was hungry too but she wanted some time alone to think about what they would do next. Cadwallader's plan was to fly to a place called Martha's Rest, a well-known trading hub. It was far away but they had just enough fuel to reach it. There, he hoped he would be able to sell the *Duchess*.

Bryce closed the door after the children left and sat on the lower bunk where Carina was lying. She'd borrowed an interface to look up information. When Bryce sat down she laid the device on her chest.

"Not hungry?" she asked.

"I thought it would be good to have some time alone together."

"I guess it would," said Carina, smiling.

Bryce took her hand. "When that destroyer was attacking us I thought we'd had it."

"Me too," she admitted, covering Bryce's hand with her free one. She'd explained to Bryce about everything that Lomang had told her and Cadwallader in the mission room.

"You know," she continued after a pause, "it didn't even occur to me to ask Darius to Cloak the *Duchess* while we were being attacked."

"I don't think it would have made any difference," Bryce said. "The destroyer's crew would have seen where the pulse cannons were firing from."

"Yeah, but we could have moved, though I don't know if Darius could have Cloaked both ships. Still, it's something to remember if we ever find ourselves in a similar position."

They lapsed into silence again for several moments.

"When I thought we were all going to die," Bryce said, "I tried to say sorry for being an asshole."

"I know. It's okay. I think I kind of understand, and, you're right, I've been difficult to live with. I didn't realize how much I'd slipped back into being a merc once I was around them again."

"It was strange, seeing you change. You weren't different all the time. Not around Darius, for instance. And it wasn't like the changes were that bad. In fact, in some ways..." The corner of Bryce's lip lifted into a half smile. "...It was pretty hot."

Carina raised an eyebrow. "Is that so?" She lifted herself up on her elbows. The interface slid onto her stomach and she moved it onto the bed. "How about you show me how hot I was?"

Bryce leaned down to kiss her. After a moment he pulled away and said, "Do these room doors lock?"

"Huh," said Carina. "What do you think?"

"Hmm, that's a pity." He kissed her again.

"Not that it usually stops people," said Carina after a while. "I mean, if someone were to come in and catch us it wouldn't be the first time it's happened. Not by a long shot."

"But if it were one of the kids that would be traumatic for everyone concerned."

"Ugh, good point." Carina lay down and picked up the interface. "We'll just have to wait a little bit longer."

Bryce sighed.

"I'm trying to figure out what to do when we get to Martha's Rest," said Carina. "I can't decide if we should continue on to Ostillon and try to find out how to get to Earth, or if we should try to reach the inter-sector vessel Lomang gave me the coordinates for. We need a ship like that so badly, and we could try to figure out how to get to Earth later. That's where *Lomang's* going the first chance he gets. No doubt about it. Though I don't know how he'll get there with no creds and no ship. Unless his wife decides to forgive him and finds him again."

"She'll have a hard time doing that now that Darius is Cloaking the *Duchess*."

"So maybe we're safe going to Ostillon for a short time before setting out for the inter-sector ship."

"I don't know if *safe* is the right word," said Bryce. "But, yeah, maybe. Unless Lomang left a skeleton crew behind with instructions to leave or do something else if he isn't back within a certain time."

"He might have," said Carina. "It would be risky to leave a ship like that entirely unmanned, even if it was in the middle of nowhere."

"We have a lot of time to think about what to do next," Bryce said. "Let's go and eat."

THE MESS WAS EMPTYING when they arrived. The kids were sitting together at a table, three on each side. Carina and Bryce filled plates from the buffet food that remained and joined them.

"This food is disgusting," Castiel said as they sat down.

"Welcome to the military," Carina said. "And don't say that around Lieutenant Colonel Cadwallader, or he might decide to halve your rations as a punishment."

"I'll eat yours if you don't want it," said Ferne. He'd recently started eating everything he could get his hands on, and shooting up before Carina's eyes.

Castiel pulled his plate closer and folded a protective arm around it. "Get your own."

Carina began to eat. The food wasn't really that bad and even if it were she was in no position to complain. She would be relying entirely on Cadwallader's generosity all the way to Martha's Rest. She would have to think of a way to show her gratitude somehow. Perhaps she could perform some Casts that would increase the final payout to all the Black Dogs before they disbanded.

She looked up and noticed Bryce was staring at something behind her. She turned and saw Stevenson walking over.

She tensed. Was Bryce going to get all jealous again?

He wasn't taking his eyes from the pilot. Then he seemed to come to some sort of decision. As Stevenson arrived he stood up and held out his hand across the table.

"I don't think we've met," he said.

Stevenson shook his hand a little warily as the two men introduced themselves.

"Is it okay if I sit down?" the pilot asked.

"Sure," Carina replied. "We're nearly done anyway."

"I bet this brings back some memories," said Stevenson.

Before she could reply, he went on, "I was talking to Cadwallader just now about what's in store when we reach our next destination."

"Yeah," said Carina, "He and I had a similar conversation. I wanted to thank you for forcing him to wait for us on the rogue planet, and apologize for the fact you're losing your job. Only it turns out everyone's losing their job anyway."

"Don't speak too soon," he said enigmatically.

Parthenia stood up. "We're going back to the cabin."

"Okay," said Carina. "Thanks for looking after the children, Parthenia. Try to get them to keep the noise down, all right? The mercs aren't used to having kids around."

"It's more likely the mercs will disturb the kids," Stevenson joked. "Hey, Nahla. Could you stick around?"

Carina shared a glance with Bryce. What could the pilot want with the little girl? It wasn't likely she'd been naughty while he'd been looking after her during the rehearsals. She was the best-behaved of the whole set.

Stevenson said, "Cadwallader happened to mention something Lomang had been talking about after he brought him aboard. Something about some jewels."

At the word 'jewels', Nahla gasped and turned scarlet.

"It's okay," said Stevenson gently. "You aren't in any trouble. Well, maybe just a little bit. But it's all going to be fine."

Nahla's hands rose to her face and she began to cry.

The pilot touched her shoulder. "Don't worry. Just show Carina and Bryce what you showed me."

"I just wanted to look like Mother," Nahla sobbed. "They're pretty."

"Stars alive," said Carina. "Nahla, show me what you have."

The little girl reached under the neck of her dress and pulled up a string. Hanging from it was a pouch of soft, fine, rich material typical of the stuff Lomang carried on the *Zenobia*.

"I really don't think she thought she was doing anything wrong," Stevenson said, "or she wouldn't have shown them to me."

Carina wasn't so sure. Nahla's behavior indicated she knew she'd done something that wasn't quite right. But none of that mattered if the contents of the pouch were what she thought they were.

Nahla handed it to Stevenson, who pulled open the top. He looked around the mess, which had emptied. Only the four of them were there to witness the reveal. Stevenson upended the pouch, and a mess of silvery chains and precious stones spilled out.

Carina lifted a chain out of the pile, disentangling it from the rest. It was a necklace, probably made from platinum, but it was the stones that drew her attention.

From Lomang's description she'd expected them to be bigger, but most were only about the size of her thumbnail. She rested the mounted stones in the palm of her hand and held them up to the mess's poor lighting. She'd never seen anything like them. Light seemed to emanate from within—firelight that flickered and shifted as she watched.

"They're so lovely," Nahla said. Her tears had dried and the stones held her gaze as if she were mesmerized.

"Nahla," Carina said, taking the girl's arm. "Where did you find these?"

"I saw a funny sign on the map of the ship."

Carina recalled the hours her sister had spent poring over the *Zenobia's* blueprints, apparently fascinated by the ship's design and engineering.

"I wondered what it was," Nahla continued, "so I went to take a look. I found a secret cupboard in the back of another cupboard in the passenger galley. When I saw the pretty stones someone had hidden there, I thought I'd done something wrong so I didn't tell anyone. But I liked them so much I didn't want to put them back either. I'm sorry."

"She showed me her secret find while you were away on the first rehearsal," said Stevenson. "I thought the jewels were probably worth something but I didn't want to get her into trouble so I didn't tell you. It wasn't until Cadwallader mentioned Lomang's claim that something valuable had been taken from his ship, some jewels, that I put two and two together."

"Nahla, sweetheart," said Carina. She held out her arms. "Come here." As she hugged her sister she said, "I think you might have saved us all."

36

The jewels had changed everything. Carina felt kinda bad for not giving them back to Lomang, but not bad enough to actually hand them over. Besides, technically, they weren't even his.

Though she had never heard of the precious stones, they were apparently famous and highly prized throughout the sector. Called 'ember gems', their rarity had lent them an almost mythical status. At Martha's Rest, Cadwallader had paid for repairs and refit of the *Duchess* with just one of them. Another gem had bought fuel, supplies, and the latest weapons and armor for the entire merc band. Carina had given Cadwallader one more in payment for the Black Dogs' upcoming service on Ostillon and then kept the rest. She wore them around her neck as Nahla had done, sometimes shuddering at the thought that for a time they had been a little girl's playthings.

Carina was sitting with Stevenson in the *Duchess's* cockpit after another lesson in flying starships when her hand strayed to the pouch around her neck. At the same time her mind strayed to the question of how all their lives might have turned out differently if Nahla hadn't been curious about that symbol on the *Zenobia's* blueprints.

"Do you believe in fate?" she asked the pilot. "You've mentioned it a couple of times but I didn't know if you were being serious."

"Uh..." Stevenson made an adjustment on his flight control panel before replying, "I believe there's more to existence than we currently understand. Look at you, for instance. What explanation is there for what you and your sibs do?"

"Nai Nai—my grandmother—and Ma told me the explanation accepted among mages. It makes sense, in a way, but it doesn't explain it properly."

"No kidding," Stevenson said. "What does mage lore have to say about what you do?"

"That most mages' energy to Cast comes from the stars. And the mages who derive their energy that way are called Star Mages. Parthenia, Oriana, Ferne and I are all Star Mages. Darius is a Spirit Mage. His energy comes from living things. As for Castiel, I'm pretty sure he's a Dark Mage. Dark Mage's energy is hidden in the universe."

"That does make a little sense," said Stevenson. "And there's no doubt that what you do is real so there has to be an explanation for it."

"I might find the answer on Earth," Carina said pensively. "That's where mages originated so it stands to reason that's where most research was done."

"But, assuming you're right about mages originating there and that you manage to find the planet, is it likely any of the information still exists after all this time?"

"Who knows?" Carina asked. "But at least I will have tried."

More important to her than information about mages was the dream that Earth would be somewhere people had learned from their history of persecuting mages and grown more tolerant and accepting. All she wanted was for her and her family to be left alone and to live without fear. It didn't seem too much to ask.

"Your boyfriend, Bryce," Stevenson said. "He's going with you?"

"He says he wants to. I hope he does."

"That's quite a commitment."

"He's quite a guy," said Carina, somewhat flippantly, but she meant it.

"He is?" Stevenson said. "I mean, if you say so, but he seemed the jealous type for a while there."

"He was, but he got over it."

"I'm glad, for your sake."

"So am I," Carina said. "I think I figured out where he was coming from. You see, he got really sick one time, and his entire family abandoned him. They just went off and left him to die, alone and homeless. He says he forgives them and he's gotten over it, but I don't think he ever has. I think deep down he's worried *I'm* going to abandon him too."

"That must be hard." Stevenson's attention returned to the *Duchess's* flight controls.

Carina snuck a glance at the man's profile as he worked. Bryce hadn't been wrong when he'd sensed something between them. The pilot had been a port in a stormy sea for her when she'd first joined the Black Dogs. After years of homelessness, she'd been well-fitted to the name of the band. She'd been feral, scared, determined to prove herself, desperate for and terrified of companionship. She'd been a mess.

She'd bounced around the other mercs, not knowing who was friend or foe, who was genuine and who wanted to take advantage of her. And the mercs themselves were almost as much of a mess as she was. The lifestyle attracted the worst and most damaged of humanity. At times, Stevenson had seemed the only sane, normal one among them with the exception of

Cadwallader and Speidel, whose higher ranks prevented them from having much to do with her.

The pilot had helped calm her down and reassure her that she was doing okay, that she wasn't about to be kicked out of the band. He'd warned her of the mercs to stay away from and who she could trust, to an extent.

They had never been exclusive. That wasn't how it worked when you didn't know if you would still be alive at the end of the next mission. But they had been more than friends, and Bryce's gut had told him so.

"You'd better go ask your little brother begin Cloaking the ship," Stevenson said.

"What?" said Carina. "Are we nearly there?"

"Uh huh. It would be better if the Dirksens didn't know we were coming."

Carina got up to leave, but she paused and turned. Bending down, she gave Stevenson a hug.

"Not unwelcome," he said affectionately, "but why?"

"The last time we parted ways I didn't get to say a proper goodbye. After this mission's over we probably won't see each other again. I just wanted to say thanks."

"For what?" He had drawn back and was looking Carina in the eyes.

"I don't know," she said. "Just being who you are, and for being there for me when it counted."

"I could say the same." He gave a soft smile. "Good luck, Carina. I hope that if fate does exist it leads you where you want to go."

37

The *Duchess* sat on the dark side of a gas giant in Ostillon's system, gathering data on the state of affairs on the Dirksens' former hideaway planet. The ship's scanners had been set to pick up signal leakage. Media reports, private conversations, and comms on domestic matters would paint a picture of what was happening on the planet's surface.

It had been months since Carina had left, or rather, had been kidnapped and forced to leave. Were things still as dire? Perhaps the Dirksens had closed up shop and left. That would be ideal, but Carina had a feeling things would not be so simple and easy for her.

They never were.

But she was in a better position than she'd been for a long time—ever, in fact. After plenty of practice and meditation, the kids' Casting had improved enormously, and the Black Dogs were equipped with state-of-the-art weapons and armor, and were battle-ready. It would have been good to carry out more rehearsals, but this was her chance and she was going to take it.

She was on the bridge with Cadwallader when the latest

computer analysis of the scan data arrived. He was first to check it.

"It's the same." He sighed.

"The same?" she echoed. "Nothing?"

"Not a thing."

"And you're sure it can't be an error?"

"We ran diagnostics on all the scanners like you asked," Cadwallader said. "They're all functioning perfectly. They're just not picking up any signals from Ostillon."

"It doesn't seem possible," said Carina. "The situation was bad when we left, but it's hard to imagine things going so far south that no planet-wide comm systems are working."

"We can send out probes to gather more data. Maybe get some visuals of the surface, especially that mountain range where your brother says the Dirksen headquarters is situated."

"Yes." She nodded. "Please do that." Another six or twelve hours' wait wouldn't hurt. She was fairly confident that due to Darius's regular Cloaking of the *Duchess*, they had slipped into the system unnoticed. Providing they remained in their current position they shouldn't be detected. A departing Dirksen vessel might happen to pick up on the *Duchess's* presence, but the chances of that were slim.

"This gives me an idea about what to do with Lomang and his little brother," Cadwallader said.

He and Carina had been debating how to get rid of the smugglers for some time, without coming up with a solution. Murdering the two men in cold blood seemed harsh, yet if they allowed them to go free there was little doubt Lomang would come after them—perhaps in his wife's destroyer. The fact that Nahla had taken his jewelry from the *Zenobia* had never been divulged to him in the weeks he'd spent in the *Duchess's* brig, but the man wasn't stupid. He would know the money for the complete refitting of the mercs' vessel had to have come from somewhere.

"You think it's safe to abandon them on Ostillon?" Carina asked.

"If we're going to maroon them it seems a good place to do it," replied Cadwallader. "Assuming they survive it'll take them months to leave."

"Okay, let's do that." She thought for a moment. "But not until the mission's over. I want Lomang safely confined here in the meantime, out of danger of interfering I can't stand the sight of the man's hat. It's way too distracting."

She spent the next few hours double-checking the provisions and equipment they were taking along on the mission. A plentiful supply of elixir was paramount. Each mage would carry two large canisters and the shuttle would carry a small tank full of the precious liquid. She had also packed ingredients so they could make more if necessary. She'd gathered wood and soil at Martha's Rest.

When the data from the probes arrived, it was shocking. No aircraft were plying its skies, no ships sailed its seas, and very little traffic traveled along its road systems. Over the cities the atmosphere was hazy, as if smoky from intentional or accidental fires. Ostillon appeared to have reverted to an early settlement state.

Even more pertinent and shocking was the fact that no starships appeared to be in orbit around the planet. It was conceivable that one or more could have been orbiting sunside and thus not visible, but the probes hadn't even picked up traces from starship engines. It seemed that no space vessels had been on site for several weeks at a minimum.

Could the Dirksens really have abandoned the planet? It was more than Carina dared to hope.

"I know what the data says," said Cadwallader, "but we should proceed as if the planet and the Dirksen headquarters remain heavily defended."

"Agreed," Carina said.

"And, on the chance we've arrived at an opportune moment but Dirksen starships are on their way," Cadwallader continued, "we should commence the mission as soon as possible."

"Also agreed. I'll break the news to the kids."

THE MAGES PUT on their armor in silence. It had been custom-made for them at Martha's Rest. These were no cut down EVA suits, potentially with vital components missing. The mages wore the same state-of-the-art reinforced plexi-silicon as the mercs. It would protect them against direct hits from highest-energy pulse rounds, though not at close range and not forever. No armor protected you forever.

As Carina also got ready to go to the shuttle, she recalled her argument with Bryce in their cabin, when their anger had visibly hurt Darius. Bryce had implied that what she was trying to do wasn't worth risking the lives of her siblings. At the time she'd dismissed his words, telling herself that she was doing the right thing, the best thing for all of them; that finding the way back to Earth could be the only solution to all their problems.

But, in truth, she had to admit that reaching Earth was her dream, not her brothers and sisters'. Everything they did and were about to do was her idea. Though they'd mostly gone along with her, she didn't know if that was because they really wanted to, or if they were doing it out of gratitude for her rescuing them from the Sherrerrs, or because they were too submissive or scared to say no.

"Kids," she said suddenly. It was somewhat late in the day to be putting the question to them but this would be her last opportunity.

The mages paused in their movements.

She took a breath. "If you don't want to do this you don't

have to. You can stay on the *Duchess*. All of you. I can go down to Ostillon by myself."

"No!" Darius exclaimed. "I want to come with you, Carina."

"I know you don't want me to leave," she replied, "but that doesn't mean you have to come on this mission with me. I'll be coming back whether I find the coordinates for Earth or not." Her last statement was less certain than she made out but she didn't want to frighten her brother.

"I still want to come with you," Darius declared.

"So do I," Parthenia said gravely. "This is family business. We have to stick together."

"That's right," said Ferne. "You need us. We all need each other if we're going to survive."

Oriana said, "We couldn't allow you to do this by yourself. Besides, I want to see where the early mages lived."

Carina was also curious to see the mountain castle. She knew she could be wrong about it being the place the mages on Ostillon had built to live in when the newcomers began to persecute them, but something told her she was right. If only she could ask Jace, the tall, black-bearded Ostillonian native, descendant of those first mages to arrive from Earth.

She noticed Castiel had said nothing while the others had given their assurances they wanted to take part in the mission. She still didn't trust him even as far as she could hoist his scrawny body. He hadn't done anything to draw attention to himself since he'd been threatened with being left behind on the first rehearsal, and the other kids seemed to have forgiven him if not forgotten his past despicable behavior. But Carina had a long memory. She would be keeping a close eye on him.

Finally, they were ready.

They walked through the *Duchess* to the shuttle bay. Stevenson would be flying them the remaining distance to Ostillon.

The mercs who would accompany them were already

boarding. Atoi would be their CO for the mission as they would be out of radio contact with Cadwallader, who was remaining aboard ship.

Bryce moved out of line to join the mages and Carina. It would be several hours' travel to Ostillon.

Everyone's visor was up so they breathed the starship's atmosphere and conserved their suits' gases. As Carina sat down she noticed Chandu had taken a seat in the shuttle. Her gut rebelled at the thought of the man taking part in the mission but there wasn't anything she could do about it now. It was too late to ask Cadwallader to pick someone else a as substitute.

Then Chandu turned in her direction and she saw he was sporting a black eye.

"What happened to him?" Carina asked Bryce softly, nodding her head in the scarred man's direction.

"Didn't you hear?" Bryce asked. "He got too familiar with Parthenia."

Anger rose in Carina but then she chuckled. "She punched him? I guess I shouldn't have worried about the mercs taking advantage of her after all."

She opened a private comm to her sister. "I forgot to warn you to watch out for Chandu, but it looks like I didn't need to."

Parthenia leaned forward to give Carina a smile.

The cabin Stevenson's announcement the shuttle's hatch was about to close. His co-pilot would be responsible for the *Duchess* while they were gone.

In another few seconds they were sealed in. The rumble and roar of the shuttle's engines firing vibrated through the vessel.

They were on their way.

38

Castiel took the lead as the mercs and mages advanced along dusty mountain tracks toward the Dirksen hideout. Atoi walked directly behind him, followed by most of the mercs. The mages walked to the rear of the group with a few mercs at the very back. Nothing moved in the slopes around them. It was night time on that part of Ostillon, and everyone was relying on night vision to see the way ahead.

Carina hoped it didn't make too much of a difference to her brother. According to what he'd said, he'd always approached the Dirksens' headquarters in a skimmer or similar vessel and usually during the daytime.

He'd seemed confident about where to set down in the *Duchess's* shuttle, however, so she guessed she had to trust to his judgment.

She'd asked Bryce to stick close to the mages. They needed the additional firepower—they couldn't Cast and shoot at the same time—and once they were inside the two groups would inevitably split up and she would stick with her siblings. If things didn't go their way she didn't want to be separated from him.

As before during the rehearsals, Nahla had remained behind with Stevenson. The mission was simply too dangerous for a nine-year-old girl with no way to protect herself. As consolation, the pilot had promised to teach her about the shuttle's controls.

Not a single sign of the Dirksens' presence had been spotted. Flying down in the Cloaked shuttle had given a close up of the state of things on the surface. Everything the vessel picked up confirmed the data from the *Duchess's* scanners and probes. No electric lights shone in the darkness and the planet's communications networks seemed dead. No signals were passing to or from its satellites. Ostillon was in a dire state.

Carina recalled the young woman, Asha, who had helped her when she was in need. She hoped her short-term friend was doing okay.

Ferne opened a private comm to Carina. "Can't we Transport in?"

"No," she replied. "Think about it. We don't know what or who is there. If a bunch of people in armor suddenly appear from nowhere and the Dirksens are still at the castle they'll shoot us to pieces. And where would we Transport to? Only Castiel knows exactly where we're going."

"Okay," Ferne sighed. "I guessed there was probably a good reason."

Carina was gratified to hear his mature response. The days of dealing with whiny kids appeared to be finally passing.

The rough mountain path dipped into a hollow and began to rise again, winding its way across the steep slope. She wondered what had made it, people or animals? And if it was people, had it been Dirksen troops? The area was so remote it made more sense to fly troops in and out but perhaps the Dirksens had once stationed lookouts and guards among the peaks.

If so, it hadn't done them any good. For their purposes, Ostillon was a dead planet. The Sherrerrs had discovered the

Dirksen presence there and their attack had devastated the place, collapsing its infrastructure. The land and people would not recover for a long time. The Dirksens turning up had been the worst thing that could have happened to them.

But so it was across the galactic sector. The warring clans exhausted resources, exploited populations, and wreaked havoc wherever they set foot.

Carina recalled the words of Calvaley, the high-ranking Sherrerr officer she'd encountered on Ithiya and then again on the Sherrerr flagship, *Nightfall*. He'd opined that the clan's influence brought control and order to chaos, and with them came civilization. Ostillon was testament to his delusion.

Atoi raised a hand and the line halted.

Castiel opened a comm to Carina. "It's around the next bend. I'm sure of it."

Atoi said, "Car, you, me, and the kid should go take a look."

"I'm coming up," Carina said. She edged passed the mercs in the line along the narrow track. When she reached the front she joined Atoi and Castiel as they split from the group to walk the final few meters.

At a sharp edge of the protruding slope, Castiel squatted down. "This is the place the skimmers would turn before heading directly into the mountainside." He spoke in an unnecessarily soft tone. "Or at least that was how it seemed. In fact, they passed through the illusion and landed in the bay. There were always guards around but not many."

"Never any outside?" Atoi asked.

"No," Castiel replied.

"I'll send in a fire team," said Atoi. "See what they find."

"Wait a minute," Carina said. "I just thought of something." She comm'd the whole platoon and her siblings. "There's gonna be some noise. Don't panic."

Scanning the canyon, she found a boulder. Then she closed her eyes and sipped elixir. After sending out the Transport

Cast, she opened her eyes. The small shift in the boulder's position was all it needed. The rock fell, bouncing down the canyon wall, scattering stones and vegetation, and making enough of a racket to attract the attention of anyone nearby.

They waited. No one appeared through the illusory wall Castiel claimed to exist or from anywhere else.

Assured they wouldn't be ambushed, Atoi picked her fire team and sent them in. Castiel directed the men and women to an exact location, but when they arrived there they stood still, looking around as if confused.

"Castiel," said Carina, "you're going to have to find the wall yourself. I'll come with you."

"But if Sable or Kee see me they'll recognize me immediately."

"Your visor is down, dummy," Carina replied.

Castiel still seemed reluctant but he got up. Atoi waited with the remaining mercs while he and Carina walked down toward the supposed opening to the mountain castle.

When she arrived there, she could see the source of the fire team's confusion. The division between the real mountain and the illusion was invisible to the unknowing eye. Even Castiel couldn't find it at first. He moved sideways, pressing his hands to the upright surface as the trail faded away, leaving nothing except vertical slope and a deep drop to rocks below.

Then his arm slipped into nothingness.

"It's here!" he exclaimed. "I found it. I *told* you it was here."

The invisible entrance was almost impossible to walk through. It was easy to understand why the Dirksens had used skimmers to enter and leave the headquarters. Only a tiny fragment of path remained at the edge of the illusion. They were already down to single file. In order to go into the headquarters they would have to walk on tiptoes.

"Is it solid floor once you're through?" Carina asked Castiel.

"Yeah, we'll enter into a large bay."

"All right, go around me. I'll go in first, followed by the fire team. You return to Atoi and the others."

Castiel didn't need to be told twice. He ran up the slope and disappeared around the rocky protrusion.

Carina pointed her pulse rifle forward and stepped into rock.

39

The entrance chamber of the mountain castle rose four or five stories high and was wide enough to hold five or six skimmers. The marks of that many vehicles were plain to see on the rock floor.

The place had clearly been created and hadn't formed naturally, though no marks of cutting tools or drills marked the surface. Carina couldn't imagine what had carved the chamber. The walls were smooth and polished like the pebbles Nai Nai used to make, the stone highlighted with subtle colors and grains.

She guessed that at the time the chamber had been created, the walls had been beautiful, but the dust of ages had overlaid them and skimmer exhaust had burned the floor.

The illusion was maintained on the inside, where an interior wall appeared to rise to the ceiling in the space the skimmers would enter. On closer inspection she realized the patterning was a facsimile of the right hand wall. At the rear of the chamber stood an arched doorway from which no light shone.

The fire team stepped through the wall behind Carina. She

gestured to them to halt and increased her external audio to maximum, but all she could hear was the movement of the night air.

Returning the audio to its regular setting she walked with the fire team to the far side of the cavern, where an unlit passage led upward from the arched doorway.

Carina comm'd Atoi. "The place seems deserted. I think it's safe to bring everyone in."

Was she really standing in an underground castle created by mages thousands of years ago? It was too early to tell but the thought sent her heart into her throat.

One by one, the rest of the mercs stepped through the illusory wall into the skimmer bay. Had the mages even used air transport to reach the place? It seemed unlikely so the trail that petered out at the edge of the entrance would have been only an emergency measure. The mages would have Transported into and out of the place.

Atoi walked up to Carina. "I'll send out teams to search the place. You said they should look for paper documents containing star maps, strange writing, that kind of thing, right?"

"Or anything that seems odd, I guess," Carina said. It was hard to give clear instructions when she didn't know what she was looking for herself.

"If the worse comes to the worst and we don't find what you need," said Atoi, "we might find some Dirksen intel we can sell to the Sherrerrs. I can't imagine they would have been too careful about clearing such a well-hidden site."

As she began to divide up and instruct her soldiers, the mages and Bryce appeared through the cavern wall, followed by the remainder of the mercs. The children seemed impressed, standing still and gazing at the ceiling and walls.

Carina comm'd them. "Hey, we have a job to do, don't forget. We need to focus."

She worried it was mean to hurry them. She knew how they

felt. When you grew up differently from everyone around you, separated and cut off from regular life and the dominant culture, to suddenly find yourself in the home of your ancestors, a place where you would have belonged, was an amazing feeling.

But the mountain castle had also been the Dirksen headquarters on Ostillon. It would never be safe for them to linger there.

Atoi's teams were running up the passage out of the chamber. When the kids joined Carina near the doorway, she told them to wait while the mercs checked the interior was empty.

After several minutes, Atoi said, "Car, from the reports I'm getting back this place is huge. Do you want to wait while we check it top to bottom or start searching it yourselves now?"

"I don't want to hang around," Carina replied. "We'll begin our search."

As she led the children up the passage into the main area of the castle, she said, "Castiel, are you absolutely sure you don't have any idea where something secret might be hidden?"

"I already told you I don't remember anything like that," he replied. "All I know is the older parts of the castle are different from the areas the Dirksens built."

They emerged into a second large chamber, about four times the size of the one at the entrance.

"This is the great hall," said Castiel.

Carina noticed the temperature level on her HUD suddenly drop.

"Whoa," said Oriana, "it's really cold in here."

"Yes, it always was," Castiel said.

A blackened fireplace stood in one corner and next to it a large, comfortably padded armchair and a small, three-legged table. The rest of the hall was empty.

"How many floors did you say there are here?" asked Carina.

"I didn't," Castiel replied. "Lots, though."

"Are there any below this one?"

"Yes, but the Dirksens built it. That's where they put their prisoners."

"We aren't going to find anything the mages may have left down there," said Carina. "This seems to be the hub. The mages may have created a secret safe somewhere in here. Let's start by examining these walls."

It occurred to her that mages wouldn't have needed to install a lock or any other external device to open a secret repository. All they would have required was the knowledge of where something was located. They would have been able to Transport the item in and out.

"Look for a pattern or carving on the walls that might indicate something is behind it," she added.

She jogged to the farthest wall and inspected the surface. Like in the entrance chamber it was smooth. She couldn't imagine what had created the effect. Perhaps the mages of olden times had known more Casts.

The patterning seemed natural, arising from the rock of the mountain itself, and she couldn't see any irregularity in the smoothness that would indicate carving.

She moved quickly along the wall, scanning it and running her hand over it to feel for something she might not see. The children and Bryce were doing the same, but the hall was huge. It would take them a while to check all the parts they could get to, but most of the height of the towering walls was unreachable. And the hall was only one part of the castle.

A sense of fear and defeat began to grow in her. The task she'd set seemed hopeless. Even if her guess that the mages had left something behind was correct it might take them years to find it.

Suddenly, Atoi ran back into the hall and crossed toward Carina.

"What's happening?" Carina asked her.

"I think the Dirksens may have left some prisoners behind."

"You're kidding."

"Come and see for yourself."

Carina told the others to keep looking, and if they didn't find anything, to try the next level up if it had been declared safe. Then she ran after Atoi, who had disappeared through one of the hall's openings. She found the other woman waiting in an elevator. They went down together.

When the elevator doors opened Carina saw three mercs standing in a narrow hallway. The air was hazy and her HUD told her it contained products of combustion. Opened steel doors ran across the passage but the doors in the walls on each side of the soldiers were sealed. Carina heard faint thumping and cries from within.

"Can't get the door open, Captain," said one of the mercs to Atoi. "Tried everything. We can't even blast them open. The material's too tough."

"Where are the sounds coming from?" asked Carina.

The woman indicated a door.

Carina sipped elixir and Cast Unlock. A metallic click was followed by the door swinging slightly ajar.

"Food," said a frail voice. "I need food."

The merc pulled open the door. Inside the cell, an old man lay on the floor. His body was skeletal, the skin stretched over bones that barely held scraps of flesh. The man's eyes stared from round, hollow sockets.

Despite his terrible state, he looked faintly familiar to Carina.

"Are you Sherrerrs?" the man asked. "Did we win?"

A bolt struck Carina as she finally recognized him. "Calvaley?" she said, astonished.

"I am Admiral Calvaley. Who are you?"

In answer, Carina lifted her visor.

His features remained confused.

“How long have you been here?” asked Atoi.

“I don’t know. Weeks. There is water here but no food. That bitch Sable Dirksen left us to starve.”

“Us?” Carina said. “There are more of you?”

“At least one more, but I think he’s dead.”

Carina stepped out of the cell and Cast Unlock on the remaining doors. In the cell next to Calvaley’s lay another man. He must have once been large. He was very tall, but the weeks of starvation had left him cruelly emaciated. It was the man’s thick black beard and hair—now streaked with white—that clued her in.

Jace.

40

Carina walked heavily into the hall of the mountain castle. The children were standing in a group with Bryce, their visors up.

On seeing her, Parthenia said, "We can't find anything here. We're going up to the next level."

"Not just yet," Carina said. "I have some news. When the Dirksens left the castle, they didn't take their prisoners with them. They left them to die in the cells on the lower level."

"How terrible!" Oriana exclaimed. "Those poor people."

"Well, one of those poor people is Jace," Carina said.

Seeing Parthenia's face begin to crumple, she added hastily. "He's still alive. The medic is with him now. And another prisoner survived, a Sherrerr called Calvaley. You might remember him from the *Nightfall*. Both of them are very, very ill."

"I want to see Jace," Parthenia said.

Carina knew there was no point in trying to stop her. Parthenia had formed a special connection with the ranger after he'd helped her and Darius when they first arrived on Ostillon.

"Go ahead," she said, "but I warn you he's almost unrecognizable."

Parthenia quickly stepped over to the opening and through it.

"*Shit,*" said Atoi over Carina's comm.

She thought the merc captain was going to report that Jace had died. But instead, Atoi went on to say, "Stevenson's just reported he saw five skimmers heading this way."

"Five?" Carina said. "Stars, it's the Dirksens. It has to be. Nothing else on Ostillon is moving."

"I know," Atoi replied. "What do you say? Do you want us to evacuate or defend?"

"The trail away from here is open to the sky so they'll see us if we leave. We won't have time to get under cover. There's no time to Transport everyone out either."

Carina had another reason for staying. Someone among the Dirksen party might know something about ancient documents that had been found there.

"So we stay and engage them here," said Atoi. "I was hoping you'd say that. I want a chance to face the people who did this." She'd remained in the prisoners' cells with the medic. "I'll bring everyone down to the hall and we'll give the Dirksen troops a nice surprise. You get the kids away from the battle."

"No," said Carina. "We can help."

"Up to you," said Atoi stiffly. She closed the comm.

"The Dirksens are coming," Carina told the children. "Five skimmers are on their way."

"They're coming *here*?!" Oriana exclaimed. "What are we going to do?"

"Carina will protect us," said Darius.

"Even she can't protect you from five skimmers full of Dirksen troops," Bryce said. "What do we do, Carina?"

"We should station ourselves in that corner," she replied, pointing. "It isn't visible from the door."

Mercs began to pour into the hall. Atoi emerged from the basement and her soldiers lined up along the walls nearest the entrance.

"Darius," Carina said, "do you remember when you helped me at the Mech Battle? Can you do the same again? Can you Transport the Dirksen soldiers hundreds of kilometers away?"

"I'd love to do that!"

"Excellent. The rest of us can do the same," she said. "Even if we can't Transport them as far, we should be able to prevent them from returning to the battle in time to be of any help. But wait until I give the signal."

They all nodded.

"Okay. Lower your visors."

"The skimmers are arriving at the bay, Car," said Atoi.

"Right," Carina said to the children. "Remember to stay well back and let the Black Dogs do their work. Don't Transport any of *them* by mistake, okay?"

She gasped.

"What's wrong?" Bryce asked.

"Parthenia's still in the cells on the lower level."

She looked over to the doorway that led to the elevator. It was opposite the hall's entrance. If Parthenia tried to join them she would be seen by the Dirksens and give the game away.

"She'll have to stay there until the battle's over," she said resignedly.

A man in a soldier's uniform but helmetless walked casually into the hall, his arms relaxed as he held his rifle with the muzzle pointing downward. Behind him strode a woman dressed in a simple, black, silver-edged pantsuit. Her dark brown hair was pulled tightly back in a bun. On each side of her and trailing her slightly were two more helmetless soldiers. A fourth soldier brought up the rear.

None of the group noticed the mercs or mages spread out in their peripheral vision.

Atoi was apparently waiting until the Dirksens realized they'd walked into a trap before springing it.

"Carina, Atoi," said Stevenson over comm. "Cadwallader's just told me a corvette has arrived from outsystem and is heading toward Ostillon."

"Must be a taxi for the bitch," Atoi said.

More soldiers walked into the hallway. Carina couldn't believe none of them saw the lines of people in armor stretched out on both sides of them. How couldn't they feel the tension, stretching the air so tight she could almost strum it?

The dark-haired woman was walking toward the exit that led to the lower level. Carina couldn't let her go down there, where maybe only one merc and the medic could defend Parthenia. But before she could say anything, there was a movement at her side.

Castiel was striding forward, his visor and arms raised.

"Sable!" he yelled. "Watch out! It's an ambush."

The woman, Sable Dirksen, whirled around to see where the voice had come from. Her mouth stretched wide in shock as her eyes took in the sight of a platoon of enemy soldiers in her headquarters.

The mercs began firing. Castiel turned and raised his weapon, aiming it at Darius.

Bryce shot the Dark Mage in the stomach and he doubled over, dropping to his knees then toppling to the floor. He lay still. Bryce ran up to the boy and kicked his body out of the way.

More Dirksen soldiers flooded into the hall from the bay.

"Darius, everyone," Carina shouted, "start Casting."

Sable Dirksen was backing away from the fighting, her guard protecting her.

"Don't Transport the woman in black," Carina instructed her siblings.

Though removing their leader might encourage the

Dirksen soldiers to surrender, if anyone knew where mage documents were it was Sable.

Mercs were falling, hit by close-range fire. It was typical that the Dirksens would have the latest weaponry, which would be effective against the latest armor. But Dirksen troops were falling too, and simply disappearing as the mages Transported them away from the fortress.

They were the lucky ones.

Carina realized Sable was nearing the exit to the lower level. Leaving Bryce to protect the children, she ran around the edge of the room. A pulse round hit her but only obliquely, skittering over her shoulders. She felt a flash of heat then it was gone.

The hiss of pulse fire, thud of boots on stone, clack of weapons on armor, and cries of wounded Dirksen soldiers echoed from the high-vaulted ceiling. The mercs seemed to be winning but it was hard to tell. Carina didn't know how many enemy soldiers had yet to enter the hall.

One of Sable's guard had seen Carina coming. The woman turned her focus from the mercs to the approaching threat to the Dirksen leader.

Carina fired on her before she could shoot, hitting her in the face. The soldier fell, her head a mess of smoldering flesh and bone.

Sable's wide-eyed gaze fixed on Carina. She pushed the back of another of her guards, drawing his attention. He swept around, but as he was about to fire he disappeared, Transported by one of the kids.

Two down, two to go.

The sounds of battle seemed to be lessening.

Another of Sable's guard disappeared.

The woman began to run to the exit.

Carina switched her weapon to stun and shot the Dirksen

leader in the back. Her remaining guard fired on Carina, hitting her thigh. Searing heat erupted from the muscle.

She fired back. Her shot went wide, but a pulse from another direction hit the man's chest. He collapsed, falling backward onto prone, unconscious Sable Dirksen.

41

Carina slid to the floor, the pain from her thigh felling her. Her suit's medkit kicked into action and she felt the pressure of an air-injector against her skin. An icy sensation spread from the injection site, first dulling then entirely numbing the pain. She exhaled.

The shooting had stopped. What Dirksen soldiers remained were motionless on the floor, either dead or incapacitated. The mercs were walking among them, removing their weapons and checking their statuses.

Carina got to her feet. Her injured leg felt weak but she walked over to Sable Dirksen, who lay face-downward beneath her dead guard.

"You okay, Car?" asked Atoi as she approached.

"Until the anesthetic wears off," she replied.

"Did you kill her?" Atoi gestured at the prone Dirksen leader.

"No. She's only stunned. I want to find out what she knows about this place."

Atoi paused a moment as if listening to a comm. "One of the

skimmers either didn't arrive or left after the battle started," she said. "Only four are in the bay."

"Maybe some Dirksen troops decided their leader wasn't worth fighting for," sad Carina, thinking she would never have fought for Sable Dirksen either, not after she'd tried to massacre thousands of innocent mages.

"Or they left to wait for reinforcements," Atoi said.

"I guess there might be more troops on Ostillon," Carina mused. "That corvette is probably here to take the majority offplanet along with *her*."

"Imagine being so scared of reprisals you take a whole platoon with you wherever you go."

"The Dirksens sure have a lot to answer for. Before they came along Ostillon was doing okay. Now the place is a wasteland. I doubt any Ostillonian would hesitate to slit her throat if they got the chance."

"We'd better not hang around too long," Atoi said. "Just in case the Dirksens decide to mount a rescue."

Carina walked closer to Sable and tried to move the dead soldier off of her.

Seeing Carina's struggle, Atoi stepped up and helped her roll the corpse away.

Sable appeared to be coming around.

The sound of running feet distracted Carina. A figure in merc's armor was running across the hall. The person was too small to be a mercenary, however.

After puzzling over it briefly, Carina realized the figure was Castiel.

She'd thought Bryce had killed him—and she hadn't shed any tears about it.

She lifted her weapon and aimed, but before she could get off a shot the boy had disappeared through an opening.

"Send some people after him, Atoi," she said. *Dammit.*

She wished Bryce had removed the thorn that had been

stuck in her side for so long. Now she would have to figure out what to do with the little traitor. Again. Had he really imagined the Dirksens would win against the Black Dogs and that Sable Dirksen would be grateful to him?

The boy had even greater delusions of grandeur than his father.

Bryce walked up, the children trailing him.

"I know, I know," he said, seeing her expression. "I just couldn't kill a kid."

"Castiel is *bad*," Darius said.

"I hate him *so* much," said Oriana.

Sable Dirksen groaned. She tried to turn onto her back and failed.

"Let me help you," Carina offered sweetly.

She slid her booted foot under the small woman's torso and flipped her over. Then she rested the end of her rifle's muzzle against Sable's forehead.

The Dirksen leader's eyes narrowed and focused on Carina. Then the woman groaned again, turned her face to one side, and vomited.

"Pleased to meet you too," Carina said.

"*Gross*," said Ferne.

Sable wiped her mouth on her sleeve. "Can I at least sit up?"

Carina eased the pressure of her weapon against Sable's forehead and gave a nod, though as Sable drew herself into a sitting position, Carina's weapon was never far from her face.

"You must be Carina Sherrerr," said Sable.

"My name isn't your business," Carina replied, not bothering to correct the woman's error. "You're alive for one reason. I'm looking for something here. If you can tell me where it is, maybe I'll only lock you in one of your cells with the corpse of a prisoner you left to starve. Maybe one of your officers might think to look for you there."

"You make it sound so inviting," said Sable. "Perhaps I would rather die than endure that, or help you."

"No, you wouldn't," Carina said simply. "Cowards always cling to life. No matter how many people have to die for them or what dishonorable things they must do. You'll do anything to live."

Sable swallowed and her gaze slid from Carina's to take in the state of things in the hall. Perhaps she was hoping to see some of her soldiers still standing, giving her a chance of reversing the situation in her favor. Or perhaps she was counting them, wondering if some had gotten away and might return to try to rescue her.

Carina thrust her muzzle into Sable's skull, causing her head to jerk backward. "I'm looking for documents. Ancient papers, or anything else that was here when you arrived."

Sable hesitated.

"What is it?" Carina demanded. "Tell me!"

"There's a room," Sable replied, looking as though she'd tasted bile. "We call it the Star Tower. There might be something in there."

"Show me," Carina ordered.

Atoi hauled the Dirksen clan leader to her feet. "Move fast," she said, pushing the leader forward.

The woman had no choice but to walk quickly with Atoi's gun in her back. Carina, Bryce, and the mages followed.

The mercs remained in the hall, tending to their own wounded and corralling the Dirksen wounded who could still walk toward the prisoner cells.

Sable took them up many floors to the very top of the castle. They stepped out of the elevator into a chill breeze and starlit sky. They were inside a tower with arched, glassless windows that looked out over the mountains, their peaks glowing softly in the starlight. Low seating ran around the edge of the room that was topped by an octagonal roof.

"You'll have to be quick," said Sable sullenly. "The effect disappears at dawn."

"What are you talking about?" asked Carina.

"This is hollow." Sable kicked the solid wall that ran down from the edge of the seating. "I think something's inside but it's impossible to open. I guess it's something to do with stars, but I could never create the right pattern. There are too many possibilities, even for a computer to generate."

Carina knelt down in front of the panel Sable had kicked. It was hard to see in the minimal light, but she thought she could make out some faint lines. As she peered at them more closely her heart leapt.

It was a Character, though one she didn't recognize.

She'd been right all along. Mages had lived here! Her ancestors had stood where she was kneeling.

The thought brought a lump to her throat but she had no time to indulge her feelings. The Dirksen woman had said something about having to hurry and star patterns.

However, Sable Dirksen was not a mage.

Carina sipped elixir, closed her eyes, and Cast Unlock. She opened her eyes and touched the Character.

The section beneath the seat didn't move and the lines around its periphery remained thin.

Carina stood up. "What do you mean about the stars?"

Sable began to lift an arm.

"Hey!" said Atoi.

"Do you want me to show you or not?" Sable asked acidly.

"Let her move," Carina told her friend.

Sable reached up and tapped the air above her head with a finger. A point of light appeared. Like a tiny star, it hung in the dark space below the tower roof. She touched the air in another place and a second star came to life.

"It only happens at night," said Sable. "As soon as the sun rises the stars disappear."

"I know what it is!" said Oriana excitedly. "It's the Star Map."

Carina had realized it immediately too but the realization had filled her with dread.

The Star Map was the hardest part of the mages' meditation ritual. Nai Nai had taught it rigorously, forcing her to draw it on a holoscribe over and over again. If she made one mistake she had to start again from the beginning. As a young child, she'd fallen asleep trying to draw the Star Map correctly and dreamt about being lost in it, unable to find Ma or Ba or her way home.

My way home.

If she could draw the Star Map correctly, it might unlock the door and reveal whatever secrets the mages had stored there, perhaps even the route back to Earth. But only if she could draw it correctly.

How many times had she wondered if the Map had been corrupted over the centuries and generations of mages, passing it on from memory alone?

"Carina," urged Bryce, "you have to do it quickly."

Outside the tower, the real stars were beginning to fade in the pre-dawn light.

One hundred star positions, from memory?

Swallowing her fear that she would get it wrong or that the Map she'd learned with so much effort and anguish was incorrect to start with, Carina began.

Instinctively, she swiped away the stars Sable had created, leaving a blank canvas. As always, she began from the center. The central patterns were burned into her mind like the most painful moments of her life. Like the time she finally accepted that her parents were never coming home, and the moment Nai Nai took her last breath.

When the center was complete, she moved to the right quadrant at the rear of the 3D map. Nai Nai had taught her tricks to help her remember. This set of stars looks like a scalobite tail, and they join to this set via a winding trail like a soft noodle.

Carina moved to the next quadrant, conscious of the sky lightening around her. As she worked, old memories of her grandmother surfaced. Moments she'd forgotten.

The old lady had been a fearsome force to reckon with at times but Carina had felt her love like a thick blanket surrounding her and protecting her always.

She started on the third quadrant. These stars were like the spots on a kruekin's wings, and these were regular like the windows of a three-story house.

Carina had once asked Nai Nai if they would ever live in a three-story house. Her grandmother had replied, "Probably not, but we will always be happy."

By the time Carina moved on to the fourth and final quadrant, her face was wet and she could barely see what she was doing. She stopped a moment to wipe her eyes.

The edge of the mountain range was turning rosy-red and the Map was beginning to fade.

She hurriedly created the last set of stars.

One here, another here. Five to go. Carina counted them down. She touched the final star to life and fell to her knees, grasping the flat surface under the seat.

The door didn't open.

She pressed it, then dug her fingernails into the cracks, but it remained firmly closed.

"Never mind," said Darius. "You tried."

Carina leapt up. She'd gotten something wrong, she knew it. If she could only remember.

Then she saw it. The final five stars were reversed. She'd created a mirror image of their true position.

She swept her hand through them. Beyond the space that had held the erased stars, she saw a brightness on the horizon that heralded the sun's approach.

Her hand trembling, Carina re-created the final five stars.

"It's opening!" shouted Oriana.

But before Carina could turn around to see what lay beyond the door, Sable drove her elbow into Atoi's stomach. The merc's armor protected her from actual injury but the distraction gave Sable the chance she needed.

She ripped Atoi's weapon from her hands and fired at the group of mages.

The pulse hit Darius.

Carina screamed and launched herself at Sable. Atoi was already on the woman, knocking her to the ground and wrestling the weapon from her. Carina knelt on her chest and grabbed Sable's throat with both hands.

"Don't kill her," warned Atoi.

Carina took no notice. Sable was turning purple.

"Car," barked Atoi. "Let go. We need her."

With all her strength, Carina squeezed tighter.

"Don't make me do it, Car."

Carina felt cold, hard metal against her skull. The red haze that masked her vision began to fade. The noises and sights of her surroundings flooded in.

"He's still alive," she heard Oriana say.

Somehow, Carina managed to loosen her grip on Sable Dirksen.

The woman coughed and writhed, trying to get her hands up.

"One of you take whatever's inside that cubbyhole," said Atoi. "We have to get back to the shuttle."

42

"I haven't heard from Stevenson for a while," Atoi said as they ran down the castle stairs, "and he isn't answering comms. The last thing he said was he could see that fifth skimmer that got away. Then nothing."

Carina could hardly make sense of what the woman was saying. All she could think about was Darius. She was carrying the little boy over her shoulder as they ran.

Darius. Her sweet little brother, who she was supposed to protect and keep safe. And he'd been shot, right in the stomach, by that Dirksen bitch.

But Carina knew it was her fault. Her fault for taking him into danger.

The armful of documents Ferne was carrying, the treasure Carina had worked so hard and risked so much for, meant nothing compared to Darius's life. Nothing was worth attaining if it meant she had to lose him.

"Car," Atoi said. "I need you to keep it together."

Carina hated her friend right then but she knew she was right.

"The mages can Transport the platoon to the shuttle," she said.

"I'm worried about that corvette," Atoi said. "I want to take the bitch with us." She was gripping Sable Dirksen tightly by her upper arm and part forcing, part dragging her down the stairs.

"No," said Carina. "The cells."

She could imagine worse and more suitable fates for the Dirksen leader than starving to death but she didn't have time to enact them.

"We can use her as a hostage for safe passage out of the system," countered Atoi.

Through the fog of her rage, misery, and guilt, Carina could see the sense of what Atoi was saying. Without Darius they wouldn't be able to Cloak the shuttle and sneak past the Dirksen corvette unseen. The shuttle had little in the way of defensive weaponry. It relied on the *Duchess* for its defense, but the mercs' starship was currently on the far side of a gas giant.

"All right," Carina said. "But I want to be the one who kills her when this is done."

"Just wait until we're aboard the *Duchess*," replied Atoi. "then *I* certainly won't stand in your way."

The mercs were waiting in the great hall. Parthenia was there too. She gasped at the sight of Darius over Carina's shoulder.

"He's just hurt," Oriana assured her sister. "I Cast Heal on him and so did Ferne. We can all carry on Casting it until we get him to the *Duchess's* sick bay."

The girl's tone sounded hopeful, but Carina knew that Heal wouldn't prevent death, only forestall it in decreasing increments until the Cast had no effect whatsoever. Only Spirit Mages who could prevent someone from dying and then only at great cost to themselves, usually their own death.

The little boy hadn't moved at all since Sable had shot him.

Carina knew she would never forgive herself for allowing him to be hurt, and if he died she wouldn't want to go on living.

Jace and Calvaley lay on the floor of the hall. Jace remained unconscious and Calvaley seemed coherent, but only barely. Loath though she was to take Calvaley with them Carina's conscience weighed heavily enough without also leaving an old, starved man to die alone.

"Do you know where Castiel is?" she asked Parthenia.

"No one can find him," her sister replied. "Someone told me what he did. I can't believe he still betrayed us after we'd forgiven him for so much. I hate it, but we'll have to leave him here. Carina. You take Darius to the shuttle. Ferne, Oriana, and I can Transport everyone else, then we'll come ourselves."

"I'll stay with them," offered Bryce.

Carina was in no state to argue. On top of everything, she was also concerned about Stevenson's silence. "Okay. I'll Transport myself and Darius. Send Atoi and as many mercs as you can manage with me."

The Black Dogs were carrying their own weapons as well as those they'd taken from the dead and wounded Dirksen troops. Carina cradled hers under her right arm as she balanced her brother on her left shoulder. Atoi stood beside her, her grip tight on Sable Dirksen.

Carina Cast.

A moment later, she was standing outside the shuttle. The sun was coming up over the peak of a mountain, and someone was screaming.

Atoi and Sable Dirksen appeared.

"What the hell is that?" Atoi asked.

Six mercs materialized in a group.

Carina recognized the person who was screaming.

Nahla? No!

The shuttle's ramp was up. Carina ran around the vessel to the pilot's hatch. Scorch marks ran down from the roof of the pilot's section. The shuttle had been attacked. The departing Dirksen soldiers in the skimmer must have spotted it and fired.

Nahla's screaming was an endless horror reverberating around Carina's head. She had to get into the shuttle but the hatch was closed. Only Stevenson could open it, from the inside.

"The manual's here," said a voice. A merc had arrived at Carina's side. The man felt the under carriage and popped a door. The next second, the hatch opened.

The rising sun's red beams slanted into cabin from holes burned in its roof.

Stevenson sprawled in his seat, utterly still.

It had been quick, from the look of him.

Nahla was hysterical.

"I'll get her," said the merc.

But as he approached her the girl screamed even louder and fought to get away from him. She tore at her harness, trying to unfasten it but not succeeding.

The soldier retreated, shaking his head. "I'll hold the boy if you want to try."

Carina passed her brother over to the man and then climbed into the pilot's cabin.

"Nahla," she said, her voice thick. "It's me, Carina. It's okay. No one's going to hurt you."

Nahla's wildly staring eyes focused on Carina and some semblance of recognition passed over her features. When Carina got nearer to her she stopped struggling. She allowed her big sister to undo her harness and lift her from her seat. Her screams grew quieter. As Carina carried her down they stopped altogether and she began to sob.

"It's okay," said Carina, holding Nahla tightly. "It's going to be okay." But they were just words. She had no idea how they were going to make it back to the *Duchess* alive.

More mercs had arrived while she'd been dealing with

Nahla. The news that their pilot was dead was spreading, and concern and grief were rising among the soldiers.

"Shit," said Atoi when she saw Stevenson. "Why'd the bastards have to do that?"

The answer was obvious: the Dirksen skimmer hadn't possessed the firepower to destroy the shuttle but the troops inside it had hoped that by killing the pilot they would prevent the mercs from leaving Ostillon. But Atoi wasn't speaking from a place of logic.

Carina could barely think either but she had to get Darius back to the *Duchess*, whatever it took. "I'll fly the shuttle."

"You?" asked Atoi. "Do you know how?"

Parthenia, Bryce, Ferne, and Oriana arrived. Everyone had returned from the ancient mages' castle.

"Yes," Carina replied with determination. "I can fly it well enough to get us out of here."

"But the cabin won't hold atmosphere."

"I'll breathe my suit's," said Carina.

Parthenia had walked up. "Nahla, come with me. Carina needs space so she can help us."

The little girl allowed Parthenia to take her away and Bryce took Darius from the merc's arms.

"Just..." Carina said to Atoi. She swallowed and her lips trembled. "Just help me get him down."

Her eyes wet, Atoi nodded. Together, they undid Stevenson's harness and lifted the man's body out of his seat.

They laid him down on the mountainside. Carina climbed into the cab again and opened shuttle's ramp. Pairs of mercs carried Jace and Calvaley inside first, another pair entered with Sable Dirksen, wounded mercs followed, Bryce and the children went in, and then the remaining soldiers.

Her heart breaking, Carina took Stevenson's shoulders while Atoi took his legs. The two women carried him into the shuttle and placed him in the well between the benches.

Carina had seen dead soldiers lying there before, as the mercs carried them back to the *Duchess* for a proper commemoration of their lives before they were committed to the void, but she had never once imagined that Stevenson would be one of them.

43

When Carina had confidently asserted she could fly the shuttle she hadn't known if the Dirksen attack had damaged its controls. She climbed into the pilot's cabin and Stevenson's seat, immediately closing her visor against the smell of death. Then she closed the pilot's hatch.

The sun's rays shining though the holes in the cabin roof were growing brighter. The thought that Stevenson would never see another sunrise popped into her mind. She choked and forced the thought away.

She had focus on getting Darius and everyone else back to the *Duchess*.

Carina gave a warning to her passengers over the vessel's comm and then lifted the ramp and closed the airlock. She ran through the flight checks. Nothing seemed damaged. The thick casing over the control center seemed to have protected it from the skimmer's fire.

She started the engine. Her chest heaved.

Blinking away tears, Carina flew the shuttle up into the sky, piling on as much speed as she dared to with sick passengers.

Then she comm'd the *Duchess*, briefly informing Cadwallader about the situation, Stevenson's death, and the three new arrivals. She omitted that one of the Dirksens' ex-prisoners was a Sherrerr. There would be time to explain later, provided they made it. At the end of the comm, she reiterated the need to have the sick bay ready to treat Darius upon his arrival.

Ostillon's pale blue sky faded to black, and the forces acting upon Carina's body eased somewhat. Her HUD signaled the rapid drop in atmospheric gases and temperature. As silence pressed in on her, she felt suddenly, dreadfully, alone.

She comm'd Atoi. "What's happening back there?"

"Everyone's fine. Your sibs are doing that thing with your brother and the little girl's stopped crying, I think. It's hard to tell, with her face behind her visor, but she's sitting still now."

Poor Nahla. Carina didn't even want to imagine what her sister had been through, trapped next to a dead man. She would need psychological help. Her entire family needed psychological help.

"Any sign of the corvette?" Atoi asked.

"Shit," said Carina. She'd forgotten about the Dirksen vessel. She brought up the scan data. "I can't see it. Maybe it's around the other side of the planet."

"Funny," said Atoi. "I would have thought the troops who got away would have been in contact with it."

"One would think." She closed the comm.

Bryce reached out to her.

"Hey, how are you holding up?"

"I've had better days," she replied. "In fact, nearly all of them were better than this one."

"You'll get through it. We all will. We only need to get back to the *Duchess* now."

"Easier said than done. There's a Dirksen corvette out here somewhere but the scanners aren't picking it up."

"Well, that certainly puts a downer on things."

"If I can think of anything to cheer you up," Carina said, "I'll let you know."

"Take it easy," said Bryce.

A pause stretched out between them.

Bryce said softly, "I love you."

"I love you too." The words came easily to Carina's lips, though it was the first time they'd said them to each other.

An alert sounded in Carina's helmet and a message from the *Duchess* flashed up on the flight console. She opened it.

"We're coming out to meet you," said Cadwallader's recorded voice. "It'll bring forward your ETA, and you may need our firepower. The Dirksen corvette is coming toward you with the sun at its back, probably scrambling the data your scanners are picking up."

Dammit. Carina checked the data again. There *was* an anomaly in the readings in the direction of Ostillon's star, but the shuttle's system hadn't flagged it as a ship.

She warned the passengers she was going to increase the shuttle's speed.

Atoi's plan to use Sable Dirksen as a hostage was sound but they couldn't tell the Dirksen forces too soon. Until the shuttle came under the protection of the *Duchess* the enemy would be able to board her and rescue their leader. If Carina could *just* make it within range of the *Duchess's* weapons they would be safe. After its recent refit, she was confident the mercs' ship outgunned the little corvette.

The additional acceleration forced Carina into her seat. She hated to think what it might be doing to her passengers but if she didn't get away from the corvette they would all be dead anyway.

A hail arrived. With no other starships in the vicinity, there could be no doubt where it came from.

Carina ignored it, buying time, glad that whoever was in

command wanted to speak before firing. Did they suspect Sable might be aboard?

The hail sounded again. Carina coaxed a smidgen more acceleration from the shuttle's engine.

The scanners finally picked up the corvette and the flight console announced its presence.

"Gee, thanks," she muttered.

The kilometers between the shuttle and the *Duchess* melted away.

A third hail sounded.

Carina gritted her teeth.

Patience aboard the corvette would be wearing thin.

Whoever commanded the vessel wouldn't wait much longer.

Suddenly, a clanging alert rang in her ears. The shuttle was under attack! The corvette had fired. A pulse was streaming across space toward them.

Shit.

This was it. All it would take to finish them was one direct hit.

Carina's muscles turned rigid...but nothing happened. The shuttle flew on. The corvette's pulse had missed, but that seemed an unlikely accident.

It had been a warning shot.

Where is the Duchess?

Carina sought out the mercs' ship on her display. As she saw the vessel it fired, but the distance was too great. The energy would dissipate before it reached the corvette, having little effect.

It was time to go to the next stalling tactic.

She opened the hail from the corvette.

"This is Commander Kee of the *Tumult* to the starship shuttle departing Ostillon. Reverse thrust immediately and prepare to be boarded."

Carina responded, "This is the shuttle departing Ostillon. Under whose authority do you command us?"

"Under the authority of the Dirksen clan."

Carina thought she'd heard the man's voice before but she couldn't remember where. She hadn't met many Dirksens, only Reyes and his awful mother, Langley.

"Really?" she said in a mocking tone. "I have it on good authority we shouldn't stop."

"Reverse thrust immediately or we will fire." The man sounded unusually calm given the circumstances.

Then she placed it. Commander Kee was the dark-eyed, shaven-headed officer who had taken her prisoner when she'd first arrived at Ostillon. He was smart and effective.

She would have to be careful.

The *Duchess* was nearly within range. Just another few minutes.

"Go ahead," Carina said. "But you're gonna get into a hell of a lot of trouble."

"You're that Sherrerr girl," Kee said. "Or, no, not a Sherrerr. You were working for them as a merc. Makes sense. You have ten seconds to slow down or we *will* fire."

"So you aren't too fond of your precious leader?"

A long pause.

Carina counted down from ten. She got to three before Kee answered.

"Is Sable Dirksen aboard your vessel?"

"She is. We'd rather not have her, though."

"I want proof," said Kee.

"You mean a finger or something?"

"I want to speak to her."

Carina checked the time remaining until they reached the *Duchess's* protection.

"Atoi," she said in a private comm. "The commander of the corvette wants to speak to the bitch. I'm going to put us all on a four-way comm. If she refuses to talk, encourage her."

Once the group comm was initiated, Carina addressed the Dirksen commander.

"Okay, she can hear you."

"Ma'am," said Kee. "I need to verify your presence aboard the Sherrerr shuttle."

"Yes, I'm here," Sable replied through gritted teeth.

Still clinging on to your life, Carina thought.

She smirked and closed the comm.

"If you fire on us, Kee," she said, "you'll be putting her life in danger."

The commander didn't respond.

Carina checked the time again. They were nearly safe. It was almost all over.

The *Tumult* fired.

Carina tensed. Had Kee decided to sacrifice Sable? Did he want a chance to be leader himself?

But, again, the pulse sped by the shuttle. She checked its trajectory. It was heading for the *Duchess*! Kee's plan must be to defeat the mercs' starship and prevent the shuttle from reaching a safe haven.

The two starships were in range of each other's firepower so Carina altered course. A stray pulse could destroy the shuttle.

The *Duchess's* four cannons returned fire.

"What's happening, Car?" Atoi asked.

"The boys are fighting it out."

"But our boy is bigger."

"You betcha."

The *Duchess* scored two direct hits on the corvette, but at the edge of its range the effect wasn't devastating. The *Tumult's* pulse had also hit, with similarly minimal effect.

The two ships drew closer.

The *Tumult* and *Duchess* fired simultaneously.

Kee's bravery was mildly impressive. Or was he only foolhardy? The corvette would never defeat the larger ship.

The *Duchess's* pulses impacted the nose of the *Tumult*, sending the ship veering off course. The *Duchess* also received a hit but sustained no obvious damage.

Surely Kee will give up now?

But the corvette came around as if to continue the battle.

Madness!

Then the ship slowed, continued on its circular path, and flew away from the *Duchess*. Kee had finally come to his senses.

Carina breathed out heavily, and then guided the shuttle home.

44

s soon as it was safe to leave the shuttle, Carina leapt out of the pilot's hatch and ran to the back of the vessel, where the ramp was still lowering.

Bryce emerged first, carrying Darius in his arms. Carina stopped him, drank a mouthful of elixir, and then Cast the most powerful Heal on the boy she could muster.

Then she grabbed her brother from Bryce's arms and ran to the sick bay.

The door was open and the medics were waiting.

Carina laid Darius down on the examining table and began to remove his armor.

"Let us do it," said one of the medics. "Out of the way."

Carina backed off, her arms wrapped around her chest, every muscle and fiber tense as she watched the woman and man work.

Darius's eyes were closed and his little chest rose and fell.

Carina told herself that was a good sign, that he would live, but she didn't dare to really believe it.

Hands touched her shoulders—Bryce's. Then they rose to the clasps on her helmet. She'd forgotten to take it off.

When he'd removed her helmet and put it down Bryce wrapped his arms around her. "I think he's going to be okay," he murmured. "He's small but he's strong."

The door to the sick bay opened and Parthenia, Oriana, and Ferne came in, their faces ghostly white as they took in the sight of the burn to Darius's chest and stomach.

"Right," said the female medic. "That's it! Everyone out. This isn't a performance."

Bryce pulled Carina out of the room last. When the sick bay doors closed behind them they stood in the corridor.

"Where's Nahla?" Carina asked.

"Atoi is bringing her," Bryce replied. "Her case isn't so urgent, but I think she'll take longer to heal."

"Stars, that poor girl," Carina whispered. The mission's events were catching up with her. The starving prisoners, Sable Dirksen shooting Darius, Stevenson's death.

She began to shake.

Bryce's arms tightened around her.

"We had a look at the stuff we found at the mage castle," said Ferne. "It's cool."

Parthenia put a hand on Carina's arm. "We saw a set of coordinates. We think you found the way, Carina. We can go back to Earth."

But it didn't matter any more. She didn't want to go to Earth. All she wanted was for her brother to not die.

Cadwallader walked up to the group. "What's the situation with the little lad?"

"They're still working on him," Bryce replied.

"We have the best medics with the best equipment," Cadwallader said. "If he can be saved, they'll save him."

Parthenia started to sniff. "We shouldn't have been so nice to Castiel. He was pretending all the time, planning on betraying us the first chance he got."

"I told you we shouldn't trust him," said Ferne.

"I certainly won't trust him again," Parthenia said.

"You probably won't get the chance," said Bryce. "He won't be getting off Ostillon for a while."

"Yes he will," Oriana said. "That corvette will go back for him."

"Not any day soon," said Cadwallader. "The corvette is sitting on our tail, just out of range of our cannons."

"Waiting for a chance to get their leader back?" Bryce asked.

"So it appears."

"That doesn't matter," said Ferne. "Darius can Cast Cloak and...oh." He looked down.

There was a brief, uncomfortable silence.

"When Darius is better," Oriana said carefully, "he can Cast Cloak on the *Duchess* and we can lose the nasty corvette."

"What have you done with Sable Dirksen?" Carina asked.

"She's on her way to the brig, of course," replied Cadwallader. "Where did you think I would put her? She can swap stories with Lomang and his twin."

Carina marched away from the sick bay.

"Where are you going, Lin?" Cadwallader called out after her.

A pair of mercs guiding an a-grav medi-bed came around the corner. Jace lay on it, finally awake. His hand lifted slightly at the sight of Carina but she didn't acknowledge him.

She could talk to him later. She had a task to carry out.

"Lin!" came Cadwallader's shout. "Answer me."

Carina broke into a run, worried that Cadwallader would find a way to stop her.

She met a second medi-bed carrying Calvaley. He stared at the ceiling passing overhead, deep in thought.

Carina skirted around him and the mercs bringing him to the sick bay.

Years of living aboard the *Duchess* meant she knew its layout well. That was good. Cadwallader was smart. He would guess her intention.

She turned down a corridor. The new route to the brig would take her longer but she would approach it from the other direction, where she wouldn't be expected.

She broke into a sweat though she was hardly panting. Everything that had happened was passing through her mind. Scenes she would never forget as long as she lived.

The odd soldier she passed simply stared at her.

Good. Cadwallader hadn't put out a shipwide comm...yet.

She still had time.

She turned into the final corridor. Ahead lay the brig.

"Hey, Lin," said the guard, cautiously. "I'm not supposed to let you in. Cadwallader's orders."

"That's okay," she replied. "I don't want to go in."

"I hate to refuse a fellow merc," said the guard as she reached him. "But order's orders." He sounded relieved.

Carina peered over the man's shoulder. "I know how it is. You don't need to worry."

The cell walls in the brig were transparent. In one cell Lomang sat on a bunk in his hateful hat, talking. His enormous brother sat at his feet like a child listening to a story.

In the other cell was Sable Dirksen.

Sable stood facing the transparent wall, looking out. She'd seen Carina. As her eyes met Carina's, the color drained from her face.

"I don't *need* to go in," Carina explained to the guard .

She sipped elixir from the reservoir in her suit, and closed her eyes.

"Wait," the man said. "What are you doing?"

As she had done since she was a little girl, more times than she could remember, she wrote a character in her mind. With a feeling of joyful relief she sent it out.

"Stop," said the guard. "You aren't supposed to do that."

Carina opened her eyes and smiled. "And yet, I did."

She looked at Sable's cell. It was empty.

Lomang had stopped talking. He was staring at Carina, his mouth a dark hole filled with shiny teeth. His younger brother looked puzzled. He stood up and walked to the wall of their cell, peering into Sable's.

Sable Dirksen was floating about three meters outside the *Duchess's* hull—just three meters, but it would make all the difference. Air was forcing its way out of her lungs, bursting through tissue and bone, sinew and vein, to erupt in a bloody, bubbly fountain. Her skin was freezing. The saliva in her mouth was boiling and evaporating into the void. Within minutes she would be dead.

Carina's only regret was that it would all be over too quickly.

"Dammit, Lin!" Cadwallader yelled as he came running up. "What the hell do you think you're doing?"

He ran to Sable's cell, looked inside, and then turned back to Carina. "You do *not* have the right to execute prisoners!"

Carina shrugged and walked away.

"The Dirksens already hated us," he shouted. "Now they'll hunt down everyone on this ship. You've signed a death warrant for us all!"

Carina continued to walk away.

Cadwallader's yelling faded. She wandered, not knowing where she was going.

Then something snapped.

She found she couldn't move any farther.

When Bryce arrived, she was sitting against the corridor wall, staring into the middle distance, unable to think, unable to feel. She had a feeling Bryce might have been comming her for a while but she wasn't sure.

All she knew was that she had killed Sable Dirksen in cold blood, and that she had *enjoyed* it.

He squatted down. “Carina, why didn’t you answer me?” he asked gently.

She could only look at him.

“I wanted to tell you the good news. Darius is going to be okay.”

The dam broke.

Carina collapsed into his arms.

She clung to him for a long time. She didn’t know how long. Eventually, she found she could speak again.

“What am I, Bryce? What have I become?”

CARINA’S STORY CONTINUES IN...

ACCURSED SPACE

Sign up to my reader group for an exclusive free copy of the *Star Mage Saga* prequel, *Star Mage Exile*, discounts on new releases, review crew invitations and other interesting stuff:

https://jjgreenauthor.com/free-books/

Printed in Great Britain
by Amazon

59764983R00168